Mrs. Milner Gets a Kitchen
A Midcentury Modern Romance
Jane Hadley

Mrs. Milner Gets a Kitchen

Copyright © 2023 by Jane Hadley
Cover art by Jane Hadley

ISBN 979-8-9913918-5-6

All rights reserved.

No portion of this book may be reproduced in any form without written permission from the publisher or author, except as permitted by U.S. copyright law. Any use of this work to "train" generative Artificial Intelligence technologies is strictly prohibited. Be a part of celebrating and protecting the intellectual property of authentic human creators. Creation isn't just about the product; it's about the process. We lose much more in skills, processing, and practice than we gain when using AI technologies as a short-cut.

This is a work of fiction. The story, all names, characters, and incidents portrayed in this work, while inspired by the historical record, are entirely fictitious.

Content Notice: Internalized misogyny, body image/size discussion, period-typical misogyny (especially among women), divorce/fractured family, co-dependent/passive-aggressive family dynamics, gratuitous use of the word "panties" (it's the historically correct US term, I'm sorry, take it up with the Silent Generation). I promise you, the dog will be fine.

To the ghost that haunts my kitchen

Chapter 1

Marion Milner lifted a dark eyebrow as she peered sidelong out the window of her heavy front door. Mrs. Dvorak was hovering on her front porch across the street holding a paper plate laden with cookies and Marion prayed that those morsels were not for her. No tray of cookies was worth the price of Mrs. Dvorak's simpering brand of passive-aggressive interrogation and besides, Marion's kids got enough sweets as it was without errant plates of cookies showing up in their kitchen.

The kitchen. That was why Marion lurked in the entry, impatiently watching the corner of the frosty street. The General Electric salesman was due at any moment and she could hardly wait. Finally, all those nosy women at Sokol would have something to whisper about other than Joe leaving. Rather than being the poor, unfortunate divorcee, Marion could elevate her reputation to the aloof, elegant housewife with a fully modern, fitted, *electric* kitchen. All she would have to do was sit back, read a magazine, drink a cocktail, and then she'd be swanning through potlucks with a rotisserie chicken automatically cooked to perfection through the miracle of modern living. She'd be the envy of the entire neighborhood.

Just then, the gleaming, white truck appeared through the snow flurries, with General Electric emblazoned in crisp letters along the side. Marion grinned to see Mrs. Dvorak's mouth flap in the wind as the truck pulled to a stop in front of Marion's house. On cue, Marion swept the door open, the cold metal weather stripping giving a crack, and stood confidently in the entry in spite of the chill. She wore her rust-colored rayon dress — not so fancy as to look like she was trying too hard, but nice enough for an independent woman of means to welcome the sale of a significant home upgrade. Thanks to the settlement, she wouldn't even need to worry about convincing a bank to give her a loan. She could pay for the whole thing out of pocket without even needing to wait for Joe's next alimony check. She supposed there were silver linings to one's husband being so wracked with guilt for leaving her. It made him very generous with his pocketbook.

Two men climbed out of the truck. One was tall, his dark hair slick with pomade, a fine wool coat over his navy blue suit. If the first man appeared to be auditioning for the General Electric spring catalog, the second man, who drove the truck, appeared to be shooting for John Deere. He had a red check flannel coat over brown overalls, a flat cap with fold-down ear warmers, and a knit scarf slung over one shoulder. The salesman and the contractor. Marion slotted them neatly into the roles their uniforms denoted and felt her heart flutter as she opened the storm door for them.

"Welcome, gentlemen," she called as they made their way carefully up the icy front walk and mounted the stoop steps.

"Mrs. Milner, I presume?" the salesman said, shining a

row of straight, white teeth at her. He was tall and sharp and dashing. Magazine ready. Nothing like Joe's quiet, bespectacled lankiness. This man stood straight like he had nothing to hide.

"That's right," Marion replied and allowed herself to enjoy the fellow's attention, even if he was only there to make a sale. "Please, come in out of the cold."

She ushered the salesman and his shorter contractor into the entry. Before she shut the door, Marion met Mrs. Dvorak's dumbfounded gaze across the street with a gracious smile. It was deeply satisfying.

When she turned back to the crowded entry, the two men were stomping their feet on the rug and shrugging off their coats. Milly, the family's dopey elderly cocker spaniel, snuffled around their ankles, and the contractor bent to give her a scratch behind her floppy ears. Marion imagined the swelling violins of the dramatic, daytime infomercials about electric kitchen appliances as she slipped past them, gathering their coats to hang on the hat tree. "Thank you so much for coming out in such chilly weather."

"Oh, it's our pleasure," the salesman replied with another toothy smile. He had a narrow, Clark Gable mustache. "After all, there's no such thing as bad weather—"

"—Just bad clothes," Marion finished for him with a knowing nod. "Can I get you any coffee?"

"No, that's alright," the salesman said, just as the contractor, pulling his cap off to reveal a shock of red hair, replied in a surprisingly deep voice, "Yes, thanks."

The salesman, whose hair was a much more dignified shade of brown under the fedora he'd hung on the hat tree, glanced at his companion. "Well, I suppose if you're serving…"

Marion glanced between the two of them, then smiled.

"Of course. Make yourselves comfortable, and I'll be right back."

She swept through the sitting and dining rooms and into her miserably outdated kitchen with Milly at her heels. It hadn't been updated since 1928. She knew this because Joe's grandmother had been the one to do it. Marion filled the coffee pot with water from the hulking enameled sink under the window and set it to heat on the free-standing gas stove at the far end of the small room.

She chided herself; she should have started heating water before they arrived. This was going to take too long. While she waited for water to boil, she snatched out a serving tray from the hoosier cabinet opposite and arranged coffee cups on saucers, along with the sugar bowl. As she filled a pitcher with cream, she wondered if these fellows were going to insist on speaking with her husband before beginning work. Christmas was only a month and some change away, and she wanted her kitchen finished before the Sokol Ladies Auxiliary Christmas party in mid-December.

When the coffee was ready, Marion swept out with her tray to the sitting room where the salesman and the contractor perched together on her sofa. The salesman's legs were so long, he looked a bit like a spider on her little settee. Marion gave a coquettish smile as she set the tray on the coffee table. She bent and carefully poured out three cups before she sat down in the armchair across from the settee. Milly settled carefully at her feet with a wary woof, though Marion was certain if the contractor offered the dog any further attention, she would readily abandon her master for the fleeting pleasure of getting a good scratch under her chin.

"Lovely home you have here, Mrs. Milner," the salesman said, his eyes casting appreciatively over the woodwork. "It's a wonderful Craftsman. Duplex?"

"Yes," Marion replied, crossing her ankles daintily. "It was built in 1915 and has a kitchen to match."

"Oh my, it's a good thing you called us!" the salesman laughed. "I'm Gerald Stinson, by the way, and this is Mr. Harry O'Conner, our contractor for West Side installs."

"Nice to meet you, ma'am," Mr. O'Conner said, tipping his ginger head respectfully before he reached for a coffee cup. He was short, maybe only a few inches taller than Marion's five and a half feet, and square in all the ways that Mr. Stinson was long. He didn't add anything to his cup before he took a sip.

"Have you had a chance to look through the catalog we sent you?" Mr. Stinson asked as he spooned sugar into his cup.

Marion grinned, her heart leaping at the chance to answer a set of questions she knew all her answers to. "Oh, yes." She pulled the catalog out from her dress pocket. "I'm interested in a total remodel."

She spread the catalog out next to the coffee tray and pointed out the spread she had been admiring for the last two weeks. "I want everything fitted, with built-in cabinets and sink. I would love a double wall oven, and the electric stove. I saw one of your commercials where the refrigerator's shelves swing out and can be adjusted, so everything can fit without too much trouble. And I want to make sure it's got frost protection on it."

Mr. Stinson raised his eyebrows at Mr. O'Conner with a playful grin. "My, I'm not sure I even need to be here. Mrs. Milner, you'd have me out of a job."

Marion tucked her chin to hide a sheepish smile. She thought to say something modest, but what came out was, "Nonsense. Without you, how would I see a sample of the teal finish?"

Harry hated going on sales calls. Hated it with every fiber of his being. It wasn't just because Gerald was an ass who always made him drop the financial bricks on the customers (he could say that because they'd been friends since grade school). He just wasn't very good with these housewives. They always seemed worried he was going to get engine grease on their upholstery or something, which was ridiculous because he was a carpenter, not a mechanic, but that didn't seem to make a difference to the neurotic ladies up on Crocus Hill.

There was something different about Mrs. Milner, though. Probably because she was the first customer they'd had who lived at the bottom of the hill, in the Little Bohemia area of the West 7th neighborhood. Most of these folks were laborers or clerks; they couldn't afford the Kitchen of the Future G–E was hawking. And even if they could, their older houses didn't have the electrical capacity to support them. (Harry hoped Gerald would make sure to touch on the electrical sooner rather than later.)

Gerald was laughing again and drew samples out of his briefcase for Mrs. Milner to consider.

"Now," he said as Mrs. Milner flipped through them, "the matching steel cabinets can be an investment, and somewhat difficult to install in these older houses. Do you have lathe and plaster?"

"Oh, yes," Mrs. Milner replied dismissively as she chewed on her lower lip. She'd put on lipstick for this occasion. Harry wasn't sure who she meant to impress — maybe it was the appliance suite itself — but, well, she did look rather impressive. She was all mahogany hair with a square face slashed with thick, arched brows and dark, full-lashed eyes. She had to be Bohemian — most of the people in this neighborhood were — but she couldn't be first-generation by any means. She had no accent and seemed to be putting on a sort of air that he usually associated with actresses in the movies. It was obviously an affectation, but, well, it was also working for her. Harry felt a little bit stupid every time he looked at her. Which was extremely rude and unprofessional, for multiple reasons.

"Sometimes," Harry said, clearing his throat roughly, "the lathe and plaster can't support the steel cabinets with the same integrity as —"

"— I thought the steel was lighter than wood cabinets," Mrs. Milner interrupted. "That's what the catalog says."

"No, you're right, of course," Gerald chuckled amiably. He was very good at affecting amiability, which was why he was the salesman and Harry was not. "You've done your homework."

"It's not a matter of wood or metal," Harry cut in. "It's that a lot of the houses in this neighborhood cut their plaster with other materials to cut costs when they were built, so their plaster just crumbles whenever I drill into it."

Mrs. Milner raised that arched slice of eyebrow at him and blinked. "Have you done many kitchen installs in this neighborhood?"

Harry shifted uncomfortably. "No, but I did a fair amount of handyman work around here before the — before I did kitchens."

"Oh good," Mrs. Milner replied, "because I have my heart set on being the envy of the neighborhood."

Gerald glanced between the two of them before he

exclaimed, "I have no doubt that you will! We scarcely ever make sales calls down the hill."

Harry bit the inside of his cheek to keep himself from bringing up the electricity as Gerald leaned over the catalog, discussing oven models and features. Mrs. Milner's fingers curled around the edge of the coffee table as she leaned in and Harry noticed, very much in spite of himself, that she wasn't wearing a wedding ring. He frowned and took another sip of coffee. That was utterly irrelevant information. The cocker spaniel nosed his other hand just then, so he settled into petting the dog while he waited for Gerald to wrap up his sales pitch.

After about fifteen minutes of discussing which features would be most advantageous to Mrs. Milner's workflow, Harry couldn't take it anymore and suggested they take a look at the room before they started talking specifics. All the conceptualizing was moot to him if he didn't know what kind of space he was working with.

Mrs. Milner led them through the dining room and into a cramped, unfitted kitchen with a free-standing stove and icebox taking up most of the space on either end.

"Oh, Mrs. Milner," Gerald said in his most sympathetic tone. "This is worse than you made it out to be."

Harry tried very hard not to roll his eyes. If he had a nickel for every time Gerald gave out that tired line…

Mrs. Milner looked at Gerald sidelong. "What part of 'utter disaster' did you think I was exaggerating?"

Harry snorted and then tried to cover it up by coughing. Mrs. Milner tipped her pointed chin at him and smirked.

Gerald and the lady of the house went to stand in the center of the room and talked at great length about minimizing steps and stooping and triangular floor plans while Harry took the liberty of measuring out the room.

"For greatest efficiency, you'd have to have your refrigerator against this wall," Gerald said emphatically. "Right now, with it across the room, you are walking actual *miles* more than you need to just traveling back and forth across the room all day."

Mrs. Milner tipped her head and gave a slow smile. "No wonder I wear out all my shoes."

Harry couldn't help himself. He grunted.

Gerald grimaced. "Uh oh, that's never a good sound."

"No, I can't imagine it is." Mrs. Milner straightened. "Is there something very wrong, Mr. O'Conner?"

Now Harry felt stupid. "No, ma'am," he said. "It's just the model of refrigerator you're talking about is too deep to fit on this wall." He pointed his tape measure against the wall in question, on the far side of the radiator. "If you put it where he says, you'll cut off traffic to the stair door."

"How deep?"

Harry touched his tape measure to the wall and stepped back to indicate the depth of the model in question. "If you got your double ovens perpendicular, you ain't gonna be able to pass through."

"I see." Mrs. Milner pursed her lips and stood for a moment with her arms crossed over her chest. Her dress must have had a crinoline beneath it, because it perfectly accentuated the supple hourglass of her figure. Which Harry certainly wasn't admiring. How could he be? He was too busy raining on her parade.

"Well, you could just knock out the wall and bump out into the dining room a bit," Gerald suggested helpfully.

Mrs. Milner frowned, her lips pursed into an endearing little frown. "Wouldn't that take quite a lot longer?"

Harry set his jaw and focused his eyes on the wall in

question (and resolutely away from the mouth of their latest client). "Yes. I don't think I'd be able to get the job done by Christmas if we rebuilt the wall. And of course, it would be more expensive."

Mrs. Milner flapped her hand dismissively at him like she was some Summit Avenue princess, and Harry felt like he had to check again to make sure he was indeed at a house on the bottom of the hill.

"The price isn't an object. It's just — I'm hosting a party on December 17th and I need the work to be done by then."

*

Marion served lemon bars when they sat at the dining table after Mr. O'Conner had taken every possible measurement known to man inside her cramped kitchen. She'd almost cracked a line about how he'd be measuring her next, but it was clear after fifteen minutes of him being much too serious for his years that he was the kind of man who would not appreciate the joke.

"Well, Mrs. Milner, I think I have a really good idea of what you're looking for," Mr. Stinson said with an easy smile. She only felt a little sorry for herself when she'd noticed his wedding ring. (It wasn't like it would change anything anyway, but it was nice to dream.) "Will your husband be home soon? Or is there a number I can reach him at?"

Marion's stomach dropped out from under her, even though she knew to expect this. She tipped her chin up more defiantly than she felt. "I don't have a husband."

Mr. Stinson was taken aback. "Oh, I — I'm terribly sorry, but ... ah, what?"

"I said I don't have a husband," she repeated through a tight jaw. "I will be taking care of this expense on my own."

"Uh…" Mr. Stinson snapped open his briefcase and started rustling through his papers. Avoiding her eye contact. "I'm not sure we can get financing for a … well, do you work? Sorry, I just thought, since you're *Mrs. Milner*—"

"No," Marion interrupted crisply. "I don't work. I am newly divorced and I have come into some money. Financing won't be necessary."

Mr. Stinson forgot all his manners and stared at her. To his credit, Mr. O'Conner was very focused on his lemon bar instead of studying her like she was some sort of carnival sideshow. Milly, unaware of the awkwardness of the situation, whined at his feet, begging for a morsel.

"I will pay in cash," Marion clarified.

"Are you sure you can afford it?" Mr. Stinson blurted out. He looked horrified at himself for saying it, but he also didn't hurry to smooth it over.

Marion glowered. "Yes, given my calculations from your promotional materials. Provide me with your estimate, Mr. Stinson, and I can confirm."

Mr. Stinson, inexplicably still flustered, rustled through his papers some more. "I, um, certainly. Give me a few moments and I can draw that up for you."

Mr. O'Conner, who was holding half a lemon bar between his teeth, scratched some numbers on the back of an envelope with a carpenter pencil he drew from his breast pocket and slid it around Mr. Stinson. Marion picked up the paper. Oh hell, that was *a lot* of money. Even so — it wasn't beyond her means. And she had her renters upstairs and Joe's alimony besides. She did her very best to conceal her response, straightening her shoulders with great dignity as she said, "Yes. That will do."

Mr. Stinson regarded her for a long moment. His mouth flapped for a moment like a beached codfish before he said, "Very well, let's get down to brass tacks, then."

✦

Harry and Gerald made their way down the icy walk toward the truck.

"What did you write on that envelope?" Gerald asked as he climbed into the passenger seat and pulled a pack of cigarettes from his breast pocket.

"Twice as much as you would have," Harry replied, turning the key in the ignition, and releasing the parking brake.

"What!? And she didn't even bat an eye. Astonishing."

"Guess she's loaded," Harry shrugged as he pushed the clutch and shifted into first gear.

"I wonder what the hell her ex-husband did?" Gerald mused. "Because if she's newly divorced and rolling in it, you can bet he did something pretty rotten."

Harry pressed his lips into a grim line and turned left on St. Clair Avenue. He couldn't imagine the kind of man who could be married to a woman as pretty and decisive as Mrs. Milner and spurn her so horribly that she'd get enough in the settlement for a whole new kitchen. But then again, what did he know? Given how things had gone with Alice, he was a pretty poor judge of character.

Chapter 2

The next time the General Electric truck pulled up in front of Marion's house, only Mr. O'Conner emerged from the cab. She supposed since the sale had already been clinched and the paperwork signed, there was no reason for Mr. Stinson to come back. But it still made her gracious smile a little stiffer as she ushered an unmarried man (presumably; he wore no ring) into her home, where she, an unmarried woman, was alone until her children came home from school. It felt like the beginning of either a cautionary tale or a pulp dime novel. And the fact that Mrs. Dvorak was definitely peeping out the window behind a corner of her curtain just sharpened that edge a little more finely.

"Good afternoon, Mr. O'Conner," Marion said as she stepped onto the front porch, holding the storm door open for him. "I've got some coffee inside, if you'd care for a warm drink."

Mr. O'Conner stepped into the front hall and pulled off his flat cap. His hair was coppery red and shorn short and tight — perhaps a vet. He was of an age with her, so most likely he'd been in Korea. Mr. O'Conner's eyebrows flew up as he regarded her with mild surprise and Marion realized that she had, in fact, mused quite aloud.

"Yeah, Korea," Mr. O'Conner said with a tight smile.

"Oh, well, thank you very much for your service," Marion blurted, her thumbs twiddling in her clasped hands as she fought to regain her composure — and her control over her interior monologue. "My father fought in World War II, and my uncle too, though he was in Japan. He served during the occupation as well. He's got a Japanese wife now, lives in San Francisco. He says the seafood is much better than here in the Midwest." Oh hell, here she went again. She could see Mr. O'Conner's fingers fidgeting with the brim of his hat as he waited politely for her to finish. "D-do you find that to be true?"

"Hm? Yes, seafood here is horrible," Mr. O'Conner replied in that deep, resonant voice of his. He bent to give Milly a scratch on the ears as she sniffed him, detecting him for possible threats. Which was endearing, because the dog was so old she could scarcely smell anything anymore. The kids could drop a scrap of chicken right next to her and she wouldn't notice.

"Taking our lives in our hands," Marion agreed as she absently wiped her sweaty palms on her plaid skirt and led the way into the sitting room. "Lake fish, though, that's different. Fresh out of the lake, fried walleye is the taste of summer. Would you care for coffee?"

Shut up, Marion thought to herself. But she didn't. She never did. Especially not when she was nervous. *There's no good reason to be nervous*, she told herself as Mr. O'Conner nodded and she tipped the spout of the coffee pot to his cup. Just because the fellow didn't have a wedding ring didn't mean he harbored any kind of interest, other than the desire to get his work done. He certainly hadn't given any indication he'd noticed her at all on his last visit.

"Do you have any connections with any lake cabins in summertime, Mr. O'Conner? We have gone up every summer since the children were little, though I imagine now I won't be joining them anymore…"

Marion gave a weak little chuckle, a truly pitiful whine of a sound. She hadn't really thought about that before, but it was out of her mouth before she could realize that she'd managed to uncover yet another fresh piece of grief, another scrap of what she'd lost this year. She swallowed against a lump in her throat and blinked the sting from her eyes. She sloshed some coffee into her cup and pressed its edge to her lips, just to shut herself up.

"My old man's from up near the Cuyuna Range. He belongs to a hunting club with lakefront property," Mr. O'Conner said, graciously ignoring the fact that Marion's eyes were a bit watery. "I've been a couple of times, but it's really not my thing."

"What, deer hunting?" Marion could see it. The plaid flannels, the overalls. It wasn't much of a stretch.

"Yeah. It's mostly sitting in a deer stand doing nothing."

Marion hummed. The joke was out of her mouth before she could determine if it was funny or mean. "I suppose that goes to show the caliber of hunter you are."

"A bad one?" O'Conner replied with a smile. "Yeah." There was a pause as he sipped his coffee. "But not as bad as that pun."

The relief that she hadn't inadvertently offended him was palpable even as she felt her cheeks heat. She forced a genial chuckle. Her fingers tapped at the sides of her cup.

"So I've been thinking a lot about the metal cabinets," she said. There was no whiplash quite like the fling of a patented Marion Milner non sequitur. Marion stood and looked toward the kitchen. "Maybe you can tell me what you think."

✦

Harry followed Mrs. Milner into the kitchen, wondering at the display of, well, flightiness she hadn't exhibited during his previous visit. But then again, she wasn't quite as put together as she'd been the other day, either. She wore a wool skirt and sweater over a plain, white blouse that looked soft with wear. The dark brown curls that skimmed her shoulders were looser and pinned back with combs on either side of her head. Regardless of any apparent nerves, she was still very pretty, even without her red lipstick and affectations. Maybe especially without those. It pleased him to see her come apart a little in front of him. It allowed him to make believe he was being treated to something she didn't show everyone.

"I kept thinking about the teal cabinets in this room," Mrs. Milner said as they entered the kitchen, which looked to be in the middle of a baking day, ingredients and flour dusting over the hoosier cabinet and a loaf pan with a kitchen towel over it set to rise on the side of the stove. "Do you think it might be jarring for someone to come into a Craftsman home and then enter a fully modern kitchen? I'm worried it would feel like they're walking into a time warp."

Harry stood in the doorway and crossed his arms. "That's a good point." He frowned and considered the hoosier. Painted pine, simple design. It suited the Craftsman woodwork well, even though the built-ins in the dining room were oak and much more carefully crafted into their geometric, utilitarian style. "But I also don't think Craftsman is too far removed from the modern design. There's a lot of sleek, straight lines in both."

"So … you don't think people would feel like they just walked into a spaceship that landed in my kitchen?"

Harry couldn't help but smile. "They might. But then, if you want the status of the fully fitted kitchen, it would truly be a spectacular reveal."

Mrs. Milner mirrored his posture, her arms crossing over her sweater in a way that accented her figure. Harry found it a little difficult to concentrate.

"But don't you think it'll look awfully dated in ten years?" Mrs. Milner asked, chewing on a fingernail as her eyes skittered across the dim room, rosebud lips pursed in thought. Good heavens. Harry quickly averted his gaze before he could complete any further musings about her figure or her mouth. *Kitchen install. Kitchen. Focus on the job.*

"Well, yeah. I do." Wow, A+ salesmanship there, O'Conner. "But I'm sure G-E will have another state-of-the-art kitchen to sell by then."

The words tasted sour on his tongue. Mrs. Milner frowned with similar distaste, and it made him want to snatch the notion out of the air, run outside, dig a hole in the frozen ground, and bury it forever.

"I don't expect I'll have another opportunity like this," she said, shrugging wistfully, "and I don't want to mess it up."

"That's a lot of pressure to put on yourself," Harry murmured. "But I think … if you want the fitted cabinets with the matching appliances, you should get them. It's not about how it looks to everyone else. It's how it works for you. And if you want teal cabinets, you should have them. But if you want wood cabinets, I could build the fittings you need. There's no pressure."

Mrs. Milner paused, regarding him for a moment. Her eyes were dark, chocolate brown, like swimming in a pool of hot fudge. Harry wanted to touch her arm, encourage her, let her know that her vision was worth fulfilling. That there wasn't a wrong answer and she didn't need to worry about regrets. He'd get her the kitchen that worked for her, because … well, because it was his job, but also because it would make her happy, which would make him happy and oh, dammit, he had barely known this woman for a handful of hours and he could already feel himself trying to fix everything for her, as if it were she, not the kitchen, that was broken.

She eyed him sidelong. "Won't Mr. Stinson be cross with you for talking me out of the prefabricated cabinets?"

"Probably, but he don't have to cook in your kitchen every day."

"You're not much of a salesman, are you?"

Harry shifted his weight, arms still crossed. "Nope. 'Bout as good of a salesman as I am a hunter."

Mrs. Milner gave a chortle and the bells of her laugh splashed off the plaster walls. Harry stuffed his hands tighter in the crooks of his elbows and swallowed any thought that wasn't kitchen related. Squashed them all down tight, to wait until it was an appropriate time to be considered. Which was never. He even furrowed his brows as if they could force his eyes to take stock of the kitchen he'd been hired to install and not the lovely woman who owned it.

He imagined the room without its furnishings and tried to unveil its potential. It was small, but one didn't need a large room to make it functional. It could be so neat and efficient with a fitted set-up. As much as Gerald's lines about triangle layouts drove him nuts, it wasn't because the idea was a bad one. It was because Gerald made them sound like some sort of new space-age technical innovation when it was nothing more than common sense. And the layout they'd discussed a few days ago was fine once they'd settled on a smaller refrigerator model. "Let me run something by you."

"I'm listening."

"What if you did wood cabinets?"

Mrs. Milner sighed. "Wouldn't that take a lot longer?"

"Well, yes."

She pursed her lips. "They wouldn't match, either. Not like in the catalog."

"No, they wouldn't. Though there is a wood brown color for the appliances —"

"Heavens no. I have my heart set on the turquoise green."

He stood quietly and waited, even though he desperately wanted to launch into a dizzying array of encouraging options that might suit someone whose heart was set on turquoise appliances. He'd said it was up to her. It would not do for him to try and influence her decision, even with the best of intentions.

Mrs. Milner tapped her mouth with her finger. Harry reminded himself not to stare, but this time, he didn't manage it. She had the most adorable mouth, like a little pink bow on a gift he would be truly delighted to open. *Hell*. The way his imagination kept running away with him was unacceptable. Mrs. Milner had enough to worry about without a common grunt fresh off a discharge giving her puppy-dog eyes instead of doing the damn work she paid him to do. It was just … he really couldn't imagine the man who'd pay out that much money to be rid of such an attractive woman.

"You're right," she said finally. "It doesn't matter what

other people think. I want the kitchen of the future, and if it looks like someone slapped a showroom into my house off the dining area, then so be it. I like the look of it, and I'm not gonna settle for less."

Harry grinned. He couldn't help it. Her certainty was infectious. "Let's go over the layout, then. I put together some drawings based on your measurements."

✦

Marion wondered if G–E knew the diamond in the rough they were sitting on in the form of Mr. O'Conner. His large, blunt fingers pointed out a diagram of her kitchen drawn with surprising elegance, bringing to life the lay-out Mr. Stinson had tried to explain to her last time. But his sketch included so much more: a sliding hatch for food scraps in the countertop, a lazy Susan in the corner cabinet, a built-in light fixture above the sink. As he walked her through several drawings of slight variation, he explained all the different ways the spaces would be optimized for the greatest efficiency, and for a moment, Marion thought about proposing to him as a joke because she had never met a man quite this domestically compe-tent before in her life.

"It's a tight space," he concluded. "You might want to think about some cabinets in the back hall for pantry items and extra storage."

"Oh, now he brings the hard sell," Marion teased.

"No, it wouldn't be any extra. The estimate has plenty of padding for adjustments to the design."

Marion peered at him. "I'm beginning to think you're the brains behind the operation. And Mr. Stinson is just the shiny, good-looking fellow who secures the sales."

Mr. O'Conner pressed his lips into a tight smile and nodded. Marion resisted the urge to assure him that he was also good-looking, but in a gruffer, strong-silent-type way. Because he was. And he was kind to her doddering dog. One could always pick out a man's character by how he treated an animal.

"How much longer to do the pantry cabinets, then?" Marion asked, leaning toward Mr. O'Conner so she could see the paper better. And maybe to enjoy how her elbow brushed against his. (What? She was only human. And divorced, so she had better take whatever scraps she could safely scavenge without any further damage to her reputation.)

"A couple weeks, maybe? Your room isn't plumb, so it might require some finagling, but we don't have so many installs scheduled this month that I can't fit it all in before Christmas." He looked so earnest when he said that, Marion couldn't help but believe him.

"Well, that sounds wonderful. Even if we can't get the pantry cabinets done before the Christmas party on the 17th, maybe you could build them after. When can you start?" She grinned, then stopped. "Wait — if you're going to be building in there," Marion jerked her thumb behind her at the kitchen door, "where shall I do all my cooking?"

O'Conner hesitated and Marion suspected he was trying to find the best way to break some bad news. "We'll have to move some of your current kitchen furniture into the dining room. Maybe get a hot plate to cook on."

"And the sink?"

"Do you have a sink upstairs?"

Marion looked up. "Well, yes, but it belongs to the tenant up there. I suppose I could use the bathroom sink…"

"Yeah, that'd probably be best."

Marion looked through the kitchen door to her tiny bathroom, where a toilet, pedestal sink, and bathtub were all crammed into six square feet. "Won't that be a little adventure," she murmured.

"I'll do my work as fast as I can," Mr. O'Conner said as he scooched his chair back and stood, all ninety degree angles and rumpled utility in a pair of brown twill overalls. "Once the sink is installed, you'll be able to at least do the washing in there again, even if the appliances haven't come in yet. I'm sure I'll be out of your hair by your party, as long as we don't run into too many set-backs."

Marion considered him for a moment. He wasn't ever going to be in a G-E catalog, not even as the contractor model. He was broad and blunt, but his twinkling blue eyes and lopsided smile were endearing. And he knew enough about housework to know what made a kitchen work for a housewife. Yes, she didn't think she would mind having him around. Not at all.

"I'm looking forward to it either way."

Chapter 3

Tuesday, November 22, 1955
26 days until the Christmas party

Marion blinked. Who on earth thought it was a good idea to manufacture five different brands of catsup, and who thought it was an even better idea to put them *all* for sale on the same shelf? Right next to each other? How on earth was she supposed to know which kind would taste best in a meatloaf? It wasn't as though she could sample them all here. She just had to buy whichever one seemed the best based on the packaging. And, she supposed, the price. How did that make sense?

"Is that Mrs. Milner I see?"

Marion flinched and snatched one of the catsups off the shelf, throwing it in her basket. She wondered if she could feasibly pretend she hadn't heard her name as she turned in the opposite direction and tried her darndest to escape the condiments aisle before one of the four horsewomen of the Sokol Ladies Auxiliary descended upon her.

"It is! I would know that green coat anywhere! Oh, Mrs. Milner!"

Whoever it was — it had to be Helen Blaha at that volume — was so loud the entire grocery store must have heard her. Marion gritted her teeth and braced herself as she turned on the heel of her winter boot.

"Oh, Helen! Hello!" she said with a wooden smile. "I must not have heard you."

Helen laughed, a big, loud guffaw that would probably shake the bottles of catsup right off the shelves. "Off in your own little world again? You always were so imaginative."

"Yes." Marion's smile petrified a bit. Helen was only five years older than her. It wasn't like she was an aunty who had watched her grow up or something.

"What have you been up to? I didn't see you at the Thanksgiving pageant."

Marion's smile was so stiff now it might crack. "Yes, Charlie was sick." He wasn't sick. Unless one counted sick with worry about encountering a certain brood of bullies he'd been trying to avoid at school. Things weren't easy for a child whose parents were the object of relentless neighborhood interest.

"Well, you sure missed out. The children were just darling in their little play, and of course, the Ladies Auxiliary sold perogies afterward."

"I'm so sorry I missed it." It was hard to train her voice to sincerity.

"I noticed there was a General Electric truck outside your house the other day." No, she didn't. Helen lived on 7th Street and had no cause to wander deeper into the neighborhood to see what vehicles were parked outside Marion's house. Mrs. Dvorak must have called her.

"Oh, yes," Marion said, keeping her voice light. Wasn't this what she'd been waiting for? "I'm getting a new kitchen."

"Oh, Marion! One of those new-fangled metal monstrosities?"

Marion did an excellent job of not rolling her eyes.

This was for the notoriety, she reminded herself, not the approval. It didn't matter if they liked the kitchen. The point was for them to talk about it instead of Joe. The kitchen itself? That was just for her.

"The very same."

"Well, you sure are lucky," Helen replied. "My Monty would never let me rack up such an expense."

Marion deserved a gold medal for not slapping that stupid expression right off Helen's little pug-nosed face. Instead, she felt her smile turn vicious. Words charged into her mouth, and she opened it before she could think too hard about it. "Yes, it is rather nice to be the master of my own money for a change. I think divorce rather suits me. Maybe you should try it?"

Helen's chin dropped halfway to the floor. Marion grinned and took the opportunity to make her escape. "I'll see you at the Sokol Ladies Christmas party at my house. Maybe then you can see my new metal monstrosity!"

She waved and hurried toward the cash register before Helen Blaha could get another word out (and before Marion herself lost her last scrap of dignity by crying in the middle of the grocery store). The register and the teenaged Biederman kid seemed like an insurmountable hurdle to get through with her eyes prickling, but she managed to dig in her purse long enough for all her items to be rung up and placed in a paper bag for her convenience. Then, when she had two bags in the crooks of her arms, she set out to walk the six blocks home in peace and quiet. Hopefully. Providing no other neighbors decided to pop up out of the snowbanks.

Marion made it round the back of the grocery store before several errant tears leaked out. She let herself breathe for a moment, standing still across the street from the Sokol Hall while she waited for the emotion to pass. The kind of comments Helen made were nothing new. So why did every insinuation still feel like a twist of the knife in her chest?

She juggled her bags and pulled out a handkerchief to dab at her eyes. She'd done her face up before going to the store and she didn't want makeup running all over just because she was still inexplicably raw about being alone. It had been six months since she and Joe had settled everything. Over a year and a half since it all started. So why was this still so hard?

Marion shook her head and hitched her grocery bags onto her hips. She'd made it this far. Besides, Mr. O'Conner was due to arrive before lunch to start taking everything out of the kitchen so he could get started laying some brand new linoleum tiles. She had to make some decisions on the pattern before he started installing.

The trek back to her house was pleasant enough, and thankfully free of any more nosy neighbors. The weather was just above freezing and the light drizzle was melting the thin layer of snow on the ground, creating small pools of water draining across the sidewalk toward the street. The streets themselves were a sloppy mess, slush sloshing under the tires of passing cars, but the neighbors were good about shoveling the sidewalks, so her path was clear.

When Marion turned the corner onto her street, she was startled to see the General Electric truck parked at the curb already. She quickened her pace, gripping her hands tightly around the sides of the paper grocery bags. She was about halfway to her house when she realized with a start that Mr. O'Conner was sitting inside the cab of his truck, waiting. Oh hell. Not only was she late — was she late? — but she didn't have any refreshments prepared. Maybe she should have gone to the Thanksgiving pageant. Then she'd at least have perogies to serve. Dammit Helen Blaha. (Somehow, this was all *her* fault.)

Mr. O'Conner saw her coming and hopped out of his truck as soon as Marion was within earshot. He had his flannel coat and a toolbelt on, with a satchel slung over his shoulder.

"Here, let me help you with those," he called and strode toward her, not noticing whether he stepped on the cleared sidewalk or through the several inches of wet snow. He skidded to a stop in front of her and she let him take one of her bags.

"Thanks," she said, using her free hand to push her hat up out of her eyes.

"It's no trouble at all," Mr. O'Conner replied with a crooked grin and led the way to her front porch. He stood aside as Marion wrested her keys out of her pocket and pushed open the brass handle of the Craftsman door.

"I'm so sorry I'm late," Marion apologized as she let them into the front entry. She wished she was less flustered, but Helen Blaha had thrown her off-kilter. "I got waylaid by one of my neighbors at the grocer."

"That's alright," Mr. O'Conner said genially, taking her other grocery bag with such easy presumption that she scarcely noticed. "I was early."

Marion checked her watch as she hung her coat on the coat tree. "Oh, so you are. I don't suppose you'll mind waiting for refreshments. I had planned to brew coffee before you arrived."

"You don't have to fuss on my account."

"It's no bother." She toed off her boots and slipped into her house shoes as Milly wound clumsily around her ankles in greeting. As she walked through the living room, she resisted the urge to adjust the crocheted antimacassar that was once again half folded and sliding down the back of the armchair. It was Charlie's favorite reading perch and it was always in disarray. It wasn't until she was in the dining room that she realized she had no bags in her arms. She turned, and Mr. O'Conner, carrying both the bags, almost collided into her.

"Oh, Mr. O'Conner, you really don't have to —" she nattered as she tried to take one of the bags.

"It's not a bother," he replied, his shoulders bristling pridefully. "And most people just call me Harry. Mr. O'Conner is —"

"Your father?" Marion finished with him. He flushed and it made a grin stretch across Marion's mouth. "Heard that one before."

"There's no reason to argue about these bags," Harry O'Conner said. "I'm going to pull all the kitchen furnishings out into the dining room, so they might as well stay here."

Marion smiled and then mentally flicked the uncomfortable reality of having to cook in her dining room off her shoulders. "Oh, I hadn't really thought of it that way," she murmured.

"Don't worry, Mrs. Milner," Harry replied bracingly. "I got a good idea of how to arrange everything so it won't be too in the way. And I brought you a little something to make things easier."

"A gift?" Marion frowned as Harry dug in his large satchel. "Is this a bonus service?"

"No," Harry laughed as he proffered an electric hot plate. There was a scratch in the shiny chrome and it had some sort of dried scrap of food caked on it. "Just something I thought would make it a little easier with two kids running around."

Marion stared at him for a moment, at the way his smile made his cheeks crease and his blue eyes crinkle.

She didn't know why she was so touched. It wasn't like it was new or even freshly cleaned. She reached out and took the hot plate.

"Thank you." It came out dazed. "General Electric, huh? Is this how you all make additional appliance sales during the install?"

Harry's brow furrowed. "Not at all. I got it as a bonus when I signed on and I figured you could do a lot more with it than I can."

"It's yours?"

"Well, yeah."

Marion regarded the hot plate with a measure of guilt, "Don't you need it? You must have a stove too, if you're willing to part with this. Otherwise, how will you cook your dinner?"

Harry shrugged easily. "I'm rubbish at cooking. I basically live on bologna sandwiches anyway."

"Oh," Marion frowned. "No, I can't accept this—"

"Come on now, Mrs. Milner. You need it much more than I do—"

"I can buy my own, though. I don't need to take yours—"

"Take it for now, then. As a stop gap. I can let Gerald know to order one for you. But this time of year, it ain't gonna get here until after your kitchen is installed anyway."

"Surely Donaldson's has something—"

"Or you could just borrow mine," Harry shrugged with an amused smile.

"Heavens to Betsy, are you a contractor or a lawyer?" Marion huffed, setting the hot plate on the dining table in defeat. "Fine. Thank you for your thoughtfulness, I suppose, but know that you will be getting dinner to go every day you're here. Don't think I'm going to just let you get away with this."

Harry burst out laughing, the deep, resonant sound saturating the room. "I'm not sure I've done you a favor or a crime."

Marion glowered, even as she soaked in the satisfaction at having made him laugh so freely. "Is there a difference?"

Harry bit his lip and let his smile hang crookedly on his square face. Just then, despite the bright hair and the short build, he was enigmatically handsome. Marion was horrified to discover she was staring.

"Um, well, thank you, I suppose," she grumbled at the floor.

"Don't fall over yourself," he teased. She pressed her fingers to her forehead and hummed a weak, helpless laugh. Somehow, when she'd imagined her new kitchen getting installed, she'd thought there'd be a group of fellows quietly hauling her new fittings through the back door, drilling things into the wall, and generally trying their best not to make a racket as they installed everything as quickly as they could. She had not imagined a charming bachelor in overalls and a tool belt trying to take care of her instead of doing his damned job.

Some of what she was thinking must have shown on her face, because when she looked up at Harry again, his countenance had sobered.

"Let me run this layout past you before I get started moving everything," he said, his tone taking on the no-nonsense tone he'd had during their first meeting with Mr. Stinson.

"Thank you," Marion said and tried hard to press down the tingling awareness that she was alone in her house with a charming man. And also that all of her neighbors knew it. She glanced over her shoulder as she followed

Harry into the kitchen. The dining room windows faced the sidewalk that ran directly along the side of her corner property. People frequently walked right past those windows on their way here or there and she would do well to remember that. Gossip traveled fast and she was loath to allow anything else to be leveraged against her kids on the playground.

Harry showed her a neat pencil drawing of his thoughts for where her unfitted kitchen furnishings could be moved to make her dining room a small but efficient eat-in kitchen. The gas stove could not be temporarily moved, of course, but the hoosier cabinet and the icebox could, as well as her work table with the folding leaves.

"What about the hutch? I need that for storing all my dishes," Marion said, pointing at the dining room wall where Harry had designated the hoosier cabinet to go.

"I thought it could move to where the piano is."

Marion stared at him for a moment. "And where do you suggest the piano goes?"

Harry grinned. "Under the piano window, of course, in the living room."

"And you propose to move this yourself?"

"It's got wheels, don't it?"

"Yes, and a cast iron soundboard."

He shrugged. "Do you play?"

Marion rather felt he was avoiding her line of questioning but couldn't resist the chance to brag a little. "Yes, I do. I taught lessons before the kids were born. Actually, I thought I might do that again this spring."

Harry wore that slanted smile. It made him look at once both cocksure and impish. The kind of fellow who wouldn't think twice to ask a girl on a date and who'd laugh it off if she turned him down. It held no trace of that crotchety seriousness he'd exhibited in previous meetings. She wondered which was more authentic and immediately felt certain that the smile was something special.

"You should do that. Not enough people play anymore," Harry said and his smile grew almost wistful.

"Do you play?" Marion asked.

"Oh, no," he chuckled. "My fingers are too stubby." His eyes hovered on her hands.

"I could teach you a little something."

He shook his head, and she could have sworn his cheeks were a little red. "That's okay. If you're alright with the plan, I'll get things moving here."

"Thanks so much," Marion said uselessly as he shouldered the hoosier cabinet away from the wall. "Should I pull everything out of there?"

"No," he grunted. "I've got it."

"I don't want it to scratch the floor."

"It won't."

Marion felt relatively certain it would, but wasn't sure how to convince him otherwise. "At least let me help you move it."

"Not necessary," he grunted again as he picked up one end of the cabinet, swung it a foot or so out, and then set it down again. It appeared he intended to move it the entire way to the dining room in this manner. Marion lifted a brow and went to the other side of the hoosier. She lifted that end the same way before he could sidle round. It was heavy, but it wasn't anything she couldn't manage.

"Hey—" he started with a frown.

"No," Marion cut him off, "I am fairly confident that you do not normally move furniture as a carpenter, so since you are going above and beyond, I had better too."

"But—"

"Don't give me any of that outdated nonsense about

female constitutions. I fend for myself and I do just fine. If I can pick up my six-year-old, I can help move a cabinet. Besides, you made me accept your hot plate. It's only fair you accept my help too."

Harry studied her for a moment and then mumbled something that sounded a lot like "You're something else" before directing her in his full voice, "Alright, on the count of three."

Chapter 4

Mrs. Milner was something else. She helped Harry get the hoosier cabinet placed in the dining room, as well as rolling the piano into the living room in great heaves over linoleum samples to save the floor from getting scratched and then shifting the hutch to its place. She was strong, no doubt about it — Gerald couldn't have done better. It never occurred to him before, but it made sense. Lifting two rapidly growing children certainly had to count as weight training to some degree.

After all the moveable items from the kitchen had been squared away, Mrs. Milner set straight to sweeping all the dust and lost jacks and matchbox cars that had been revealed. When Harry returned from shoving the dining table under the bay window, she was on her hands and knees scrubbing at the floor with a wash rag. The way she curled round herself, with her hips up and her skirt draped over her rear end … oh, it sparked something in the pit of Harry's stomach that he immediately and very firmly smothered, averting his gaze well away before his more primal urges could manage to shame him.

"You really don't need to worry about that," Harry said as he busied himself clearing pans from the metal cabinet in her range. "We're putting down new linoleum."

"I know," Mrs. Milner replied. "It's just I won't be able

to unsee it until then. Besides, it's already done."

Harry dared to look back. The floor was shining, but all he could focus on was the perfect hourglass shape of her, sitting back on her heels. The way her shoulders sloped, the way her waist nipped in, the way her hips spread wide seated as she was on her knees. Oh, Jesus Christ. He'd need an extra-long confession if he kept going at this rate. He cleared his throat and asked, "Where do you want these pans?"

Mrs. Milner got to her feet in a very utilitarian, rather inelegant way and replied, "Oh, I don't know. There's no storage left to speak of."

Harry considered the pan in his hand. "I'll figure something out." If he was going to entertain dirty thoughts about a client, the least he could do was overcompensate as far as his industry knowledge could manage. He went to the dining room and set the two skillets and a soup pot on the dining table. He took a long breath in and applied himself to the task of making this temporary kitchen as efficient as he possibly could.

"You got a very nice house," Harry found himself saying as he shifted some dish towels aside in the bottom of the hutch to make space for the pans. The cocker spaniel was sitting on the floor next to the dining table and he swore the dog lifted a disdainful eyebrow at him. He grimaced.

"Thank you," Mrs. Milner replied easily. "It helps not having a husband to pick up after."

Harry was really not sure what to make of that. It hit him in three different ways at once: *I'm sure the kids are more than enough on their own; Not all men are lazy slobs;* and *So you don't want no husband, huh?* He took the latter to heart, shored up his finer feelings, and articulated the first.

"I'm sure the kids are more than enough on their own," he delivered rather well. "You have two, right?"

"Yes. My son is eight and my daughter is six," Mrs. Milner said, her voice growing clearer as she reentered the dining room. "Do you have any little ones?"

"No," Harry replied, not turning to face her. "I'm a bachelor."

"Ah, the good ol' days," Mrs. Milner sighed wistfully. "Enjoy it while you can, Harry."

He frowned. "It really ain't all it's cracked up to be."

There was a long silence in which it occurred to Harry that while Mrs. Milner had made a comment that had effectively conveyed she was uninterested in a partner, he'd very clearly articulated the opposite. He could feel his cheeks flush hot. He whirled on his feet and grimaced at her. "I'm very sorry, Mrs. Milner. I don't mean to take your time with my troubles—"

"—No, it's alright," she replied. She regarded him with a serene expression and a slight, curious tilt of the head. "I'm used to everyone being interested in my own troubles, so this is quite refreshing."

Harry pressed his lips together. He knew better than to take her words as *carte blanche* to talk about himself. But the curl of her lips sliding into a slow smile made him weak in his damn knees.

"My kids are going to be home soon," she said.

"Sorry, I'll get out of your hair—"

"—Oh, not that soon," she corrected. Harry's heart lurched for a moment and he watched her very carefully. "Do you want to have a cup of coffee before you go?"

Harry had a distinct feeling that their conversation was dancing over a whole bunch of different meanings, but he couldn't hash out what they were. He could reasonably imagine that she was being a gracious hostess, a sympathetic mother-figure, or coming onto him, all at the same time. And none of the options seemed particularly more or less likely than the others.

"Sure," he said warily.

Mrs. Milner was a very fine woman. If he'd met her on the street, he'd have asked her on a date immediately with no compunction. But he hadn't. She was a client. A particularly unusual one at that. Harry knew that there was a strange intimacy of working inside someone's house that made them act in all sorts of strange ways (usually of the variety of overcorrecting his work or otherwise patronizing him). So he sat down at the dining table covered in neat stacks of kitchenware and clutched the cup she'd given him tightly in his hands. He pointedly did not watch her crawl back on her hands and knees under the table to plug in his hot plate.

✶

It was about when Marion sat back on her heels after plugging in the hot plate that she recognized Harry's expression. His parted lips, pink cheeks, furtive eyes. He was interested in her. And despite the fact that he was a stranger and they were in her house all alone, she realized she had no scruples about it. In fact, she was rather flattered. It had been a long time since a man had looked at her like that. She'd forgotten what it felt like to be wanted and remembered just as suddenly how much she enjoyed it. Her greatest anxiety was whether anyone was walking by her bay window presently to see her rise from the feet of a strange man inside her house.

"Pardon me," Marion murmured as she got back to her feet. "I spend too much time with small children.

I sometimes forget what normal polite behavior should be."

Harry shrugged and averted his eyes. "Ain't no skin off my back."

Marion busied herself with the percolator, fumbling at the hoosier cabinet to get the beans ground before dashing into the kitchen to fill it with water. Once she returned to the dining table-turned-range, she turned the dial on the little electric hot plate and could not help but fill the silence.

"Oh, isn't that something," she exclaimed. "That heats up neat as a pin. Thank you so much for bringing that along. It will make everything that much easier. Is there a particular use they market it for?"

"I think Gerald usually tries to pitch it to bachelors and housewives keen on entertaining."

"The bachelors I understand," Marion replied, "but entertaining?"

"Yeah, so you can serve something hot and keep it hot on the dining table from the start of the party till the wee hours."

"Oh, I see," Marion said. "That is clever. So you don't do a lot of cooking, then?"

"No, I never learned."

"Lucky you," she drawled, then doubled back. "I mean, don't get me wrong, I enjoy cooking just fine. I love a hearty meal and it's fun to try new recipes from magazines and all. It's the cleanup I hate. The drudgery of dishes makes me rethink the whole endeavor. You know, when I was a child, I was confident that cooking and washing dishes was my mother's favorite thing to do. I would try to get her to play with me, but she never wanted to leave the kitchen. She's a good cook too, so I suppose she does love it, but goodness, she basically lived her whole adult life in her kitchen. I guess that's part of why I want to replace mine. If I'm going to live in it, I'd better like it, right?"

Marion risked a glance up at Harry as the percolator began to shudder with a boil. She expected his eyes to be bored and half-glazed over after that patented Marion Milner soliloquy, but they weren't.

"Hopefully, your new kitchen will give you enough efficiencies you don't have to spend all your time in there," Harry replied with that half smile. God, he could turn heads with that smile. Marion fumbled with the percolator and poured the coffee into the two cups.

"That would be ideal," she said feelingly, watching the steam come up off the surface of their cups.

"The drudgery of housekeeping is going to be a thing of the past," Harry asserted as he accepted his cup. "Things that used to take all day are going to take only a couple of hours. There's all sorts of new stuff coming out of G-E research and development that'll make as big an impact on the lives of housewives as the washing machine did for our mothers."

"Oh heavens, can you imagine? Washing all the laundry by hand? I could never."

"It's no wonder everyone used to send their laundry out."

"I would if I didn't have my machines."

"Do you have a clothes dryer?"

"Oh yes. It's sublime," Marion sighed.

"I'm stuck at the laundromat again. For now."

"Did you used to have a clothes dryer?"

"Before the war. I had — well, I had a lot of things before I joined up."

Marion tipped her head to the side and blew the steam from her cup. Too hot to drink. "Like what?"

Harry had keen blue eyes that sliced cleanly when he was focused. Marion was fascinated to see them blink hesitantly.

"A wife, I guess," he said finally with a sigh. "I'm, uh … newly divorced as well."

"Oh!" Marion almost dropped her cup. "I'm sorry, I shouldn't react like that. I hate it when people react like that. But, wow, I just didn't expect … Hm. Well. Congratulations, Mr. O'Conner."

Harry was taken aback for a moment. His lips parted. Then he said, "I — no one has ever said that to me before … Thank you."

"It's called a breakup because it's usually broken," Marion replied with a flick of her hand. "By the time folks go through with it, it's usually not something anyone would mourn losing. Not to say it isn't hard, of course it's terribly hard. But everyone always acts like it's the end of your life and it's not. It's a relief, in a lot of ways."

Harry nodded and leaned against his elbow on the table in a way that Marion's mother would have frowned deeply at, which made it entirely endearing to Marion. He shoved his thick hand through his coppery, close-ly-clipped hair.

"Was it the war that did the two of you in?" Marion asked, and then pressed her lips tightly together. "I'm sorry, it's rude to ask. You don't have to answer that."

"No, it's alright," Harry replied. "It was, in a way. I was gone, and she didn't end up missing me much. I sent a lot of unanswered letters."

"Oh, that's horrid," Marion exclaimed, hand on her chest. "A man goes to war and his wife can't even be bothered to write him back?"

Harry shrugged long-sufferingly. "She'd already met someone else by the time I finished up basic and got deployed. I fought in Korea a year and a half before I came back and found out she'd filed for divorce without me."

"Without telling you?!"

"Yeah. I was shut out from our church, too."

"Oh heavens to Betsy, because of a divorce?"

"I guess when you promise forever to the Catholics, they intend to punish you for going back on your word."

"Yes, but *you* didn't go back on your word. *She* did!"

"I know." He sighed. "St. Patrick's didn't see it that way. As far as they're concerned, I'm still married. I can't marry again in a Catholic church unless she dies."

"That's ridiculous. I'm fuming on your behalf." Marion tried to huffily take a sip of her coffee, but it was still too hot. She set the cup on the table.

"What about you?" Harry asked. "Did you have any troubles like that?"

"Not particularly. It would be different if my family were part of St. Stanislaus', but my father is a free-thinker, so our community is pretty much entirely the Sokol Hall."

Harry tipped his head to the side for a moment and paused. "So no church ... at all?"

Marion shrugged. "My mother was from a Catholic family and still goes to St. Stanislaus on Christmas and Easter, but generally, yes."

It appeared that the notion of not attending church at all hadn't occurred to him before. "Huh," he said, picking up his cup and taking a sip. He flinched.

"Don't burn your tongue," Marion chided and laughed, reaching to take the cup from his hand. Her fingers curled over his and he froze, his keen blue eyes cutting right through hers, like he could see inside her mind and scrape all her thoughts out with a spoon. They caught her breath in her chest, those eyes.

"Say, uh," Harry's voice sounded new; fresh and deep and velvety. It was like Marion was hearing it for the first time. "I hope I'm not being too forward or nothing, and please feel free to say no. If you aren't interested, it won't make any difference to the kitchen job. It's important to me to be professional. But I, um, I would like to take you out sometime. If you'd like to."

Marion's cheeks blazed hot. Her heart kicked in her chest. And she was reluctant to admit she felt a curl of pleasure unfurl between her legs at the suggestion of his interest. All this put her on her back foot enough that when she opened her mouth, a giggle exploded out of her.

"Oh, I, um, I'm sorry, that was horribly rude," she babbled, horrified. "That is to say, um, I don't think I can right now. It's not anything against you—you're very charming—I'm just not, well, in a position to be stepping out with anyone just yet."

Her face had to be bright, fire-engine red. Harry's was flushed too, come to think of it. Marion quickly snatched her hand away from his coffee cup and pushed her fingers together in her lap.

"It's the children," she nattered on, helpless to stop it. "They are only just beginning to understand what's going on and why their father's not here. And folks in the neighborhood will talk and then the school children will tease and I just — I can't let them get kicked around any more than they already have been. It's not easy to have divorced parents. I mean, you know how hard it is just being divorced. It's really not you, Harry. If it weren't for the kids, I'd love for you to take me out. You're very nice and handsome and—" *Oh god, oh god, oh god, shut up, Milner,* "—such. You don't need me to tell you. I'm sure there's plenty of girls out there who would like to be on your arm. Oh, god, I'm so sorry. I can't keep my mouth shut when I'm nervous and I don't want you to think I don't care about your feelings after all that you just told me —"

"That's alright," Harry cut her off mercifully. He shrugged. "It's just a date. Don't worry, I'm not so knocked around by life to take it hard if a gal ain't interested in dinner. Besides, it is an awkward situation."

Marion pressed her lips together to try and quell the onslaught. It didn't work. "Ask me again after the kitchen is done, okay?"

That half smile twitched up and it was a balm to her dignity to see it. "Okay."

✦

The rain was starting to turn to snow, pricking at Marion's skin as she stood on the corner of Michigan and Oneida Streets to wait for the school bus. She huddled against the dropping temperature in her green wool coat. After picking out linoleum in a catalog from Mr. O'Conner's satchel, he had departed with an easy, reassuring grin. Marion couldn't really get herself to think about anything else. God, what she'd give to be twenty again. Carefree and untethered, happy to walk out with whatever fellow seemed like he'd show her a good time. Instead, she'd married Joe and wasted her youth on an endless daily regime of cooking, dishes, and laundry. Marriage. What a gilded crock of dirty dishwater.

Marion was sure about one thing, though. Stepping out with Mr. O'Conner would be a grievous mistake. Even if he took her across town, she was sure it would somehow get back to the Sokol Ladies and then she'd be sunk. She'd get a reputation for being easy, her kids would get teased even more at school, and most devastating of all, her mother would probably disinvite her from Sunday dinners.

She was nervously picking at her fingernails as the school bus turned the corner and slowed to a stop before her. The door opened and down the steep steps hopped two children.

"Momma, I made a snowman today!" Linda crowed, waving a blue sheet of paper above her head as her dark braids flapped behind her.

"It's not a actual snowman," Charlie corrected. "It's a picture of a snowman."

Marion reached out and tried to take the paper Linda was waving in front of her. "Oh, this is wonderful, darling! We'll have to put it up on our new refrigerator when it comes."

"The green one from the picture?" Linda asked, bouncing onto her tiptoes. Marion nodded as she waited for the bus to drive away before herding the kids across the street toward home.

"The very same."

"When is it going to be here?" Charlie sighed. Since Joe had gone, her serious son had become positively stony.

"I'm not sure yet," Marion replied as easily as she could. "The handyman is coming tomorrow to put in the floor, then we'll have to wait until after Thanksgiving for him to be able to come back and start putting in the cabinets."

"Oh! Are we going to Grandmother's tomorrow?" Linda asked.

"Yes, you are," Marion smiled. Unlike Charlie, Linda had a laugh that could light up a room. Charlie doted on her. She was the only one who could pull a laugh out of him these days. It weighed on Marion, that she and Joe had done that to him.

"Will you come with us?" Charlie asked.

Marion sighed as she unlatched the picket fence that surrounded their postage-stamp sized backyard. "No, I can't. I have to be here to supervise the floor installation."

This was not necessarily true. In fact, Mr. O'Conner had told her to feel free to go elsewhere as he cut and glued and fitted the new tile. But the thought of spending the afternoon with her mother the day before Thanksgiving made her feel like she was going to crawl out of her skin. She'd be run ragged doing chores to prepare for the meal and get corrected with great forbearance every time her children did anything outside of what her mother thought they should be doing. Why would she do that when she could pull up a chair and chat with Mr. O'Conner while he worked? Watch his eyes linger on her and enjoy the attention? Not have to worry about where Charlie's laugh went or wonder whether Linda will develop some sort of complex from growing up without a consistent father figure? It shamed her to feel this way, but she couldn't help it. She so rarely felt sufficient. Was it so awful to steal a few hours to feel wanted?

"Marion!" It was Edna from across the street. Well, across the street from the side of the house. Having the corner lot, Marion had a lot of across-the-street neighbors, and to be honest, Edna was the best of them. She was a stout, no-nonsense mother of four boys and she resented Mrs. Dvorak's gossip almost as much as Marion did. "Do you want some of these Little Golden Books? I'm trying to clear space on Hector's bookshelf!"

Marion saw Linda's eyes light up and called back, "Oh for sure!"

Edna jogged across the street and proffered her literary offering over the fence. Linda pulled on Marion's skirt and craned up to see.

"Momma! *The Poky Little Puppy*!"

Marion just handed the whole stack to Linda, who was grappling for them anyway. "Thanks, Edna."

"No, thank *you*. I'm running out of space for all this kids' stuff. They just keep *growing*."

"You're telling me."

"How's your new kitchen coming?"

"Slow. I've got my little makeshift kitchen in the dining room now."

"Yes, I noticed that when I walked by. Where did you put the piano?"

Damned bay window. "In the living room."

"I always hate when the weather gets cold and we can't hear you playing all winter long."

Marion scoffed, shaking her head. "Oh, stop. I'm sure you're all just grateful for a little peace and quiet."

"What's that?" Edna quipped. As if on cue, two of her boys came tearing round from the backyard. One had a football under an arm and the other was yelling like a mad rebel before he tackled the elder to the ground.

"Mother, I'm cold," Charlie declared, standing on the step and waiting for Marion to come and unlock the door.

"Momma, will you read me the *Poky Little Puppy*?" Linda asked.

"Of course, I'll read it at bedtime," Marion replied. "Thank you, Edna!"

"My pleasure!" Edna strode back across the street. As she turned to her boys, her easy smile turned flat and she bellowed, "You stain those new trousers, John William, and I swear to the Holy Trinity I will end you!"

"Momma," Linda warbled. "I wanna read it now."

"Oh, honey," Marion said, squeezing her chubby little hand. "I have to make dinner. Charlie will read it to you."

As she walked up the steps, she was struck by yet another forgotten promise. Damn. She'd swore she'd make Mr. O'Conner dinners to go, but she'd been too busy flirting with him to put anything together. Now she was going to end up doing canned soup and grilled cheese again. Her mother would be horrified, but what she didn't know wouldn't hurt her.

Chapter 5

The next day dawned frigid cold and clear. Marion dropped Charlie and Linda off at her mother's bright and early huddled in their warmest coats. Her sister Evelyn's kids were there too, so she didn't feel too badly about not staying. When all the cousins were together, the children formed a veritable horde that required little to no supervision by virtue of the fact that they were so happy to have novel playmates. That done, Marion went back home, put on a record, and took her sweet time at her vanity, all the while murmuring to herself things she might say to Mr. O'Conner when he arrived at ten.

Marion had a green sweater that she scarcely ever wore because she thought it made her chest look too large. It would be unseemly to flaunt her bosom at Sokol events or at the playground with her children. But it was just a sweater. There was nothing inherently lewd about it. It covered her fully and while snug, it certainly wasn't so tight that the edges of her brassiere showed through or anything. Actually, it was very flattering. It emphasized the hourglass proportion between her bosom and waist. It just ... it made her feel a certain way, and that wasn't a way she wanted to feel in the presence of her children.

Judging from Mr. O'Conner's expression when she opened the door, the effect was not entirely in her head.

"Oh, wow," he said, then flushed a deep red. "You look, uh, nice."

Marion grinned indulgently. "What, this old thing?" She smoothed an invisible wrinkle in her pencil skirt like she was completely ignorant of the fact that it was the sweater doing all the work. "Thank you."

Over Mr. O'Conner's shoulder, Marion caught the flutter of a curtain in Mrs. Dvorak's window. Goddamn that spying little snake. "Come in, you'll catch your death out there." It wasn't that cold, but Marion hurried him in anyway, before Mrs. Dvorak could gather too much intelligence as to the degree to which Marion had primped before her extremely mundane and utterly unremarkable renovation work was scheduled to begin.

Mr. O'Conner stepped into the narrow vestibule and looked over his shoulder at her as he unwound his scarf. "What's the occasion?"

It was Marion's turn to flush. "Oh, you know, just trying on some things for Thanksgiving tomorrow, see what I feel my best in."

One side of his mouth twitched in amusement and his blue eyes narrowed appraisingly, but he didn't say anything. Incomprehensibly, this made her flush drop between her legs. Marion blinked and looked at her hands for a moment. She spun her bracelet on her wrist while she got a damn hold of herself. There was no shame in enjoying a little attention. The percolator, which she'd had the presence of mind to set on the hot plate in advance, roiled urgently.

"Coffee?" she squeaked and swept by him in a charade of breezy confidence, like she was well accustomed to turning heads.

"Yes, please," he replied and followed her into the living room, Milly at his heels. Marion busied herself at the hoosier cabinet, whose looming presence in the dining room she was still getting used to. She poured two cups of coffee and set them on saucers.

"Cream or sugar?" she called without looking up. She wasn't sure she could keep her cool if she met those eyes again.

"No thanks. I like it black."

"Oh, yes, that's right. Of course, I knew that." She glanced at him in spite of herself. He grinned as he sat back on the sofa and stretched his arms over the back, pulling his flannel shirt taut over his shoulders. Shoulders which were, well, noticeably *there*. She supposed she wasn't the only one who could exploit the merits of a tight shirt today. Marion was mortified to find herself staring and quickly averted her eyes to something more appropriate, like the little woven cornucopia she'd put on the table for a bit of fall festivity. Was it a bit phallic? How had she not noticed that before? Her face flushed as she fumbled the milk. She tried to duck her head to hide it as she quickly dropped sugar cubes and a slosh of milk into her own cup and carried the two saucers to the living room.

"So, how did you get into this line of business?" she asked as she set the two cups on the coffee table, then perched on the seat of the wingback armchair.

"Installing kitchens, you mean?" Mr. O'Conner leaned forward to take his cup. Marion silently grieved the loss of that delicious display of his arms and shoulders.

"Yes, I suppose so." She blew steam off the edge of her cup and wondered if he usually had social time with his clients before getting to work. Did the housewives on

Crocus Hill serve coffee to their hired laborers? What had seemed a matter of basic good manners was now tinged with uncertainty.

"Gerald pulled me in after I got back from Korea."

"That sure was nice of him. Did you have previous experience in construction?"

"A bit. My father is a cabinet maker. My brother and I grew up helping him with the business as soon as we were big enough to be of any use."

"That's so wholesome." Marion's lips curled up with amusement. His eyes dropped for a moment from her eyes to her mouth. Clocking the response set off a bloom of satisfaction in her gut. She crossed her legs and leaned against the arm of the chair to set the curve of her hip to its best advantage. "Do you work for GE or are you a contractor?"

"Technically a contractor, except I am on their payroll for the sales calls." He was looking into his cup with the same serious expression he'd had that first day when he measured her kitchen. "They only sell the appliances and cabinets. But most folks want some paint or flooring too, plumbing installed and all that, so it's helpful to have someone on hand who can make that happen instead of folks having to coordinate all of that as well. It's a bit of a hard sell, since these whole kitchen renovations take up so much time and make such a big mess, so having everything taken care of in a package deal helps Gerald make the sale."

"Does he make good money doing that?"

"I expect so. More than I do, anyway."

"What? That makes no sense. You're the one doing all the work."

Harry frowned. "No, Gerald does good work. He vouched for me, which was more than my old man was willing to do."

"Oh, I'm sorry. I didn't mean anything by it." Oh hell, he probably thought she was some sort of insipid gossip. Marion felt her flush go to her ears. She had to stop spending so much time with her sister and all the other Sokol ladies.

"I know." His eyes were kind, patient with her shallowness. He shrugged. "But any old ham can put glue on the floor. Getting people to trust you with their money and their home? That's a special skill."

"I guess. I was just much more willing to trust my home with Gerald when he had you with him. Don't tell him, but I didn't have any use for him — I already knew what I wanted and what I could afford. You came in with the practical knowledge that helped me see how it'd all come together."

"Well, thanks, that's very flattering." Milly nudged her head between his hand and his thigh. Marion was sort of strangely jealous as Harry stroked the dog's ears with his heavy hand. Not that she wanted to be on her knees next to him. *Oh heavens to Betsy, shut up.*

"I'll make sure to send a note to your boss." Marion laughed a bit too loudly and took a sip of coffee to steady herself. Watching him over the edge of her cup, she asked, "So, do your clients usually serve you coffee before you start work?"

His blue eyes looked up at her and slid over the curve of her hip momentarily before snapping back to her face. "Uh, no, not usually. I count myself lucky you're such a gracious hostess."

Marion grinned. His gaze was like a caress and it made her feel powerful. Strange how confirmation of his interest had put her more at ease with being alone in her house with a bachelor instead of less so. She decided not to interrogate that too deeply. "Thank you. I've got to get some practice in before my new kitchen makes my house the premiere dinner party location."

It had sounded amusing in her head, but the flippant response was more dismissive than flirtatious when she said it aloud. Mr. O'Conner looked into his coffee cup and gave it a wry smile.

"Well, thanks anyway," he said, setting the cup on the table. He gave a gruff sigh as he gently pushed the dog's head off his lap and stood. "I better get to it. We got a lot of tile to set today."

Marion hastened to her feet too. She felt like a boor. She didn't want Mr. O'Conner to think she was some sort of highfalutin social climber who scorned laborers to bolster her own self-importance, but that was sort of exactly how she'd sounded, wasn't it? She couldn't let him think that was what she was like. "How can I be of help?"

Startled, Mr. O'Conner regarded her with a puzzled expression. "You're paying me to do this work, so it don't make sense for you to help me."

"I suppose." Marion fiddled with a loose thread on the cuff of her sweater. "But what if I were … what if you were to teach me? Then I don't just get a new kitchen, but a bunch of knowledge and experience I can leverage to…" she laughed as her thoughts clicked into place, "to slowly put you out of a job if I need repairs in the future. In fact, the only person who is really losing out by letting me help is you."

"Hm." He blinked at her. That smile was teasing at the edges of his mouth again. "I'm definitely not going to undermine myself like that. I have every intention of making myself extremely useful to you for years to come."

Marion felt herself flush from her nose to her toes. He

grinned satisfactorily, and she couldn't help but grin back. "Oh, that is a good point. Well taken. In that case, I'll just find some laundry to fold. Please, carry on."

*

That. Green. Sweater.

Harry heaved a package of linoleum over his shoulder from the bed of his truck and tucked another one under his arm. He'd run early this morning because he was so eager to see her again, so he'd stopped off at the Tick Tock Diner for a breakfast sandwich and some much-needed self-upbraiding. It was embarrassing. He spent the last two years working on establishing his professional reputation, laying the groundwork for his own handyman business apart from Gerald and his father both. But apparently, all it took to throw a wrench in the whole thing was a glance from a pretty woman and he was blurting out an invitation for a date before he could even think better of it. He'd talked himself into a state of respectable professionalism over his breakfast at the cafe. He'd promised himself as he drove up to the Craftsman on the corner that he'd get straight to work this time and leave impulsive infatuation for younger, more foolish men. He'd really believed he could do it, too, until Mrs. Milner had opened the door in that goddamned green sweater.

While Harry had been convincing himself that the key takeaway from their flirtation yesterday was that she'd turned him down, he couldn't help but notice she'd been careful with her appearance. Her hair was set, her makeup pristine, and she'd dressed in painstaking compliment to her figure. She said she'd been trying on an outfit for

Thanksgiving, but that felt like a flimsy excuse. Was he entirely egotistical to imagine she'd worn it for him?

He stilled as he passed through the living room carrying the linoleum. Mrs. Milner was standing next to the sofa, folding miniature clothes from a basket on the coffee table and listening to a Dean Martin record. Her figure was lush, smooth curves enticingly flaunted by the snug stretch-knit. She might as well have worn a wiggle dress for all she was showing off her assets. (Maybe she would when he finally got the chance to buy her a proper dinner.)

Mrs. Milner turned and caught him staring. "Do you mind the music?" she asked. God, but she was a vision, even when folding laundry. A rippling knockout with a sly mouth. He suspected she was enjoying what the sight of her did to him.

"The Rat Pack's swell. It's nice to have something to listen to while I work."

She set the trousers she'd folded on the coffee table with a flicker of concern. "Oh, that looks heavy."

Harry straightened. Firmed up his hold on his load. "Not at all."

He strode into the dining room and dropped the linoleum on the floor with as much control as he could muster. He felt the heat of her gaze on his back. He imagined her hands on his shoulders, skimming over his arms like her eyes had done when he sat on the sofa earlier. He could enjoy what the sight of him did to her too.

Dean Martin continued to croon drunkenly while Harry dropped to a knee and sliced the linoleum packaging open. It was a honeycomb pattern, in a saturated golden yellow that would contrast brightly with the teal appliances she had chosen. Bold and stylish. Harry lifted a stack of tiles and went into the kitchen, dry fitting them roughly on the floor. He'd already laid plywood over the original floors to protect them from the glue, just in case Mrs. Milner ever decided to change her mind.

"Do you ever get bored?"

Harry looked up and saw Mrs. Milner hanging on the frame of the swinging kitchen door. He must have appeared puzzled because she clarified, "I mean, doing the work all by yourself. I spend a lot of time doing housework while the children are at school and sometimes by the time their bus comes, I think I might explode if I don't talk to another human being."

"I suppose I don't mind it," he replied, sitting back on his heels. "I like working with my hands."

Her eyes narrowed and she gave him that sly smile again. The one that felt like a challenge. He wished she would say it out loud: *I have some work for your hands to do.* He was grateful he was sitting down because he had several specific ideas of work his hands would like to do and all of them threatened to tent his overalls.

She didn't say it, though. She paused for a moment, her eyes casting over the tiles arranged roughly over the floor. Harry tried to clear his throat as inconspicuously as possible and said, "I like the honeycomb."

"Yes, I thought it might make it feel sort of like a beehive in here," she mused. "It's already as busy as one, at least when the children are home."

Harry had noticed the framed photograph of her children on the top of the piano in the living room. A girl and boy, both with the same round face and determined chin as their mother. Harry couldn't imagine their father. He couldn't imagine a man who would leave those adorable kids, or their headstrong mother.

"Do you like to talk, Mr. O'Conner?"

Harry refocused his eyes on her. "I suppose I do."

"I love to talk," she replied, her chin set. "Most people think I'd do better to be more considered with my words, but I find I don't quite know what I think if I don't say it aloud. Besides, quiet is overrated as far as I'm concerned. I'd much prefer a busy hive to an empty one."

She said these things in a flippant, conversational tone. But Harry could sense there was vulnerability behind them.

"Quiet is overrated," he agreed. "It doesn't just represent order and serenity. In my experience, quiet is often what comes after tragedy."

Mrs. Milner's expression softened. "Do you mean the war?"

He nodded.

"In Korea," he found himself saying, "the worst part wasn't the noise of the bombs. It was the quiet afterward."

It was definitely not the same thing as a quiet household. Harry feared he'd ruined the easy banter by bringing up the war. His eyes met hers. He thought he'd see discomfort there, but he didn't. He just saw himself, reflected in her dark eyes. He hoped she similarly saw herself reflected in his.

"What else do you have to get done today?" he asked, clearing his throat.

Mrs. Milner shrugged. "Not much. I was supposed to bake a pie for tomorrow, but now that my kitchen is out of commission, my sister is doing it."

"Why don't you pull up a chair?" Harry said as he pushed himself up to standing. "I don't need help with the work, but I wouldn't mind some company."

Chapter 6

Friday, November 25, 1955
23 days until the Christmas party

"How was your holiday?"

Two days later, Marion was sitting in a dining chair she'd placed near the doorway of the kitchen, her knitting needles clicking merrily away at a pair of mittens she was making for Charlie. The children had the day off of school on Friday as well, but Marion had managed to convince Evelyn that their brood of kids were actually less work when they were together and was again able to spend her day in blissful peace, chatting with Mr. O'Conner as he finished laying linoleum in her kitchen.

"Nothing too special," Harry said as he slicked the plywood with glue in a way that was misleadingly haphazard, given that the resulting application was so damn precise.

"Your family is Irish, right? O'Conner?"

"Yes. Christmas is the real to-do. Thanksgiving is more an excuse for my brother and dad and I to impose on my aunt's family for a bonafide home-cooked meal."

"Oh?" Marion's needles stilled as she sensed a need for care. "If I may ask, what happened to your mother?"

Harry shrugged and carefully set the linoleum tile in

perfect alignment with its neighbors. "She passed away when I was sixteen."

"Oh, I'm so sorry."

"Don't worry, it was a long time ago. Point is, none of us can cook, so we grab any opportunity for a good, old fashioned home-cooked meal." He chuckled. "My aunt was accommodating at first, but now she's just sick of us. Three hungry men added to her table? Even though it's just her family of four and us, she has to cook a meal for twelve. My brother can put away a whole chicken all on his own."

Marion laughed.

"'Course, we don't just eat and run. At least, not anymore. Aunt Mary put her foot down on that one. We get dish duty after everything's done, and I'll tell you what — Aunt Mary does not skimp on her pots and pans when she knows we're coming over. I thought she might just cook like that all the time, but my cousin said she's usually obsessing over using as few pans as possible. I want to say she pulls out all the stops for us, but I think she just enjoys making us work for our dinner."

Over the past few days, Marion had learned some things about Harry. She learned he was a stickler for details and that he took his time to get things right. She learned that he was patient and curious, eager to understand what made other people tick. But best of all, she learned that working with his hands made his words flow like water. He put on a nice show, pretending to be the strong, silent type, but once he got going, his chattiness gave Marion a run for her money. There was something deeply validating about that.

"Dishes are a *pain*," Marion said, flipping her needles as she started a new row. "If you told me as a young girl how much of my life I would spend doing dishes, I would have laughed in your face and called you a liar."

"Good thing you're getting a dishwasher."

"I am *counting the days*, Harry," she replied. He grinned up at her. She was experimenting with calling him by his first name today, and he seemed to be enjoying it just as much as she was.

"And your holiday?" he asked.

"Oh, you know, probably surprisingly similar to yours, actually. I got stuck with the dishes because I couldn't bring anything for the menu, but that was alright. I got the kids to do most of it. I just handled the pots and pans. I'll tell you what, baked-on turkey drippings are a *bitch* to get off." Marion's hands were occupied with knitting, but if they hadn't been, she would have clapped them over her mouth. "I'm sorry, pardon my French."

"You're right. It's a damned bitch," Harry replied with another haphazard squeeze of glue. Marion found herself grinning at him like a loon and wondering why on earth swearing like a couple of teenagers had her squeezing her thighs together. Him kneeling at her feet wasn't helping.

Some people, when they're discomfited, clam up. Marion was not one of those people. "Maybe when I get my dishwasher," she gushed into the thick silence, "I'll be able to convince my mother to let me host a Sunday dinner once in a while, and then they can all experience the high life for themselves."

Harry must have been picking up on the heat Marion was unwittingly generating. Why else would he bite his lip like that, if not to torture her?

"Of course," Marion went on, fumbling her stitches and finally setting the needles down in her lap before she dropped one, "knowing my family, as soon as I get a dishwasher, they're going to start in on how noble they are for not having one and how new-fangled appliances are for lazy housewives who don't know the value of hard work. My sister is constantly bragging about how little sleep she gets, how messy her house is even though it's pristine — you know, just how much more difficult but also more successful her life is than everyone else's. I swear, she could turn a bunion into a trophy."

Oh, there she went. Her mouth tensed, and she watched Harry carefully for some indication of his disapproval. He did frown at her, but when he spoke, he said, "That sounds awful."

"I'm sorry, I know I shouldn't talk like that about my sister—"

"No, I mean, that sounds awful to listen to. Suffering isn't a competition." He sat back on his heels and cocked his head back, studying her down the line of his nose. "You shouldn't have to feel bad about trying to make your own life easier. No one gets a medal for being miserable."

Marion still sort of wished she could shrink into her shoulders like a turtle into its shell. She nodded slowly and let out the breath she hadn't realized she was holding. "We sure as hell know that better than most." She sighed and was grateful for the back of her chair. "Sometimes I can't stand her. Her husband follows her around like a dog and just dotes on her. Brings her gifts for no reason. Compliments her, even when she's on a rant about how inadequate he is. She doesn't understand how good she's got it."

Harry's hands stilled. "I don't know. I ain't got no kids, but I know what you mean about folks taking their partners for granted. Sometimes I just want to box their ears and tell them to get their heads out their own asses. Look up and see what they've got in front of them."

Marion laughed because if she didn't, she thought she

might cry. And that would be extremely not cute and she very much wanted Harry to continue to regard her as cute.

"You're pretty swell," she said. "You know that?"

Harry grinned. "I do now."

*

"I'm so sorry I let you leave without dinner yesterday," Mrs. Milner said as she toasted grilled cheese over the hot plate. It was idiotic how gratifying it was to watch her use it.

"Not to worry, Mrs. Milner," Harry shrugged off from his seat at the side of the dining table-cum-kitchen counter.

"Oh no, you can't call me that anymore. It makes me sound like my ex-mother-in-law. It's high time you just call me Marion."

Harry's mouth quirked up into a smile. "Okay. Marion." It felt nice on his tongue. He sat a little straighter, growing increasingly confident of his post-kitchen renovation date.

"Well, what did you end up eating?"

"Oh, Oscar Mayer saved the day."

"You had a bologna sandwich?" Marion crumpled. "Now I feel even worse."

"Hey, bologna is delicious and nutritious," Harry argued. "But I actually had a Coney dog at the bar near my apartment."

"That doesn't make me feel much better." Marion flipped the sandwich and then turned for a moment to butter the bread for the next one. The cooked surface was a glistening golden brown. "Not that I'm proving much with grilled cheese sandwiches."

"I love grilled cheese sandwiches."

"That's the spirit!"

"Who doesn't love grilled cheese sandwiches?"

"My mother, for one, but she was born in Europe and has a very particular understanding of what constitutes an actual dinner. She'd be horrified that you consider a hotdog a meal."

Harry shrugged. "My mother wasn't like that. Of course, her family had been in America for a few generations, but regardless, she wasn't much for cooking. She made it into a mindless routine. Corned beef Monday. Pork and potato Tuesday. Shepherd's Pie Wednesday. She would have loved the new deep freezers they have now. She would have made monstrous servings of it all and pulled out pre-prepared meals all month."

Marion smiled feelingly at him. "Food is important, but it isn't everything."

"It's wild, because now I have these very strong food memories around things like canned beans and tough meat. The Depression wasn't kind to our family, but even when it was over, she still would buy just the worst meat."

Marion laughed, then abruptly sniffed the air like a hound. "Shit."

"Uh oh, the French are back."

"Sorry, I burned it. That always happens, I swear, I stand here and stare at it and check it every minute and then it just catches the moment I think I've got it figured out this time." She slipped the sandwich onto a plate. It was black all around the edges. "Here, I'll eat that one. This one—" she shook a finger as she scooped up the buttered bread waiting on deck, "—*this one* is gonna make it."

Harry leaned forward and slid the plate with the burned sandwich towards himself.

"Harry, come on, it's burned."

"I like burned stuff, remember? Burned, tough, flavorless food. It's nostalgic for me. You wouldn't cheat me out of a bit of nostalgia, would you?"

Marion laughed. "No, I suppose not."

After lunch, Harry got back to systematically laying tiles. Marion sat and chatted with him a bit longer, but after a while she wandered off to tidy the house and give all the rugs a once-over with the carpet sweeper. After perhaps a half hour, he heard a few plunks on the piano.

He stopped what he was doing and sat up to listen. The plunks turned into a couple of jaunty chords, which turned into a polka. He wondered if Marion had one of those fetching traditional costumes some of the Sokol ladies wore in the fall at their harvest festival.

The polka transitioned into a piece that cascaded the minor melancholies of an Eastern European composition. It was dynamic, soft and tender, then loud and insistent, and if Marion thought he wasn't going to stop what he was doing to walk through the dining room and listen, she had another thing coming.

She noticed him after a minute, crossing his arms and leaning against the built-ins that separated the dining room from the sitting room. She smiled as her fingers raced down the keyboard on her upright piano. She didn't even need to look at the keys. Harry's mouth turned up into an astonished smile. Marion preened under his attention and turned back to the keys as another movement of demanding, dramatic-tension-filled music reverberated off the soundboard. When the piece turned soft again, he said, "What is this?"

"Dvořák, of course," she replied, both hands crawling

in utter opposition up and down the board as if it were the easiest thing in the world. "The natural choice for a good Czech girl."

Harry did a damn good job, he thought, of not audibly choking. It helped that she had reached a crescendo. He generally thought of himself as a thoughtful, temperate man. He was tidy, organized, respectful, and gracious. But goddamn, that comment fed something in him that was just the opposite of temperate and measured.

"Ooh, that's a dark expression," Marion chided, her hands slowing to a gentle interlude. "You look like Brando in Streetcar or something."

He felt like Brando in Streetcar. It was terrifying, because Brando was a monster in that film. He forced himself to look at something innocuous, like the elderly cocker spaniel sprawled at Marion's feet.

"A perfect expression for Dvořák," she added with a flourish, her chords coming to a satisfying resolution. She withdrew her agile fingers from the keyboard and set them gently in her lap.

"What do you mean?"

"Oh, you know, dark and broody. He's not a Russian by any means — heaven knows those composers would like nothing better than to suffer — but of that ilk."

Harry couldn't help but laugh. "Me? Dark and broody? With this hair?"

Marion grinned. "Well, red and broody then. Bright and broody? Hm."

"A clown haunts the desolate moors looking for his long lost love," he intoned.

"No," Marion considered, standing. "Not a clown at all. A Highland warrior, maybe?"

Harry snorted — that was patently ridiculous. "I'm Irish, not Scottish."

"Same difference."

"How *dare* you?"

Marion burst into a laugh that seemed to propel her right back onto the piano seat with its force. "My apologies for my ignorance."

"Damn right," Harry muttered. His feet were drawn to her, so he walked to her side and plunked one of the lower keys. "How long have you been playing?"

"Oh, forever," Marion waved dismissively. "It was the only thing Evelyn didn't excel at, so I did it to spite her."

Harry frowned. "I don't think someone gets this good at piano just on spite."

Marion shrugged. "No," she sighed, "I do love it. It's just hard to love anything around my mother."

She glanced up at him. "I'm sorry, that's such a ratty thing to say. I love my mother. And she loves me too. She helps me practically every day, with the children and my house and the endless fallout from my divorce. But I … I'm kidding myself if I said she respects me."

Harry tilted his head towards her, leaning a bit on the piano. He wasn't sure what to say, so he waited. When she looked up at him, her brown eyes were round and a little defeated.

"I think…" she said, "I think she's fearful. Most of the time. Fearful that the other foot will fall, that something bad will happen. Fearful that if left to my own devices, I'll mess up my life or my kids even worse. So she steps in, takes control, tries to protect me from myself. But I … I don't really think I'm in jeopardy in the first place, you know?"

Harry nodded. "My dad's like that too." He lowered himself to the piano bench and Marion shuffled over to make space for him. His shoulder and thigh pressed against hers. "I think that happens sometimes. When someone's been hurt. They get scared. Try to protect others from hurting themselves the same way."

Marion nodded and nudged the old spaniel with her foot. The dog grunted in its sleep, but made no other response. "My dad should be that way, too. He was in France during the war, saw all sorts of misery. But I feel like he's the only one in the family who *doesn't* get all worked up trying to control everything."

"Control makes a hard sell," Harry mused. "It makes a lot of promises. It feels good, safe somehow."

Marion nodded, and the back of her hand nudged against his knuckles. "I'm beginning to wonder if it's all snake oil, though."

"Control?"

"Yeah. Or maybe I just want it to be, because I can't seem to hang on to it no matter how hard I try."

Harry distantly wondered how they'd ended up exchanging such personal truths when he was supposed to be finishing a linoleum floor. Probably because of his own lack of control when it came to Marion Milner. He wanted to tell her that she was wrong, that she had everything well in hand. Money, a home, her family. But despite how drawn to her he felt, how natural it was to talk to her, the fact was that he barely knew her. He had only the barest of notions where this talk was even coming from. And it felt dismissive, somehow, to reassure her.

So he just nudged her and said, "Guess that's why they say we can't let perfect be the enemy of good."

Platitudes. Wonderful.

"Guess so," she hummed. Her pinkie finger hooked round his. Harry cast a startled glance down at their joined hands. When he looked up again, his face was warm enough that he felt compelled to pull at his collar.

He glanced at the clock.

"I should, ah, get back to it. I want to get this floor done and out of your hair before your kids get home."

Marion's finger slipped away from his. "Yeah, thank you." She shook her head and stood resolutely. "I'm going to make sure you leave with a real dinner this time."

She marched off to the makeshift kitchen and pulled open the hoosier cabinet. "How do you feel about boiled potatoes?"

Harry stood and carefully pulled the fallboard back over the piano keys. "Excellent, like a good Irish boy."

It was satisfying to see the turn of phrase make her flush just as red.

Chapter 7

Thursday, December 1, 1955
16 days until the Christmas party

The cabinets came in the next week. Harry met the delivery truck at Mrs. Milner's house bright and early on Monday morning. She pressed herself against the wall and watched with a spark in her eyes as Harry and the delivery boy carried the pieces inside one by one through the front door. The pieces fitted into an L-shaped counter configuration with lowers and uppers, then there was another set of uppers that would go above the fridge on a third wall. All of the prefabricated metal cabinets were the same turquoise green that the appliances would be with a glossy shine that contrasted well against the golden honeycomb floor tiles. It was a bold choice, but the pieces sang together. Harry had the delivery boy help him place all the lower cabinets in a rough dry fit before letting him be on his way. Marion tipped the boy generously on his way out.

Harry was shoving the sink module up against the wall when her voice unwittingly turned his head.

"Oh my goodness, Harry," she purred. She had one hand on the doorframe and was admiring the turquoise cabinets arrayed in bold uniform along the wall. "This is incredible. Wow!"

Harry grinned at her, then stepped back to admire the effect. "It's pretty bold."

"I love it." She pressed her lips together and wiggled. "I love it!"

Harry loved it too, mostly because it made her smile like that.

Installation was a tedious business, but Marion kept him company as he systematically shimmed everything square cabinet by cabinet and used his electric drill to set screws into the plaster and lathe. Usually, she sat in a dining chair on the kitchen threshold, but today she was hovering, running her hands over the glossy enamel like she was trying to convince herself it was real. He drank in her smiles like fuel against the tedious task of fitting square, prefab cabinets into a decidedly not-square space.

"Where do you think everything should go for maximum efficiency?" Marion mused as he laid awkwardly under the sink, pipe wrench at the ready to reattach the drain pipe to the new sink drain.

"What do you mean?" he grunted as he shimmied himself deeper into the cabinet.

"Oh, just where the dishes are going to go and that," she murmured. He could see her toe tapping on the new linoleum near his feet. "You're so good at figuring that stuff out, though I can't figure out why, since you don't even cook. I suppose the uppers over here would be the best spot, since they'll be closest to the dishwasher and it'll be easier to put everything away."

Harry positioned the fitting at the base of the sink and juggled the pipe wrench precariously one-handed.

"But then the serving platters should be by the range, so that when something is done cooking, I can grab the platter easily. Maybe in the uppers, then the pots in the lowers."

Harry couldn't see her face but he imagined she was tapping her pointed chin with one long finger. He grunted as he got the fitting in place and felt its threads catch smoothly.

"I'm going to need a spice rack. Say — what are you doing down there? Wrestling a Kraken?"

"Not. Quite," he ground out and wrenched the fitting snug. "Water's all hooked up and the drain should be good to go." He shimmied out of the cabinet. When Marion came into full view, she smiled and offered her hand to pull him up. He gratefully accepted it. It was soft and smooth, slightly chilled. She did little to physically pull his greater weight to standing, but her grip was steadying, her touch exceedingly welcome. On his feet, his hand lingered on hers as he met her eyes. "Are you cold?"

"Maybe a little," she admitted. She glanced down at his hand in hers. "Are you overwarm?"

Harry snatched his hand sheepishly away and wiped it on his overalls. "No. I'm just fine." He did have sweaty palms. But it wasn't because of the room's temperature, or even that he was applying himself to a bit of hard work. It was *her*. She made him sweat just by being in the same room. And he was letting himself enjoy it.

Harry had done installs at the homes of attractive housewives before. Good-looking girls weren't a rare commodity in the city. But Marion Milner was on another level. She was pretty, but she was also funny, sharp, and most importantly, she got it. She understood what it was to be lost in the empty promise of the American Dream. And while Harry had spent the last two years focused on working and systematically ignoring opportunities that might result in him getting a date, he was not anxious or wary of Marion. She was a breath of fresh air. She reminded him how much less lonely those last two years could have been, if she'd been around.

After Harry successfully tested the sink, Marion offered to make coffee and serve some cookies she'd got from the upstairs neighbor who'd taken pity on the sorry state of her makeshift kitchen. Harry gratefully took a seat at the dining table and wolfed down several lemon shortbread cookies and a cup of coffee while Marion talked endlessly about the different kinds of baking she was going to try when she got her new oven. It was like being nestled comfortably inside her mind as she thought aloud. Cookies, of course, but also pies, cakes, and maybe she'd even give souffle a go. She had the latest addition of the *Joy of Cooking* open on the table.

"That cookbook gets bigger and bigger every edition," Harry pointed out as he thumbed crumbs from the edges of his mouth.

"Did you ever try learning to cook?" Marion asked as she paged through the desserts chapter.

"Nah, I never had to," Harry said. "At least, not before I got back from Korea. My mom cooked, such as it was, and after she passed, Alice did it."

"Who?"

"My ex-wife." The word cut starkly through the companionable conversation and Harry regretted saying it as soon as it left his mouth.

Marion recovered quickly. "Oh, that's right. I didn't know her name."

Harry studied her, looking for any traces of discomfort or resentment and was forced to acknowledge that he very much wanted her to be envious. He wanted her to wish that he was hers and hers alone. The way her brown eyes met his, he could imagine she might want that. But he just couldn't be sure. Something was holding her back. He experimentally lifted his hand and started to reach towards hers.

"Do you regret getting married?" she blurted.

His hand froze halfway. Harry was so startled by the question that brutal honesty slipped out. "Yes."

"Oh…" Marion flushed. "I'm sorry. That's a ratty question."

"It's alright," he said and realized he meant it. It would have been an infuriating question coming from anyone else, but Marion… Out of anyone he knew, she would understand this. "I don't regret meeting Alice or falling for her. But I do regret marrying her before I left for basic. I was … my mother died when I was sixteen. Alice was the one who scraped my ornery ass off the floor and got me back on my feet again. I repaid her by enlisting as soon as I was old enough. But then, even as I was trying to run away, I didn't want to let Alice go, so I convinced her to marry me. And I wish I hadn't."

"I can understand that." Her voice was quiet, as though the Craftsman beams that crossed her dining room ceiling were the arch of a nave, worthy of reverence.

"It was selfish." Maybe it was like a church. Because like it or not, he was confessing. "The worst part is that she didn't tell me. I couldn't understand why she didn't tell me. For a long time, I thought she just didn't care, but I think she was afraid to hurt me. I wasn't at my best when I knew her. I'd lost my mother and I was really angry. All the time. I couldn't have been much fun to be around. And I regret that, I think, most of all…" He looked up hopefully at her the same way he might look for a benediction at confession. Her dark eyes glinted, at once both sad and reflecting his hopefulness. "What about you?"

"What?" She blinked.

"Do you regret getting married?"

"Of course not. If I never got married, I wouldn't have my kids." She smiled, but her eyes flickered away.

"Of course." Harry found the dog's head on his knee and gave her a good scratch. "But if you could guarantee that they would be there, if you could go back, would you do it again?"

Marion thought for a moment. "No. No, I don't think I would." She shrugged. "I don't know. Joe is a decent guy. I don't hold a grudge."

Harry didn't think the way the name of Marion's ex-husband rankled him was jealousy. He just felt very keenly that the man was an idiot. "He seems like he feels plenty guilty about something."

"What makes you say that?"

"Sorry, I don't mean to assume. I just thought since he seemed to settle a good amount of cash on you…" Harry curled his fingers in the fur of the cocker spaniel and tried not to shrink in on himself as he watched Marion carefully to track how badly he'd offended her.

"Oh. Yes. He does. Feel guilty, that is." Marion shrugged. Her face was remarkably placid. "But it makes sense. I don't know. The writing was on the wall for a long time now. Since my daughter was born, really."

"How long is that?"

She sighed. "Six years. Maybe more. Linda might have been our sort of last attempt to make it work."

"If I may ask, what went wrong?"

Marion twisted her mouth. "Well … we just didn't want the same things."

"Like what?" It was remarkable how easy it felt to be so outrageously familiar.

Marion spun her coffee cup in her hands. "Well …

Don't get me wrong, okay, he's a good father. But he was — well, is — very clinical and rational in the way he thinks. The children's behavior makes no sense to him, especially when they're upset. And as for me … well, I'm not sure I even know what I want, really. I suppose that's my downfall."

Harry gathered up his guts and reached across the table to press his hand into hers. "I think I know how that feels."

Marion gave a wry, sad smile. "Yeah. Mostly shitty."

He huffed a sardonic laugh. "That's exactly the word."

"Oh, Jesus!"

Marion jumped up from the table and snatched her hand to her chest. Harry's eyes darted up, following her gaze out the dining room window. There, just a few feet from the other side of the glass was an older woman strolling by on the sidewalk. Looking directly into Marion's dining room.

"Hello, Mrs. Dvorak!" Marion called loudly, giving an awkward wave. The woman made a show of looking startled, like she hadn't realized Marion was inside of her house living her life. Like her dining room window wasn't actually a shop window for her perusal.

"Mrs. Milner, good afternoon!" came the muffled reply. Much too distinct for Harry's comfort. Marion kept a plastic grin on her face and watched Mrs. Dvorak make her way out of the bay window's frame of view. As soon as that happened, Marion collapsed back in her chair with a huff.

"I didn't realize people passed so close by," Harry said, leaning forward to see if anyone else was peeping into the windows.

"Yes. I thought it was charming when we first moved in. I'd open my window and call out to people and we'd chat. But Mrs. Dvorak is … well, she's very nice, but she is a busybody and seems to especially enjoy digging into my business."

Harry's mouth curled. "You? Why?"

Marion shrugged helplessly. "Because I'm the divorcee. I'm an anomaly. I guess she finds me morbidly fascinating."

"The Blob is morbidly fascinating. People's lives are not entertainment."

Marion shrugged. "She's probably just trying to get a glimpse of the kitchen. Which she will have ample opportunity to do during the Sokol Ladies Christmas party, the nosy old biddy." She glanced at Harry furtively. "Sorry. I didn't —"

Harry shrugged. "If she's made a habit of airing other people's business for entertainment, I'm sure you haven't even scratched the surface of the gossip she deserves." He stood up and straightened his tool belt. "Let's get back to work, shall we?"

Hanging the upper cabinets was significantly more difficult than the lowers. Harry resigned himself to asking Marion for her help holding the cabinets level while he got the first couple screws in place.

"You know what I don't get about marriage these days?" Marion was saying as she easily shouldered the corner of a cabinet. Harry was perched precariously on the bare top of the lower cabinet, holding the other corner with his knee while he drilled a screw into the upper left.

"What?" he grunted.

"I don't understand how it's all love and romance and then boom! You get into the house and it's just laundry and dishes and cooking and 'yes darling.' Is that what we're supposed to all be longing for?"

"I mean, a house to take care of is the best kind of investment. It's the American Dream."

"I know. Don't get me wrong, this house was a dream when we first moved in. It still is. But shouldn't couples want to take care of it together?"

"Don't they?" He pushed another screw into the wall with a whirr of his drill.

"I don't know. Ope — the level's off, hold on." She shifted her corner minutely as Harry steadied his knee. "Got it. I just didn't have that experience with Joe. This house was his grandmother's and he didn't want to change *anything* about it. He wanted it to be the same as when he was a kid. So I got stuck having to do everything just so and not getting a chance to make it my own. I mean, I've been more domestic with you than I ever was with Joe." She laughed like it was a hilarious joke, but it faded as she looked up at him through those goddamn lashes. She'd done her makeup again today. She hadn't trotted the green sweater out again, but she was a vision nonetheless in a button-up shirt-dress in a shade of red that made her hair shine. It occurred to Harry that she was right. They were being entirely domestic. Almost without thinking. It was seamless, effortless, the way they cooperated.

"Go on," Marion chided. "This is heavy."

Hell, he must have been staring. Harry snapped his eyes back on the cabinet, back to the job at hand and pushed another screw in with his drill. When the cabinet was installed, Harry awkwardly climbed down from the countertop. Marion reached up and took his hand as he hopped to the floor. This time, he held on without hesitation. It took the barest tilt of his wrist to draw her closer to him.

"Marion," he said, enjoying the taste of her name on his

tongue. She stood mere inches from him, but there was no trace of anxiety or hesitation in her expression. Just open curiosity, an air of charged energy.

"I want …" Harry began, but his voice was rough and cracked. "I wish I could —"

Marion smirked, her coal-dark lashes dusting her cheeks. "Kiss me?" she supplied.

"Oh! Uh, yes. I was gonna say take you out but that, um. Yes. *Yes.*"

Her lush lips curved into a smile. "Then kiss me."

It wasn't a question. It was a command. And Harry wasn't the kind of fellow who needed to be told twice.

✦

In Marion's experience, kissing had always been a craning, tip-toes affair. Not so with Harry O'Conner. He was taller than her, but only by an inch or two. It took very little, just the tip of her chin and the raise of her heels an inch off the floor and his mouth was on hers. Five o'clock shadow scraping her cheek, breath hot on her skin. She couldn't remember the last time she'd done something that felt this *good.* She brought her hands up and pulled him nearer by his ridiculous overalls, pressing her chest flush to his and twisting her face to the side to kiss him deeper.

Goddamn, she'd been thinking about this all week. Thoughts of Harry O'Conner reclining on her couch, or holding her hand, systematically mastering the chaos of her house into the kitchen of her dreams one linoleum tile and construction screw at a time. She'd been awake at three in the morning again when she finally resolved to kiss him. Why did they have to wait until the kitchen was done to go on a date? If the purpose of a date was to get to know one another better, they had already been on at least three dates and Marion was definitely a kiss-on-the-third-date kind of girl. Well, she'd only ever dated Joe, so her experience was admittedly limited, but she fancied herself as such regardless. Regardless, they were spending a lot of time together, and it was obvious they both would enjoy it. Besides, where had doing the proper thing gotten her up until now? Feeling miserable and worthless, the butt of everyone's joke. Why couldn't she do as she pleased for once? Unlike the dining room, there was ample privacy in the kitchen. If no one would know anyway, why not kiss?

Harry's callused fingertips gripped the back of her neck. Breath hissed between them and Marion couldn't tell where his ended and hers began. His mouth was hot, his lips open and drinking her in. This was not the long, hard kisses from the movies. It was active, working and moving, increasingly filled with teeth and tongues. Oh God, Marion had never been kissed like this before. What on earth had she been missing? She melted into Harry and he wrapped one of his thick arms around her waist as she clung to his overalls.

She had the notion she might be intimidated by her own inexperience. (Which made no sense, because she'd had two children for heaven's sake. She knew what it was all about.) But she was also overwhelmed by a sense of reckless defiance. Her usually urgent concern for propriety was sliding off the edge of her mind. It was easy to dismiss any anxiety out of hand because Harry's hand was on her hip now and he tasted like coffee and lemon shortbread and cream and there were a thousand sensations sparking from every inch of her he touched.

"Marion," he rumbled as he pressed kisses along her

jaw. "God, I've been thinking about this for a week. Since you wore that damned sweater."

She grinned and tipped her head back. He licked firmly down the length of her neck and she gave a involuntarily sigh as her toes curled. God, he was bold. "I'm glad you liked it."

"I loved it," he replied with a nip to her clavicle. "I like everything you wear. You're a knock-out, you know that, right?"

She veritably preened. The skin around her mouth smarted with sensation, part from being rubbed by his stubble, part from being whetted by his kiss. Oh, but this felt so damn good. If she could bottle this energy, she'd distill it and drink it whenever a Sokol event or Sunday dinner came up. She felt so powerful in her indulgence. Her pulse thrummed between her legs and she felt heat roll through her, sensitizing her skin and clouding her thoughts. Her bed was just in the next room. What could be the harm of a little necking? No one needed to know. His teeth worried her earlobe, his tongue flicking against it. *Oh my God*. She yanked at his overalls. "Oh, God dammit, I didn't know how much I needed this, Harry. It's been too long."

It was a bold, wanton thing to say. She felt an edge of anxious tension as she slid her hands down over Harry's broad chest and gripped his hips. She pressed herself into him and felt his hard interest in response. It almost made her choke in relief.

"How long?" Harry growled, nosing her hair out of the way to scrape his teeth along the shell of her ear.

Marion whimpered. "I told you. Since my daughter."

Harry started. "Six years?"

Marion had the presence of mind to wonder if she should be embarrassed. "Yes?"

"Since … what exactly?" He tucked his chin enough to pin her with those sharp blue eyes.

Marion squirmed. "Since I've been with anyone."

His eyes widened, but not so much surprised as intrigued. "Oh." He cleared his throat and stepped back the barest of inches, but it was enough that her hips grieved the loss of contact with his. "I, um…"

A sense of timelessness fell over Marion in that moment and for some reason — perhaps it was because of this insidious recklessness that had seized upon her, or perhaps it was because he'd seen so much of the same things she had — she didn't choke down what she really thought in favor of saying whatever she thought he'd most like to hear.

"Look," she blurted, "just because it's been a long time for me doesn't mean that I'm virginal or something and I need to be handled with care. I've had two kids. I've already been thoroughly corrupted."

A sly, crooked half smile curled his lips. "Thoroughly?"

Marion flushed. "Well, maybe not thoroughly. I imagine there are many frontiers I haven't explored yet. But I'm no stranger to the … uh … more intimate dealings between men and women."

"No, I don't think you are." His lip curled beguilingly. "I bet you like it."

"What?"

"Fucking."

God, he was so crass. His voice was like gravel and his eyes were drinking her in like water. And he was parched. Hell, *she* was parched.

"Yes," she breathed, looking up at him quite openly. She couldn't believe she was saying this. "I do."

His fingers gripped her waist as he stared at her. He started to dip his chin forward, but then he snatched himself back and groaned. "God, Marion, you're so sexy. Shit."

"What's wrong?"

"I just — I want to do right by you," he said and his eyes bored into her like he meant every word. "I want it to be good and right and I want… Well, I want to take you out. Buy you dinner like a gentleman."

"You don't need to buy me dinner to be a gentleman." To hell with good and right.

"But I want to. I would want to show you that I can be civilized before I, you know, took you to bed."

A sound escaped Marion's throat unbidden and she had the grace to blush. "But we'd have to wait until the kitchen is done to step out together. People would talk if they knew I was interested in the man I had working in my house all day. And I … I don't want to wait that long."

"You've waited a long time," he agreed. A flicker of mischief played at the corners of his eyes as his hand skimmed up her arm and over her shoulder. "You can wait a little bit longer, can't you?"

"Harry, goddammit!" she swatted at him. "What are you trying to do, torture me?"

"Maybe? Depends. Do you like that sort of thing?"

Marion didn't know from experience, but judging from the wetness slicking her panties, she suspected the answer was yes. "No! I like immediate satisfaction. Preferably with a live, human man whom I can trust and not my own damn hand." Oh God, she was precisely the harlot divorced women were made out to be. But she still just couldn't make herself care.

"I don't know. The hand sounds pretty good."

Marion regarded him with an incredulous expression. Harry shrugged. "I dunno. I think I'd enjoy watching that."

Her cheeks flushed a bright red at the idea. Jesus Christ … Could they do that? Could they do that *now?*

It was at that very unfortunate moment that the grandfather clock in the living room chimed three. Marion tipped her head back and groaned lamentably.

"Noooooo."

"Is it really that late already?" Harry studied his wristwatch skeptically.

"Harry, you have to go, I have to pick up the kids," Marion whined even as she continued to clutch his overalls.

His mouth was set in a hard line, but he pulled her very purposefully towards him and planted a chaste kiss to her lips. "Don't worry. I'll see you tomorrow."

Marion sighed. "No, you won't, remember? I have to volunteer at the Sokol Christmas pastry sale."

"Oh, that's right," he replied. He kissed her again, this time more deeply. "Okay, Monday then."

"Yes," Marion breathed, tipping her head so that their foreheads touched. "Monday."

Chapter 8

Friday, December 2, 1955
15 days until the Christmas party

The first thing Marion thought the next day when she woke up was, *What have I done?* She'd never said or done anything like what she'd allowed to transpire with Harry the previous day. Not in her life had she ever thrown herself at a man like that. If people found out, *hell* — she'd have to move to a new county. Maybe another state.

Routine carried her through the morning, enough to see the children off on the school bus and to do the washing up and a load of laundry. The Sokol Koláče sale would open at 2 pm and Marion, not having an oven to contribute four dozen pastries, had been volunteered to coordinate the set-up starting at noon. She planned to get the sale kicked off, nip out to fetch the children from the bus, and bring them back to join the fun. The fire of that reckless energy she'd sailed upon yesterday had subsided and without it, she was furtive and anxious. Regardless, she had no choice but to perform her duties to the T and show everyone that a woman didn't need a husband to be an exemplary philanthropist and dutiful mother. The key was to stop getting distracted by thoughts of Harry.

As Marion stood in the half-finished kitchen with a

basket of clean laundry, staring at the spot where Harry had kissed her, she realized putting him out of her mind was a much taller order than she had previously thought. She brought the laundry into her bedroom, which was just off the kitchen with another large window that faced the side-street, and set the basket on her neatly made counterpane. She took a deep breath and sighed. When she closed her eyes, she could still feel the imprint of his hand on her waist, her arm, on the back of her neck. She tried to tint the memories with shame, because a better woman wouldn't have told him to kiss her in the first place, and it was absolutely her own fault that he did what she told him to do. But try as she may, she couldn't even manage to regret it. All she had was the decency to worry that someone would find out. Marion squeezed her own arms uncomfortably and set to folding the laundry.

Harry had probably woken up with a sour taste in his mouth. Wasn't that the thing? Men wanted what they couldn't have, so if a girl was too available, they lost interest quickly? There was no other term to describe how Marion had behaved yesterday, if not available. Extremely available. Oh God. Did she actually tell him that she liked fucking? Sweet Jesus, how mortifying. What had come over her?

Marion folded furiously as she worked her mind into a familiar pattern. She was the worst kind of woman. Worst kind of mother. Oh God. Desperate and easy. Favoring her baser whims rather than staying focused on her responsibilities. Selfish. She could only hope that Harry didn't have a loose mouth with his friends. Even stories told in the strictest confidence still made their way to the ears of the wives. He wasn't Czech or Slovak, but he might have friends who were. And if word got to any of the Sokol Ladies, she'd be doomed.

By the time she finished folding the basket of laundry, she'd thoroughly convinced herself that Harry was so horrified with her loose behavior that he wasn't going to show up on Monday anyway, and he would send someone else to finish the install. Or worse, he'd do his duty to his job and his friend Gerald and finish the work, but it would be painfully awkward the whole time, and Marion would need to find as many things as she could to get herself out of the house to avoid him.

Marion blinked, bent down to press her face into the freshly folded pile of towels, and let loose a frustrated shout. She let the soft terry cloth gently cradle her face for several long moments as she caught her breath. A gentle voice in the back of her mind made a radical suggestion. *What if you're wrong, though?*

Marion took a deep breath and got a hold of herself. She was spinning out, letting her imagination run away with her and crafting the most outrageously catastrophic scenarios she could come up with. She had no way of knowing what Harry thought. He'd certainly been a willing participant in the entire encounter and deserved just as much responsibility for it as she did. Perhaps marginally more, for being so crass. She might as well put him out of her mind and get on with her business. She picked up the basket, put the towels away in the linen closet, and then set to getting herself ready to head to the Sokol Hall.

Back in her bedroom, Marion pulled off her house dress over her head. What if she *was* being overly dramatic? What if the simplest explanation was indeed the correct one and Harry was as interested in her as she was in him? Every interaction she'd had with him up to this point would indicate that that was true. He'd told her things, about his mother and his ex-wife and his time in

Korea, that were deeply private. She had not been the only one allowing oneself to be vulnerable. Even as he left yesterday, he'd paused as he put his coat on and looked her up and down with a grin, and he'd actually hopped down the front steps to his truck like jolly old St. Nick. He liked her. He'd said so. Multiple times. He thought she was a knock-out.

She pulled on her hose and fastened her girdle and garter. She took a long look at herself in the mirror. The bra and girdle smoothed out her curves, accentuating her waist, the measure of which she'd go to the grave before she'd admit to anyone. (Evelyn boasted 28 inches like it was a death sentence, trying to goad Marion into sharing her measurement. But Marion was no fool. She knew that for the trap it was. Any idiot could tell she was the thicker sister.) Thing was, with her sizable bust and hips, her waist still looked narrow in comparison. While her measurements weren't anything to publish in a magazine, her proportions were right on the money, especially in heels. Maybe even a knock-out, like Harry had said. She liked the idea that her appearance had the potential to turn heads. Or at least, his.

Marion smirked into the mirror and ran her hands down her sides. Maybe she was wrong, maybe she should care more about her size, but she liked her lush softness. She liked the sloping lines. She *loved* her breasts. And she enjoyed having the kind of soft body her kids could snuggle into. It didn't hurt that Harry seemed to like her body well enough, too. Her smirk stretched into a grin.

She slipped a lavender rayon dress over her head and zipper it up the side as she allowed herself to admire her own proportions. She didn't bother with a crinoline. She'd be running around the Sokol Hall in her apron setting up tables and pastries; there was no reason to get in her own way with a skirt any fuller than it needed to be. She still spent the time to put on her makeup and do her hair, though. She had to appear to make some kind of effort. That was the balancing act of Sokol events. She had to try hard enough to look put together, but not so hard that she seemed like she wanted to turn the heads of everyone else's husbands. She settled her hair into a dowdy chignon at the nape of her neck and hoped it would suffice.

After a brief lunch spent reminding herself what a disaster it would be if her inappropriate behavior got out, especially to her mother, she finally gave up and donned her wool coat and hat, stalking out the door towards the Sokol Hall. Wind whipped her skirt around her knees and she could taste the promise of snow on the air. Heavens, there were so many things more important to think about than Harry's heavy hand on her hip. Christmas and its own endless pressures, multiplied by the fact that she and Joe still had to figure out where the kids were going to spend Christmas Eve and Day. Splitting the holiday was the most painful part, but Marion would be damned if she spent another fraction of a minute in the presence of Joe's resentful mother, who had managed to convince herself that everything was Marion's fault. All of these things were important and nerve-wracking. Which was probably why she couldn't focus on them. Her mind kept slipping back to the heat of Harry's breath on the tender skin behind her earlobe. Harry was an honest fellow. Surely she could trust him to fuck her with discretion?

She bit her lip to keep from grinning as she crossed the street towards the Sokol Hall.

"Look at you, Marion." Marion almost jumped straight out of her skin. She turned and saw Edna behind her. "You look like the cat that caught the cream. Lucky you don't have to do any of the baking since your kitchen is in pieces, hm?"

From anyone else, that would have been a biting comment. But coming from Edna, it was teasing and somehow mutually commiserate. Marion laughed gamely and replied, "I suppose, but I still wasn't able to get out of setup, especially if I'm not able to bake anything."

"I'd be milking that excuse for as long as I could if I was you," Edna said, falling into step next to Marion as they traversed the last half block to the Sokol Hall doors. "I'd pay that big lug to take his time, do some work in the dining room too so I could get out of making Christmas dinner."

Marion could think of several things she'd like Harry to take his time with. She swallowed them all, chided herself for being such a pervert, and agreed. "I already got out of Thanksgiving. I think my sister would murder me if I was out of commission for Christmas too."

"Did you really? You didn't even have to make a pie?"

"Nope. All I have is a hot plate right now."

"If it were my family, they'd hand me a Dutch oven and a couple logs and tell me that the pioneers made pies without ovens just fine."

"Did they really, though?"

"No, I'm sure they made pies —"

"But were they any good?" Marion leveled a skeptical expression at Edna as she held the door open for her. They climbed up the steep steps which deposited them at the edge of a large gymnasium with a stage on the far end, hung with elaborately hand-painted backdrops. The building had gone up in 1887 and reflected a beautiful nostalgia for a time long past, with high ceilings and old, polished wood. Marion used to dote upon this space, but then she had married Joe in it. Perhaps that was what made her feel like the tall ceiling was about to suffocate her into the floorboards. Either that, or it was her mother looking exasperatedly at her from the edge of the gymnasium like she'd just tracked mud inside.

"Marion, you're late." Anna Burovansky was a slight woman, short of stature and slender from head to foot, but she somehow managed to loom over Marion despite being four inches shorter than her.

Marion cast a sideways glance at Edna, then back at her mother. "I thought you said noon?"

"That was before I knew that the boiler was having issues. We can't have everyone here if there's no heat, Marion."

Marion swallowed the urge to mutter, *How was I supposed to know that?* It was just easier to apologize. "Sorry, Mother."

"Sorry, Mrs. B," Edna said over her, in a much more jolly voice. "If we had known you were dealing with so much, we would have been here in two shakes. What needs doing?"

Mother seemed to be pacified, but Marion suspected it had less to do with forgiveness and more to do with appearing gracious in Edna's presence. Mother didn't like strangers seeing her less than perfectly composed at all times.

She put Marion and Edna to work setting up tables while she went downstairs to meet the boiler repairman. Marion enjoyed a brief fantasy that Harry was the repairman, but a glance out of the towering gymnasium windows confirmed that the truck was not his and was painted with a Czech name. She would have enjoyed sharing a secret understanding with him from across the room. And he would probably have made her look competent in front of her mother. Heavens knew if he even did any plumbing work, though. Other than installing her sink drain.

"What's got you looking so dreamy?" Edna chided as they snapped red gingham tablecloths over the wooden tables lining the gymnasium.

"What? I'm not dreamy."

"You're always dreamy."

"Then why should it draw any particular mention?"

"Fair enough. I just haven't seen you like that in a while."

"Well, I've been a little busy."

Edna went off to find centerpieces. Thank God. Marion schooled her focus to the task at hand. If Edna noticed she seemed different, what on earth would she assume it was due to? Could others see it? She resolved to put Harry out of her mind once and for all.

Charlie and Linda were absorbed by their crew of semi-feral cousins and other neighborhood children playing hide and seek among the tables as Sokol members from across the neighborhood socialized, ate, and bought inordinate amounts of pastries. Marion sat at the table at the head of the stairs, set up as a hub for people to get general information and make change. The whole event seemed a bit futile to Marion, since so many of the Sokol families had made pastries to contribute to the sale, but she supposed many of the elder community members were happy to purchase their koláče rather than make their own. Anyway, this massive effort was mostly for the fundraising. And the pleasure of the gentlemen to sample a variety of pastries without offending their wives.

"You know what I mean, Marion?" Betty Schebesta was seated next to her. She was lovely, with a figure straight out of a pinup postcard, but her reputation was cleaner than Marion's gleaming new enamel cabinets. Fellows had been dogging her heels to fundraisers and volunteer events for years, even though she now was married with five children and a sixth on the way. Either she was secretly attending St. Stanislaus on the side, toeing the "be fruitful and multiply" line, or her husband was *remarkably* agreeable.

Marion nodded even though she absolutely hadn't been listening.

"I just think your kids will do so much better with a father figure."

"What?" That caught Marion's attention.

"It's too hard for a woman on her own these days, and the little ones need some masculine influence in their lives."

What was it about Marion that invited people to give her intimate unsolicited advice? Maybe it was Betty. She'd been sanctimonious for years. It shouldn't be a surprise that she was giving unsolicited advice now. "They have Joe. It's not like he died. He picks them up every other weekend, and Wednesday evenings too."

"That can't hardly be enough, though, can it? Besides, Charlie needs a positive influence. A man with loyalty and a sense of duty." Marion scowled but she couldn't help but enjoy the passive-aggressive dig on Joe. "What about Frank Hamernek? He's eligible."

Marion followed Betty's gaze across the room. Frank Hamernek was a butcher with the forearms to prove it. He wasn't bad on the eyes. He smelled somewhat, but what man didn't? Oh hell, what was she doing, she was falling right into Betty's web.

"Ah, you can see it, can't you?" Betty crowed.

"See what?" Goddamn Helen Blaha approached the table and leaned forward to try and track who Betty and Marion were looking at.

"That Frank would be a great father figure for Charlie and little Linda," Betty simpered conspiratorially.

"Oh!" Helen put her hand to her chest as though scandalized. "You're looking to get remarried, Marion?"

"Not particularly."

"But how will you afford to go on?"

Marion glowered. "Alimony, I suspect." It pleased her how this comment made Helen and Betty's eyes both go wide. She knew it was a slippery slope being shocking, but it was so satisfying sometimes. "Like I said to Betty, it's not like Joe died or something. He's still around for the kids. I see him every week."

"Oh my goodness, Marion," Helen breathed. "Do you think he wants to get back together?"

"What? No! Not at all, and even if he did, I wouldn't be so stupid as to fall for that again." Too honest? Too honest. Marion pressed her lips together as Helen let out a scandalized squeal.

"How would that be so stupid?" Betty inquired. "I think it sounds awfully romantic. Besides — I don't know if you know this, Marion, but people have been talking. It would certainly quiet those voices, is all I'm saying."

"Really? I had no idea." Marion drawled in spite of the fact that she very much did not need to dig this hole any deeper.

"I know, can you believe it? Some people have no class. But I don't see why you can't get back together. It's not as though you've even been with any other men, Marion. You're not like *those* divorcees."

Marion wished the floor would open up and consume

her. She'd take an eternity of damnation if it would end this conversation. Betty was right, though heavens knew why she would say something like that out loud. She hadn't been with anyone else. But Joe had. Not that it was anyone's business, but Marion felt sure that if they knew, the Sokol ladies would be singing a different tune. The temptation to drop a suggestion of his infidelity into the conversation surfaced in her mind, but no matter how angry Marion was about the whole thing, she'd never do anything so careless as to put Joe and Stephen in danger.

"Hello, ladies," Ed Novak said, sidling up to their table. The only possible way this could get worse now was if her mother joined the conversation. "Mrs. Milner, you're looking very well. Mrs. Schebesta. Mrs. Blaha."

Ed nodded to the other ladies and then rested his eyes on Marion again. She sneered back and tried to disappear into her chair.

"Do you need change or something, Mr. Novak?" Marion gritted out. Betty and Helen were useless friends. No, they were not friends. Friends would have diffused Ed, but they were gawking like they were on the sidelines of a particularly good football game.

"Yeah," Ed leaned in and grinned at Marion. "You got change for a twenty?"

Waving big bills around, waggling his caterpillar eyebrows at Marion even though his goddamned wife was across the room. Marion glanced over at Mrs. Novak and saw her attention had been drawn away from selling her pastries to watch her husband be a grade-A lout in front of everyone. Marion opened the cash box in front of her and tucked Ed's big show-off bill inside.

"Two fives and ten ones?" Marion asked in her most neutral, unfriendly tone.

"I'd take two tens if I could get 'em, but that's not what

we're all here for, is it?" Ed grinned and put his hand down on the table to leverage his overly familiar lean. What was that even supposed to mean? Marion glowered and removed the bills she had suggested in the first place.

"Here you go," she said, dropping the bills on the table so Ed couldn't have an excuse to touch her. "Bye now."

Ed glanced at Betty, then back at Marion. His smile wavered for a split second before he said, "Well, I guess I know where I'm not wanted. So much for the hospitality of the Sokol Ladies Auxiliary."

This son of a bitch. Marion didn't say anything and resolutely looked at the cash box in front of her until he walked away.

"Marion!" Helen hissed once he was out of earshot. "What was that all about?"

Marion sighed and shrugged.

"You can't talk to someone else's husband like that!" Helen exclaimed, standing up and looking over her shoulder at Mrs. Novak. For heaven's sake, did she need to be so damn loud?

Marion frowned and looked up at her. "Like what?"

"Like, well, you know, that!"

"Like you're available," Betty whispered between set teeth.

"What!?" Marion exclaimed louder than she'd meant to. She quieted her voice and continued, "I didn't give him an *inch*."

"Maybe so, but…" Betty trailed off and studied Marion for a moment. "Maybe you should wear something a little less form fitting. At least until you're remarried."

Marion wanted to pick up the cash box and throw it at Betty Schebesta's head. "I didn't say anything wrong," she ground out.

"Of course you didn't, sweety," Betty cooed. "But you

can't blame a lout like him for getting distracted when you look so —"

Marion stood up abruptly. Helen and Betty both startled. "I have to go to the ladies room."

She stalked off across the gymnasium before the others could say anything else.

✦

Luckily, Marion managed to shoulder the rest of the event without tempting everyone's husbands into carnal infidelity. She'd left the others to cover the volunteer table and took her reprimand from her mother in the kitchen behind the staircase. But hell if she was going to go back and listen to Helen Blaha and Betty Schebesta tell her what a hussy she was to her face all night.

Linda skipped home, hopping through an invisible hopscotch course in front of them. It was already dark and the thick clouds that had been hanging all day reflected the lights of nearby downtown back in a warm yellow-gray glow. Charlie trailed behind and Marion lagged a bit to fall into step with him.

"Did you have a good time?" Marion asked, her hand falling affectionately on Charlie's shoulders. Heavens, he was growing so fast. He'd be taller than her before long.

Charlie shrugged.

"Honey, what is it?"

Charlie shook his head. "It's nothing, Mother. Just dumb boys."

Marion frowned. "Was it Freddy Schebesta again?" One would think that the son of a saint who volunteered at the soup kitchen every month for his entire life would be the picture of philanthropic virtue, but in a twist of fate that surprised approximately no one, Betty Schebesta's eldest son was a bit of an asshole.

Charlie shrugged. "It doesn't matter. They can't bother me."

Marion felt the familiarity of her own words parroted back to her across time. At the beginning of the school year, Freddy and his idiot cronies had been harassing Charlie about his father. Marion wasn't sure of what all had been said, because the teachers either didn't know or wouldn't tell her and Charlie refused to talk about it. But things seemed to have gotten easier recently. So this was not a welcome development.

"Well," Marion said slowly. "You can talk to me anytime you want, bud. I'm always here for you."

Charlie shook his head and gave a wistful half smile. "I know, Ma."

"No, I mean it, Chuck," Marion insisted playfully. "I can take it. Lay it on me."

The look Charlie gave her as he looked up at her, at once affectionate and gently patronizing, settled heavily in her gut. She wished so much that he would talk to her, but he wouldn't. She thought he fancied himself as her protector. Which only hinted at what kind of evil vitriol these idiot neighborhood boys were spouting.

Marion nodded slowly. "Okay. But if you don't want to talk to me, know you can talk to someone else. Your friend, Robert. Or your teacher at school. Your father," she added belatedly. Actually that might be nice, for Joe to have to listen to the sacrifice his son had to take on the playground on his behalf. "You have a good group of people around you who love you and want to support you."

Marion squeezed her son's shoulders. He nodded dutifully at her and pretended to smile. It broke her heart.

Chapter 9

Monday, December 5th, 1955
12 days until the Christmas party

Harry had never known three days to last so long. He'd spent the weekend tidying up his apartment, entertaining a silly fantasy of making sure everything was spic and span in case Marion Milner found a reason to be there. By Saturday night, he'd driven himself a little wild with fantasizing so he phoned his friend Hal and went bowling. Sunday he went to a movie and wished he could have brought Marion along with him. Although — there was really nothing good out right now and the western he'd settled on was so entirely forgettable he wasn't sure he'd even be able to tell her about it.

He was early again when he pulled up to Marion's house. There was a thin layer of snow on the sidewalk that had accumulated yesterday, so he figured he'd be of use and hopped out of his truck to grab a shovel. He pulled one from the truck bed and had just started scraping the front walk when two loud, giggling children spilled out the front door.

"Hiya Mister!" the little girl called out. "Whatcha doing?"

"Hello," Harry replied. He couldn't help but mirror the

little girl's smile, it was so infectious.

"Mother, hurry up!" the boy called and cast a wary glance at Harry from the side of his eye. "There's some fellow out here shoveling the sidewalk."

"What's your name?" the little girl asked as she approached him without an ounce of trepidation. She had two curly pigtails, a little red wool coat, and matching boots.

"I'm Mr. O'Conner," Harry said, crouching to put himself on the little girl's level. "I'm the handyman that's fixing up your kitchen."

"Oh!" the little girl gushed. "I'm so glad! The cabinets are so pretty. Mama loves them!"

The storm door opened and Marion stood on the top step of the stoop. "Harry? What are you doing here?"

The sound of his first name on her lips sent a shiver down his spine as he stood. "Sorry, I'm a little early. I thought you caught the bus over on Michigan?"

Marion, to his dismay, did not seem to be nursing a shivery spine of her own. "No, they pick it up on Erie in the morning." She drew a key out of her purse and looked between him and the house across the street for a moment. "I suppose I'll just leave the door open for you, then."

"Sure, if you want," Harry replied, straightening. "There's no rush, I can just shovel—"

"—Thanks but that's really not necessary," Marion said a little breathlessly as she pulled on her gloves and dashed down the stairs. "Come on, children. We don't want to miss the bus."

"Nice to meetcha, Mr. Conner!" the little girl called as the son and Marion hurried down the sidewalk as though Harry weren't even there. He leaned on his shovel for a moment, watching them go. Damn, he understood she was concerned with appearances, but even under the circumstances, that interaction was still downright cold. He couldn't square this Marion with the one he'd held in his arms last Thursday, who'd been so warm and eager and inviting. He frowned down at his hands and then shook his head. No point worrying about it. She'd be back in a few minutes and he could simply ask her. He pushed the shovel through the truly insignificant amount of snow and let his body fall into the rhythm of it until she returned.

It was about ten minutes until she came back. By then, Harry had easily finished shoveling the walkway and was leaning against his truck, waiting for her. It felt wrong to enter her house without her there. Old Milly was staring at him out the storm door window like she couldn't see far enough to determine if he was a potential intruder or a familiar head-scratcher with the potential to bring her a treat.

"Sorry, old girl, I wish I brought you something," Harry muttered as he twiddled his thumbs. He wondered if Marion went through the back for some reason, but he figured if she had, Milly wouldn't be waiting for her at the front. And, of course, she would have come immediately to the front door anyway because she knew Harry was there waiting for her. The older lady who lived across the street was definitely watching him out her window, now.

Finally Marion appeared around the corner. He watched her walk down the sidewalk with a utilitarian stride, a trail of footprints pressed into the snow behind her. God, but she was a knock-out. A real, grade-A looker. Her cheeks were all pink from the cold and her dark eyebrows and lashes set her off in stark contrast to the rest of the world swathed in white snow. Like Audrey

Hepburn, but with Marilyn Monroe's figure.

When Marion came within earshot, Harry pushed himself off his truck and said, "Whelp, the appliances have come into the warehouse."

Marion looked up at him and an eagerness flashed across her face for a second. "Oh good," she replied as she approached. She stood in front of him for a minute, worrying her gloved thumb between her opposite forefinger and thumb. She was in her nerves. He could sense it by the way her shoulders seemed halfway up to her ears.

Harry flicked his chin at her. "You alright?"

"Of course," Marion looked down at her feet. "It's just cold. Why don't you come in? It's freezing out here."

She wasn't wrong. It was only a few degrees above zero outside and his toes felt like they might fall off. He should have worn warmer socks. The metal handle of his toolbox bit cold into his palm as he let her lead him silently inside. As he mounted the last of the steps, he looked over his shoulder and saw the curtain in the house across the street flutter. Wow, completely audacious. Marion had not been exaggerating.

Inside, the radiators gurgled and Marion set to making coffee straight away as Harry sat on the sofa and gave Milly her requisite ear scratches.

"The fridge and the stove are both in, and Gerald said to expect the ovens by tomorrow," he reported. "We can probably get them all in by the end of the week, if the countertops can be delivered."

"That's wonderful news," Marion said politely.

Harry frowned and studied her. "Is there anything wrong?"

Marion shook her head, maybe too quickly, as she carried the coffee cups over and set one in front of him. "No, of course not."

"Because when I told you the cabinets were in, you were beside yourself with excitement," he pointed out. "So I had sort of anticipated that you'd react the same for the appliances."

"I *am* excited," Marion insisted, then put on a big grin that didn't touch her eyes. "See?"

Harry lifted a brow at her skeptically and tried to take a sip of the hot coffee. "How was the pastry sale?"

Marion blinked far too many times. "Fine."

Harry sat forward with a sigh and set his coffee cup down. "Come on, Marion. I can tell something is wrong. Is it what I said to you last week? Is it the kiss? I'm sorry if it's made things awkward. Really, you don't owe me nothing, but if I did something wrong, I want to apologize."

Marion cringed and flapped her hand at him. "No, no. It's fine. I'm sorry. I was just a bit thrown off when you were here so early."

"Oh," Harry said as neutrally as he could. "I'm sorry."

"It's fine, I just didn't want the kids to meet you like that."

Harry blinked. "Meet me?"

"Well, yes. I didn't want them to meet you until ..." she trailed off.

Harry's brow furrowed. "Until what? Till the kitchen is done?"

"No…" She winced. Then, in lieu of something helpful to say, she just shrugged.

Harry narrowed his eyes as though that would help him see her better. "Marion. Are you ashamed of me?"

"What? No! Of course not!" Her cheeks flushed and he found he didn't wholly believe her.

"I know this has been a sort of awkward way to meet, but I really thought we were getting along well," he said, more to Milly than to Marion. He focused on the methodical, familiar movements of his fingers in the dog's fur as he gathered up the courage to continue. "I know you said you don't want to step out with me until after the kitchen is done, but I thought after what happened on Thursday ..." He looked up at her and hated how small it made him feel. "I just ... you're acting different and I can't figure out why, unless you're regretting that kiss."

Marion closed her eyes and sighed, leaning back into the wingback armchair. She kept her eyes closed as she spoke. "I don't know, Harry. I just thought — if I'm going to step out with you at all, I don't want the children to know you as the handyman only to realize you're something more? Their mother's ... gentleman caller? God, I'm so sorry, that sounds ridiculous. I am out of my depth here, Harry. There's no road map for something like this and I'd rather tread carefully with the children than step wrong and regret it."

"Oh." Harry blinked. "I'm real sorry. I didn't think about it that way." He huffed a weak laugh. "It is murky, I'll give you that."

"It's okay," Marion sighed and sat up. "It's just been a long weekend. It'll be good to get some work done today."

Harry nodded and applied himself to drinking his coffee more quickly. He made every effort to push the trepidation that had put him in a stranglehold aside. If she wanted to talk to him about her weekend, she would.

✦

By ten o'clock, Harry had no choice but to conclude that something was very wrong. Marion was usually talking a mile a minute by this point in the day. Not only was she quiet, but she wasn't even listening to records as she tended to her housework in the front half of the house. That was unheard of in Mrs. Milner's world. Not to mention that, for the past week, she had sat on a dining chair to keep him company as he worked and now she seemed to be avoiding him like the plague.

Harry tried to put it out of his head as he continued installing the remaining cabinets. He really tried. But he'd run out of cabinets to install on his own and now he was at a point where he could really use her help. It also didn't help that he felt like he was going to crawl out of his skin if she didn't talk to him. He peeked his head out the door to the dining room and looked down the long nave of the house at her ironing shirts near the sofa.

"Hey, uh, Mrs. Milner," he said, stumbling over her honorific. "Could you give me a hand in here?"

Marion looked up at him, her usually merry mouth a grim line, then stood. God dammit, he must have done something awful. He tried again to scour the events of their last meeting for signs, but he couldn't find any. It was like a switch had flipped in her.

She followed him into the kitchen and he showed her the upper cabinet he needed her help to hold steady while he got the first few screws in. It was the one she had proposed to store her dishes in, that also had a sliding bread box on the bottom. He climbed up on the lower cabinet and steadied the cabinet on his knee. She put her hands up and helped him get it into place while he grabbed his drill from his toolbelt and started in on the screws.

"I'm really sorry, Harry," Marion blurted.

He frowned and said through a mouthful of screws, "What for?"

"I just … I don't —" she sighed and looked askance at the cabinet. He waited. "I don't know how to go about this … this thing … with you. I've only ever dated the one guy and he turned out to be … to be … not for me. There's a lot of pressure to remarry. But I just — I don't want to. I feel … trapped."

Harry frowned and pushed a few more screws in. "Are you saying you don't want to go out after all?"

"No. Yes. Maybe."

He couldn't help but look down at her imploringly. He wanted to understand what had her so mixed up, but how was he supposed to make sense of that? She was returning his gaze with those big, brown eyes, just as imploringly. He turned back to the cabinet and let the remaining task at hand give him the time he needed to think.

When the cabinet was installed and he had climbed down from the lower cabinet, he turned and pushed his hands into his pockets.

"Look, Marion," he said. "I don't expect anything from you. We only just met a few weeks ago. I'd be a bastard if I thought I had some claim over you now, just because we kissed last week. But I do really like you. And I'm confused."

"I know," she replied. She hunched over the sink, leaning on her elbows with her head in her hands.

"I think you're confused too," he ventured as he took a slow step toward her.

"No, not confused," she replied to the sink. "I just don't know what to *do*."

"It's okay if you've changed your mind," Harry supplied, and it was okay, even though he wished with all his heart it wasn't the case.

"No!" She dug her hands into her hair, but she still didn't turn around. "I like you. I really do. I just feel like there's no way to proceed without either of us getting hurt. Or hurting the children."

"Marion." He hooked his thumbs into the sides of his overalls. "You don't have to marry me. You don't even have to go steady with me. Your kids don't need to know me as anything other than the handyman. You don't owe me anything, and you won't. Even if we …" he gestured helplessly, "...kiss again. Or more. I just don't want you to feel like you have to—"

" — I don't feel like I have to," Marion said and she turned around. Her eyes were wide, hair askew, lips pink and plump from being worried between her teeth. "I want to. Do more. A lot."

"Me too." Understatement of the century.

"Then what are we doing?" She looked up as if imploring the heavens.

Harry took a deep breath and let it out. "What do you want, Marion?"

Her eyes skittered away from his. "I — well, you know —"

"I don't."

She flushed.

"I need you to tell me."

"I just want …" she gestured uselessly. "You know, to kiss you and, um. God, must I say it?"

Harry's nostrils flared a bit and he felt a smile creep at the edges of his mouth. "I hope you will. If I'm left to fill in the blanks, I'm not sure I can resist when you look at me like that."

"Like what? No — Harry, I *want* you to fill in the blanks. You. I don't want to decide anymore. I don't want to be in charge. I'm so tired of trying to figure everything out. I don't want to think, Harry. I just want to..." She sighed helplessly. "...*feel*."

"Okay." Her words filled him up. He felt bigger, stronger, a heady combination of trust and power. "You'd let me do that for you?"

Marion leaned into the corner of the countertops. Her eyes were dark, her lips parted. "Yes. It'd be a huge relief, to be honest."

Harry approached her. Let himself reach up and smooth her hair from her face.

"Not tender," Marion murmured. He felt another surge in his chest. He pressed himself full-length against her, pinning her against the counter.

"Like this?"

"Yes." She tipped her head back, exposing her neck to him. "More. Take liberties. I want you to make me lose my mind."

He cupped her cheek in his palm, pressed his lips to hers. Pressed his tongue to the seam of her lips, pushing her. He felt drunk on her encouragement after a morning cut off from her, but there was a part of him lurking in the back of his mind that held back. Waited for her to stop him. But she didn't. She opened her mouth for him, stabilized herself with her hands on the cabinet as he pressed deeper, tongue against tongue. A soft sound hummed from her throat, and his hands grasped her waist, pressing his erection into her full skirt until he could feel the resistance of her thighs beneath. She gasped, her breath coming shallow and hot against his mouth. Harry gripped her waist, lifted her up the scant few inches to set her on the top of the cabinet. Her hands came up, pulled at his shoulders as her knees lifted, and she wrapped her legs gratuitously around his waist.

"Marion," he rumbled against her mouth. His hands shoved her skirt up and slid rough palms up her thighs, callus snagging on her hose until he pushed past the edge and reached warm, bare flesh.

"Yes," she breathed and arched her hips against his. Overalls were a *mistake*. He couldn't scarcely feel the hot, soft slip of her panties and Christ, he wanted to. Quite desperately. He growled. It was deep and rumbly and animalistic and he felt ridiculous, but he couldn't help it. It came from his throat entirely unbidden. He had to release the straps of his damned overalls, but he didn't want to stop touching her thighs. He pushed his thumbs up, teasing at the edge of her panties, slipping under the edge and feeling hot flesh and wiry hair. She arched towards his touch.

"Harry, please," Marion whined in his ear. "Touch me. I need you to. Please."

He made her like this. She was his instrument, to play as he wished. Did she understand what a gift this was? How it filled him with heady power and lust for her to plead with him to touch her. All he wanted to do was touch her, but now perhaps all he wanted to do was make her beg like that again.

His thumbs slid back and forth in the crease of her hip, teasing the touch she desired, enjoying her plush softness enveloped in rapidly moistening silk. God, she was decadent. She arched again, whining desperately.

"Please, Harry. I can't stand it." She twisted her hips and one of his thumbs slipped between her folds and the softness, the velvet heat, the slickness, flooded him as she sucked in a breath and keened. He pressed that thumb firmly against her, then pulled it away. She cried out in such a lamentable tone, he wondered for a moment if the tenants were upstairs and whether he should worry about that.

"No, please," she cried. "Come on!"

And like that, he was a wave of insatiable hunger again.

Surging desire for more. Running on instincts he didn't even know he had, he held her thighs with his hands and lowered himself to one knee. Seeing her somehow made touching her feel sharper, sweeter, realer. Her scent was heady as he leaned in to mouth over her china-silk panties.

"Oh my God," Marion gasped and arched her hips into his face with seemingly very little regard. It pleased him, and he curved one hand on her waist to hold her firmly as he inhaled her sharp, heady scent. He pressed his tongue against the already-wet silk. Her hands scrabbled in his hair, gripping and pulling in a way that might have hurt but didn't. Instead, it pumped sensation into him like some sort of wild erotic transfusion, surging through him and making him so hard it hurt a bit. With his opposite hand, he pulled her panties sharply to the side. His tongue met her flesh in a flash of supple heat. It earned him another precious cry, one he swore to himself he'd keep forever in a sensory memory with her scent, her taste, the feel of her slick, vulnerable flesh under his tongue. He tried to hold the panties aside while also pressing her folds wider, to grant himself greater access as he used his tongue to explore her. The firm nub of pleasure at the front, which made her writhe and moan when he sucked on it, the soft yielding entrance that begged his tongue to fill it.

Marion grappled at the cabinets above her. "Harry, please, God, it's too much, I can't —" She carried on, gasping words as her hips shuddered around him, as she fucked herself involuntarily on his tongue. He thought distantly if he died tomorrow, it all would be worth it to have distilled her to this. He wedged his hand in the crease of her thigh and rubbed her clit with his thumb, fast and hard and relentless. He could scarcely breathe as she rolled her hips against him over and over, shuddering.

"Oh my fucking God," she ground out, her voice cracked, the words wrested from her throat with grating effect, a sound without breath, as she shook against him. Harry tipped his chin slightly so he could drag an inhale through his nose, her scent filling him, her taste driving him with dogged relentlessness, to the point that he pressed his mouth against her hole, to lap her up as she came.

She slumped against the countertop and gasped for breath. Harry tipped his chin up and pressed her skirt down to look up into her face.

"Don't look so damn pleased with yourself," she said, her voice raw and ragged. She yanked on his overall strap and he stood compliantly. Harry had no illusions about who was in control here. Sure, he was hitting the accelerator, but Marion was steering. She just needed some sort of plausible deniability to navigate the roads she wanted to go down. She let her feet hang from the countertop as she pushed the buckles free from the buttons, freeing the straps. He pushed the overalls down along with his boxers to release his straining cock. She watched it with heated fascination for a moment before she looked up at him with deadly seriousness. "Harry. I need you to fuck me."

He was already trying to balance pushing his hand into his pocket for the tin of condoms he'd been carrying around since she'd kissed him, while also trying to keep the overalls up enough so he could reach it. He fumbled the tin onto the cabinet and failed to flick it open one-handed. Marion's hands swatted his away and opened the tin.

"My, you're prepared," she approved breathlessly as she withdrew one of the carefully pre-rolled rubbers and tore the paper label off. "I've never actually used one of these before."

"It's pretty self explanatory," he managed as she ghosted her fingertips up and down his bare length almost reverently, each touch a jolt of sensation ricocheting up his spine. Then she pushed the condom over him. She'd scarcely reached the base of his cock before he stepped forward and realized with a measure of embarrassment that he was too short to fuck her from this angle. Before he could think too hard about it, he turned, kicked his toolbox over, and stood on the metal lid. It was a big box, as toolboxes went, and it would work well as a step stool. She regarded him with an amused brow until he pressed his tip to her entrance. Then he reveled in the way it made her eyes widen with wanting.

"Tell me again," he growled as she stretched over his tip.

She looked up at him with wide eyes for a moment before she pressed her lips together and said, "I need you to fuck me."

His voice groaned his approval as relief compounded inside the squeeze of her cunt. "Again."

"I need you to fuck me, Harry."

He pulled back, letting the tip of his cock gather her ample wetness, using his fingers to keep her panties to one side, and pressed in again, a little deeper this time. "How much?"

"God, so much, Harry, I can't stand this. Please, just —" her voice unraveled as she curved her hips up to greet him. She was so goddamn tight. The knowledge that his was the first prick to breach her in over six years made him feel powerful enough to flip a truck. He wanted to drive into her full tilt, but the sounds she was making, the words that spilled from her lips as he continued to fuck her shallow were too irresistible to give up just yet.

"Please," she gasped, her hips chasing him as he withdrew slightly, letting his prick gather more of her slick wetness. "Please, I want to feel you. I want you to fill me up."

"What if I don't?" he murmured, not sure what he was even hedging for. Not even sure he was totally in control of what he was saying, really, but just knowing this tension was exquisite and all he wanted was to feed it, even if it left his dick painfully hard.

She looked up at him with wide eyes. "Don't you want to?"

That scrambled him for a moment. He blinked. "Of course I want to. I just … I love hearing you beg for it."

He pushed in a little farther and her uncertainty melted away as her breath hitched. He slid his other palm over her thigh again and let his thumb ride at the place where their flesh joined. Fuck, what he would give to see that. He tried to shove her skirt up but the damn crinoline refused to cooperate.

"Please," she whimpered, more self-assuredly. "Please fuck me, Harry O'Conner. I want you to fuck me through the countertop. I want you to fuck me so hard the fucking cabinets collapse. I would happily pay for the damage if you would just please *please* fuck me."

Well. Harry wasn't one to hold out on such a heartfelt request. He pulled back, teasing her with the shallow thrusts once, twice … then he drove into her full length, hard enough that her head smacked against the upper cabinets and she cried out so fiercely, he could feel it reverberate in his toes. So he did it again. And again. He rode her out as hard as he could manage, feeling increasingly like he might burst out of his own skin as he chased his orgasm with relentless force. Marion gripped his shoulders like a lifeline, her nails digging half-moons into his flesh. That hurt, but it didn't hinder. Pain and pleasure tangled together until soon it was all relentless sensation pushing him headlong over a precipice that cracked through him and shook him to the bones and left him wringing his cock out inside her with short, stuttered thrusts.

He opened his eyes and saw Marion's mouth open, heaving breath as she grasped his wrist, pulling his hand tighter against her. He understood in some visceral way, and pressed his thumb against the swollen nub of flesh at the head of her folds, rubbing with vigorous, unrelenting pressure until he watched her unravel for him. She spasmed around his softening prick, and he knew, just knew, now that he'd had this, now that he knew how they could be together, he wouldn't know how to do without it.

He pressed kisses to her temple, to her cheek, and to her lips. He grasped the rubber with his fingertips as he felt himself slide from her, but he couldn't step away to deal with that just yet. Her breath was warm and bittersweet with coffee, a sensation of nearness that he was loath to lose.

"So," he murmured against her mouth, "will you let me take you on a date now?"

Her huff of a laugh delivered a burst of warm air on his cheek that he wanted to sink into. "I suppose I'd better."

Chapter 10

Wednesday, December 7th, 1955
10 days until the Christmas party

On Wednesday afternoons, Joe picked the kids up from school and brought them to his new house over in South Minneapolis. It was a weekly ritual that had become routine, both for the kids and eventually, Marion too. Wednesday nights were always too quiet. But this week, she found she had something very delightful to distract her. A date with Harry O'Conner.

She wore her green sweater because she knew he liked it and snuck out the back door, then skirted the garage. She walked down the alleyway to avoid the neighbors noticing her, like she was a teenager sneaking out of her mother's house. It was embarrassing, but also kind of exciting. She found the white General Electric truck parked by the library on St. Claire Avenue and glanced over a shoulder before she climbed in.

"I feel like a getaway driver," Harry said by way of greeting as she settled onto the bench seat. The truck smelled like musty motor oil, and there was a thin layer of dust coating the dash. Marion could imagine a thousand reasons why this should be some sort of bad sign, but all she felt was comfort. It smelled like her grandfather's garage. And cedarwood. Harry must have used some sort of aftershave to get ready for their date.

"Oh, yes, you should," Marion replied as Harry kicked the truck into gear and pulled out towards Fort Road. "I am a bank robber and I'm actually in need of a partner in crime."

Maybe not her best. Harry chuckled amiably anyway.

"This restaurant is supposed to be really good," Harry explained as he headed towards downtown. "And it's on the east side, so we're very unlikely to run into any of your neighbors."

"Thank you." She felt rather guilty about needing that kind of assurance. "I'm so sorry to ask you to sneak around like this. You're really not the kind of guy who should have to reduce yourself to sneaking around to protect my reputation."

"No, I understand. It's difficult to know how to go about these kinds of things, with the kids especially."

Marion nodded and clasped her hands awkwardly in her lap. His hands on the leather-wrapped steering wheel were relaxed and sure. Made a girl get ideas. Maybe he'd invite her up for a nightcap when dinner was done, like in the movies. After their encounter on Monday, she couldn't stop thinking about all the other things she was eager for him to do. All the things she'd wondered about — fantasized about — while Joe was rolling away from her and turning the lights out early. If she'd learned anything from pulp novels in the last few years, it was that there were depths of human sexuality she could not even fathom, much more than she'd ever thought possible. She wanted to find out for herself what she liked.

She looked up at Harry wondering how one might broach a conversation about such things and noticed he was admiring her chest out of the corner of his eye.

"You look very nice in that sweater," he grumbled, eyes darting back to the road sheepishly.

"Thanks." Marion grinned. *You should pull over and take it off.* God, she was half-crazed. She thought maybe after having sex again, after all that time, it would take the edge off, but now it was all she could think about. Making dinner and remembering the scent of his sweat. Folding laundry and imagining how he looked with his stupid overalls pooled on the floor. Singing lullabies and wishing her kids would go the fuck to sleep so she could curl up in her own bed and bring herself off once or twice while imagining Harry bending her over her dining table. Just normal, everyday housewife thoughts.

She glanced at Harry again. She wanted to say some of this to him. She wanted him to take charge of her again, and she didn't really want to waste time chatting over dinner pretending like they hadn't already gotten to know one another already, because they had — in the Biblical sense. But she also understood that this was important to him. To take her out. She supposed it probably should be important to her, too. That he treat her with dignity, like a person, and not just some girl to get his rocks off with. She appreciated that about him. She was grateful that she could trust him not to fuck her and forget her (although, that would be pretty difficult seeing as he still had to come back to her house and finish all the work in her kitchen). But she was also horny as hell, and she didn't want to wait.

So she squirmed in the passenger seat until Harry broke the silence, somewhere around Wabasha Street.

"You know, I did actually get busted for stealing a car once," he said. Marion, jumbled up in inner turmoil about what she wanted and what she should want, jolted at the non-sequitur.

"You what?"

Harry laughed. "When I was in high school, I ... knew a guy who'd gone to test drive a car and ended up walking off with the key. So that night, after the lot had closed, a group of us all went to see if we might take the car for a joy ride."

Marion feigned shock. "My God, you've been a common criminal this entire time and you didn't tell me? I'm horrified!"

"Well — just the one time. So my pals are all huddled together trying to make a plan, and I could just see this wasn't gonna go well, so I says, 'Nah, I couldn't do that. I'm going home.' When I turn around to go home, it turns out the cops were watching us the whole time and as soon as my buddies drive the car out onto Grand Avenue, the cops come and arrest them. And the cop says to them, 'You shoulda been smart like that other kid and gone home.'"

"And you were the smart kid, huh?" Marion folded her arms over her chest. "Then how did you know that the cop told them that?"

Harry's cheeks went flush in the dim light of the street lamps flickering over his features. "They told me later, of course."

"Uh huh."

"Fine, the smart kid was Gerald. I was the idiot with the keys."

Marion's eyes widened. She enjoyed letting her mouth drop open and pressing her fingertips to her lips. "Oh my gosh. You're a real thief! Grand theft auto and all that! Are we gonna get pinched by the cops while we're walking out of the restaurant? I'm not ready to be tried for obstruction of justice."

Harry's head was tilted back as he laughed, full-throat-ed and deep. The streetlights backlit the profile of his throat and it filled Marion with a sort of tingling energy that made her want to do something impulsive and reckless, like lick him. She chided herself that she shouldn't distract the driver.

"What kind of kid were you growing up?" she asked instead. "I was sort of the goody-two-shoes type. I studied hard and got good grades. I was in the booster club for the football team. Hall monitor. I was good at telling everyone else what to do."

Harry grinned. "You're still good at telling people what to do."

Marion's shoulders curled around her and she looked up at him, embarrassed. They were waiting at a red light at the east end of downtown, headed towards Swede's Hollow, and Harry's eyes met hers with a heat she felt in her gut. She remembered Monday, in her kitchen, when she detailed at length how much she needed him to fuck her. And now her face was probably fire-engine red.

The light turned green, and Harry looked back to the road, a smirk playing on his lips. Marion opened her mouth to suggest he take a detour down to the train yards for some privacy. Just to take the edge off. They could still go to dinner after. But maybe they could just work up a bit of an appetite first. She started to reach across the bench seat to touch his thigh when he said, "I was the opposite. Like I said, I lost my ma when I was sixteen, so I spent junior year of high school being an ornery, no-good son-of-a-bitch and then I dropped out to join the airforce. Stealing a car was absolutely consistent with my general character back then."

"A rebel without a cause?"

"Yeah, but a sight bit gingerier than James Dean."

"That's not fair…" Marion bit her lip. "He was cute

when I was sixteen, but I think I much prefer a more distinguished man now." *One with blunt hands and kind eyes.* He laughed self-consciously and scrubbed at his hair. They pulled into a parking spot across the street from a tiny little Italian restaurant in the first level of a brownstone.

"Is that what they're calling it these days?" Harry shoved the parking gear into place and killed the engine with an impish smirk.

"Quit it, you're darling." Marion smiled and used this as an excuse to playfully touch his shoulder. He turned and seized her hand and for a moment, they both hung suspended in some space without time, where there were only dark shadows and heated gazes and the soft kiss of his breath on her cheek. Marion willed him to kiss her. *Please, just one solitary kiss.* She parted her lips in invitation, implored him with her eyes, and he inched forward. But then he stopped himself, peered at her for a moment, and grinned.

"I'm starved," Harry declared as he kicked his door open. "Don't move, I'm coming to open your door for you like a gentleman."

His door shut with a firm clunk, and Marion looked down at her hands. Starved, huh? She was *famished,* and not for Italian food either. She was wound up tight like a clock, her gears thrumming with the promise of his touch. Did he not want to touch her? Was he afraid of giving her the wrong idea? Her mouth twisted in consideration. But on Monday, he'd seemed to take some sort of sadistic glee in making her wait, making her beg, driving her to her edge. The passenger door opened and Harry grinned at her with a proffered hand. Was this all more of the same?

"Your feast awaits, my lady," Harry said with a playful

flourish.

Marion just stared at him for a moment, trying to resolve the incongruence of this man with the serious professional who usually showed up at her door for work each morning. Instead of leaving her wanting for one or the other, she found herself delighted with the prospect that both could exist inside one person. One person who was not making much effort to avert his eyes from her green sweater. The satin lining the inside of her brassiere suddenly felt like roughspun linen as her nipples tightened with sensitivity. God, this was going to be a torturously long meal.

✦

Marion Milner was uncomfortably wet. Harry would put twenty dollars on it. She squirmed in her seat as they waited for the wine to be delivered, and Harry leaned back in his chair, reveling in the way her deep, brown eyes drank him in. He wanted to casually cross his legs and run the toe of his shoe up her thigh, but he couldn't push too hard yet. He did actually want to eat dinner with her. After the car ride in, with her lingering looks and impish flirtation, he was already formulating a way he could ask her to come back to his apartment afterwards. This was an outrageous departure from how he would normally conduct himself, but propriety did not account for Mrs. Milner. He was willing to show her his creaky old Murphy bed if she was willing to ride him on it.

The waiter returned and poured red wine into two glasses. Goddamn, this was getting out of control if he was eager to show a woman he was interested in his dingy little studio. Harry scarcely tracked his meal order even as he said it. He hoped it wasn't too obvious that he was trying to undress Marion with his eyes as the waiter inquired how he wanted his steak done. Harry was going to take that green sweater off of her as soon as he got her in the door of his little shoebox of an apartment.

As soon as the waiter walked away, Marion leaned forward on the table, plucking her glass up between her fingers. Her bosom did wonderful things squeezed between her round arms.

"To second chances?" Marion suggested with a curving smile.

Harry grinned and clinked her glass. "To second chances."

"You know, I've never eaten over here before. Seems a whole lot like DiGidio's."

"You shouldn't say that here," Harry hissed dramatically. "There'll be a riot."

Marion chuckled. "DiGidio's is wonderful, and very family friendly. They're hardly involved in organized crime at all anymore." She was using her movie star affectation, and it was doing things to Harry, particularly in the pelvic area.

"What a wonderful vote of confidence."

"Oh, like you have any legs to stand on, Mr. Grand Theft Auto. You'd fit right in with the DiGidios."

"Maybe, but this place has one very important feature that DiGidio's does not."

"Oh, and what's that?"

"It's not in Little Bohemia."

Marion sighed. Harry loved how her round chin stuck out like she was in a state of perpetual impertinence. "True. I am sorry again about being so secretive. It's just … Well, I think Charlie is getting some guff in the schoolyard again, and I don't want to give those little assholes anything more to hold over him. Sorry — I really shouldn't be calling children assholes."

"Children very often are assholes. I know I was when I was in school." Harry buttered one of the complimentary rolls the waiter had delivered with their wine. "Do you want a roll?"

Marion glanced at his offering. "Thank you." She took a bite. A bit of her lipstick smeared on the crust and Harry experienced the most incongruous desire to change places with a roll. Setting lustful longings firmly aside for the moment, he focused on buttering another roll for himself and said, "What kinds of nonsense are they lobbing at him? Does he say?"

Marion sighed. "No, I think he believes he's protecting me. Which leads me to believe they're saying all sorts of nasty things about my character. And who can blame them, really, when I'm sure it's what their parents are saying at home."

"Do you really believe your neighbors are saying nasty things about you at home?"

"I'm certain they are," Marion replied, her expression a little aggrieved around a mouthful of roll. "You should hear the things they have the courage to say to my face."

Harry took the opportunity to chew his own bread for a minute and chasten himself. "I'm sorry," he said after a moment. "I sometimes forget that your experience with divorce is very different from mine. There's no children in my case, for one thing."

"I hate how difficult it is for the kids. They didn't do anything wrong, but they get punished all the same."

"Like a hostage situation," Harry offered grimly. "I had a great aunt who was a widow. There were ladies who would grab their husbands hands at church when she walked by, like if she looked at them sideways, they'd be seduced like rats to the Pied Piper."

"Holy buckets, yes. That happens to me," Marion bemoaned into her wine. "At the Koláče Sale, one of the Sokol Ladies' husbands tried to flirt with me right in front of everyone."

Harry shouldn't have been surprised by the force with which that hit him. But the anger it incited boiled immediately into his chest and he said, "What's his name?"

Marion looked up at him and absorbed his affrontedness with a dismissive glance. "Down, Tiger."

Harry had the presence of mind to be embarrassed. (And also turned on.) "That's just—" he sputtered. "I'm outraged for you."

"That's just the thing, isn't it?" she replied. "You shouldn't have to be in the first place."

Her eyes were wide, soulful. Harry experienced a sensation of deep inadequacy and a sort of shame-faced gratitude that she was here with him right now, in spite of the fact that she clearly deserved better. Had deserved better for a long time.

Harry cleared his throat. "Well, Charlie shouldn't have to suffer for it either."

Marion sighed. "I know. And I don't know how to help him. He won't talk to me and the more I try, the more he stiffens up. I hate that he feels like he has to protect me. I should be the one protecting him."

"I remember, when my mother got sick, how much I wanted to protect her. I ended up getting in fights at school, just because I wanted to fight something, do something, in the face of all that pointless tragedy."

"Charlie's really not a fighter. He's like I was as a kid, a rules-follower, and I'm afraid he just takes it all lying down."

Harry's leg jangled underneath the table. It was unreasonable how activated this conversation made him. "I could teach him some basics, if he wants."

"No! No, he's eight. I don't want you to do that."

"It could just be self-defense. Dodging, incapacitating, that sort of thing." Harry could tell he was overstepping, but he couldn't help it. He wanted to fix that miserable, lost expression on her brow.

"No. Harry." Marion looked up at him mournfully as the waiter abruptly intruded with their food, setting a plate of stuffed shells before Marion and a bleeding steak in front of Harry.

"*Bon appetit!*" the waiter said, utterly unaware of the awkward exchange he'd just interrupted (and of the fact that this was an Italian restaurant, not French). Harry poked at his steak with his fork. He'd ordered it rare to hurry things along, riding the wave of sexual tension from the truck that had crashed after them. He didn't actually prefer to eat meat this close to raw.

Marion sighed as the waiter retreated. "I'm sorry if this is awkward, but I just need to be clear. I don't want you to meet my children yet."

Harry nodded shortly and occupied his hands with cutting his meat. "Of course. I remember."

"I just don't want them to get attached to you and then have to lose another father figure if things don't work out. I'm sorry, I hope you can understand."

It was perfectly reasonable. So why did it make Harry feel so rotten?

He took a deep breath to steel himself and looked up with his most affable expression. "Of course, Marion. I understand completely. I just —" He just wanted to help. But that wasn't right. "I like you so much, and I hate that you have to go through all this on your own. I wish I could help."

Marion's smile returned and Harry sang an inward praise at the sight of it. "Thanks. That means a lot. Harry." She put his name in like it was its own complete thought. A beginning. A promise, even.

Harry took a bite of the too-rare steak and grinned. He decided to nudge her ankle with his toe beneath the table now. And just like that, the heat returned to her eyes.

Chapter 11

Harry let Marion into a studio apartment above a laundromat on the corner of 9th and Wabasha Streets in downtown St. Paul. She stood awkwardly in the entry, lights from the neon open sign at Mickey's Diner the next block over illuminating the room in red and blue as she waited for him to switch on the lights. The bulb clinked as it glowed to life in the schoolhouse ceiling fixture. The place had the feel of old St. Paul, of dingy speakeasies filled with gangsters, corrupt police, and shoot-outs in the street. A small smile crept onto Marion's lips as she watched Harry cross to the window and pull the shade down.

There was a tiny counter along the wall behind her, with a sink and a mirror mounted above it. The center of the room had a tidy desk and chair that appeared to serve double duty as both a desk and dining table. Along the left side of the room, there was a wood paneled wall with an opening at the center. Tucked behind was a dark bathroom and a clothes closet.

"Sorry, it's really not much," Harry said awkwardly, his hands twisting as he studied her face. Marion, for her part, could hardly care less what the apartment looked like. It wasn't as though she'd expected him to have some swanky penthouse or a mansion up on Summit Avenue.

He was a bachelor. He lived in a bachelor apartment. All she really cared about was that there was a bed, which wasn't presently in evidence. She could work around that if she had to. The desk seemed sturdy enough.

Marion's pumps clicked across the hardwood floors to join him near the solitary window. "Where do you sleep?"

Harry laughed. "There's a Murphy bed, just behind here."

He stepped to the wood panel that enclosed the closet and pushed at the corner where it met the exterior wall of whitewashed brick. The panel spun on a central axis and Marion couldn't help but exclaim with surprise. On the opposite side, a mattress was nestled vertically against it.

"Harry, that's the most magical bed I have ever seen!" she cried with a laugh. He still seemed embarrassed as, having reached a half rotation, he secured the wall back into place with a sliding bolt. Then he reached up and started to pull the mattress down. Metal legs with rubber on the feet cranked out. When the bed was about halfway, he suddenly turned towards her, a mortified expression on his face.

"I'm not being presumptuous," he said matter-of-factly. "You just asked where I slept so I figured it would be easier to show you than explain."

Marion grinned. "On the contrary. I encourage you to presume. If you put that mattress away, I will be very offended."

Harry held her gaze for a moment and Marion felt like she could gather up the anticipation between them in her hands, oozing between her fingers like sticky honey. He pushed the mattress all the way down firmly. Then, he turned, took two steps forward, and seized Marion's skull with two hands behind her head.

Marion gasped as he pressed his mouth against hers, firm and open. He sucked her bottom lip between his teeth and the tension that had been building through the entire night cracked open and made her legs quiver. Heat pooled between her legs and she could feel her pulse throb there. One of his hands pushed into her hair, gripping the back of her head, while the other ran down the side of her neck. He pushed his tongue into her mouth as he pushed his thumb underneath the collar of her sweater and she moaned. Aloud. Like she was in the throes of passion. But the only thing that was happening was a particularly heated kiss and the tamest form of petting. Harry turned his head slightly, breaking their kiss and pressing her cheek against his, rough with stubble.

"I need you to take this off," he murmured, plucking at the collar of her sweater then running his palm over the curve of her breast. "I need you to take all of this off."

"Quid pro quo." Marion's breathlessness gave her away as she attempted to counter. "You first."

Harry tipped his chin down and his eyes flickered from her face to her bosom and back again. He shrugged his jacket off. He had on a respectable Oxford shirt buttoned up to his chin with a nice tie whose knot he was now working loose. He looked fantastic all buttoned up. Marion grinned, delighted to be taken so seriously. She took a few steps back to admire his progress.

The tie joined the jacket on the worn wood floor. Harry watched her with those blue eyes as he pushed the buttons through the holes in his shirt. Marion pivoted to seat herself primly on the end of the bed. She smoothed out her skirt and propped her chin on her fist to watch with singular attention as Harry sidled his arms out of the shirt. He wore a thin, sleeveless undershirt beneath.

His shoulders looked just as well as they'd felt when she'd gripped them tight for leverage on Monday, broad and strapped with compact muscle down his biceps. A vein stood out against his lightly haired forearm. She could not even begin to explain why that made her squeeze her thighs deliciously together, but it did.

"Happy now?" Harry asked, his eyes heavy and expectant. He didn't even try to pretend he was looking at anything but her green sweater, which she imagined he would cause to spontaneously combust if he had the power to.

"Not even slightly," Marion replied cheekily. She leaned back on her hands and deliberately uncrossed her legs. "Keep going."

Harry glowered at her, but his heart wasn't in it and the corners of his mouth kept trying to twitch into a smile. He released his belt buckle and unfastened the fly of his trousers. Marion squirmed a bit. He let the light wool drop to the floor and stepped out of both the trousers and his shoes. His legs were shapely, which seemed odd for a fellow, but Marion's eyes drank in the curve of his calves, the slope of his thick thighs and the power they promised. Even in his socks and shorts and undershirt, he radiated a strength that made her blood thrill through her veins. He didn't look like those fatherly fellows in whimsical magazine underwear ads, even though he was dressed like them. His expression was dark, with a spark of deviousness to his mouth and if he'd been a stranger on the street looking at her like that, she wouldn't have felt safe. But this was Harry, who wore overalls and held screws in his teeth and brought her his hotplate just to ease her way a little. He always listened to her. She trusted him.

"More," Marion murmured.

Harry shook his head a little, but his mouth was twisted into a half smile as he pulled his shirt over his head and toed his socks off. Goddamn, his chest hair was redder than his hair, more of a copper, and it glinted in the glow of the incandescent bulb. His torso was long and a little soft on the belly, stretching from his waist to his broad shoulders. His nipples were tight, dark buds on his chest.

"Come on, you damn minx." His deep voice was rough and unchecked. "At least lose the sweater. I'm begging you."

The heat pumping through her limbs sharpened to a fine point on the word *beg*. Oh, that was a sweet sensation. No wonder he'd worked her so hard for it.

"Why?" she breathed.

"You know why."

"I think I do. I just want you to say it."

"I want to see you."

"Why?"

"Oh, for fuck's sake, Marion."

"Tell me. I want to hear you say why."

"Because, I want to see your body, Marion. I want to see every inch of your skin and I want you to wonder when I'm going to touch you. I want to see you strung tight waiting for it."

Marion bit her lip. Yes. That would do. She pulled the bottom edge of her sweater out from the waistband of her skirt, holding his eyes as she did it. What if he didn't like what he saw, when all the pieces were removed and she wasn't all encased and smoothed out? What if — she seized upon her doubts and shoved them away. No. As a teenager, she'd been skinny and she'd hated it. She finally had the curvy body she'd dreamed of, even if it didn't fit into the measurements the magazines and her sister prescribed. At the end of the day, she liked what she saw in the mirror, more than she ever had. He would too.

She pulled the neck of the sweater over her head. The swell of her breasts along the edge of her long-line bra rose and fell with her quickened breath. Harry's lips parted and Marion couldn't help but note that his shorts seemed markedly tighter than they had a moment ago.

"Shorts now," Marion pressed. She looked pointedly at the white cotton.

Harry pressed his lips into a thin line, his eyes skating ghosts of caresses over her shoulders and chest, then shoved the shorts down over his thighs. They dropped to the floor and his cock jutted out from him, flushed and firm. She swallowed hard. She wondered how soft and silky smooth that hot flesh would feel against her tongue. She almost lunged at him, but held herself back. There was an exquisite torture floating in the space between them, a tension so thick she could spread it on toast. It could have felt like an unnecessary barrier, or a source of awkwardness or indecision, but it didn't. It felt thrumming, alive and audacious.

Harry reached down and gave himself a firm, precise down-stroke. A sound escaped from Marion's throat.

"How do you just do that?" she asked.

"What?" He did it again. "This?"

"Yes," she moaned emphatically. "I could never just touch myself like that."

"Why not?"

"I don't know. It would feel embarrassing, with some-one watching."

"Would it? I think you might be surprised." His shaft had grown a bit under the attention of his hands. Its glistening tip seemed to reach for Marion. Desperate thoughts scrambled for her attention. She wanted him to crawl over her, wrap her knees over his shoulders, and press unapologetically into her. She wanted him to pull all her clothes off. She wanted him to kneel between her thighs. She wanted to kneel for him, lap that glistening moisture from his tip. She wanted all of these things at the same time, and so she did nothing except sit there, cunt throbbing, and whimper.

"Marion," he said, and even though he didn't move, he felt somehow closer. "Take off your clothes. Show me how you touch yourself."

He wasn't asking.

"What if I said no?"

"Then we'd find something else you want to say yes to. But I think you're tempted to do it."

She was. Before she could think too hard about it, she stood and unfastened her skirt, letting it and her crinoline drop to the floor. His eyes skittered over her girdle, the garters pulled tight over her thighs, as she released the long row of hooks that marched down her back. When that was done, she toed off her shoes and pushed everything, the girdle, the stockings still fastened to their garters, her panties, all of it down in one fell swoop. She had never felt so naked in her life and she was still wearing her brassiere. She could feel his eyes and the chill air of the drafty apartment make her skin tingle, mapping down the dip of her waist, the ample curve of her hip, the dark hair at the apex of her thighs. Her quim throbbed and she could feel the air cool the wetness that had smeared to her thighs as she removed her clothes. How could he make her feel like that without even touching her? His gaze was relentless, heated, and overwhelming. His fingers tightened around the base of his cock.

"You're not done yet," he murmured.

Marion gave a somewhat hysterical laugh as she shook

her gaze from his erection and reached behind to unclasp her brassiere. She slipped it off and let it drop to the floor, then looked eagerly to his face to track his response.

Harry's eyes dragged over her breasts. The cold air tightened her nipples, made them taut with sensitivity. She imagined she could feel his breath travel the two feet between them.

"This is …" she breathed. "This is wild."

"What do you mean?" He whispered too, like if they spoke too loud, they might break the spell.

"I've never imagined doing nothing could feel this good."

Harry cracked a smile. "Maybe doing something will feel even better, after the doing nothing." He took a step closer, packing the tension tighter between the two of them. Marion thought she might be able to feel it pressing against her stomach. "Now, lay down."

Marion obeyed. She could think of fifty things she would rather happen right now than lay down, most of them involving his tongue in some way, but he hadn't led her wrong yet.

"Spread your legs."

Marion let out a nervous giggle. "What? I can't…"

"Do it."

And like that, her knees fell open, seemingly of their own volition, even as her face burned with embarrassment. Harry grinned almost ferally. He jerked towards her and for a split second, Marion was giddy — finally! — with the promise of his touch. But he stopped. Gripped the base of his cock again in a way that made Marion choke a bit.

"Show me," he gritted out. "Show me how you touch yourself."

Mere moments ago, Marion would have been mortified. Maybe she was still mortified, which was part of why this felt so ridiculously good. But her fingers skated over the curve of her thigh and settled lightly over the lips of her folds. She pressed two fingertips into the wiry hair, pressed the folds open. His eyes widened. God, he could see everything now. She dipped the pads of her fingers into the wetness that pooled there, smeared it up to slick her way. His throat bobbed in his neck as she drew in a sharp inhale.

"Like this?" she whispered. God, the press of her fingers over her clitoris felt so fucking good. The slip of skin on skin, the touch of cool air chilling her eager entrance, the pressure as she rubbed harder.

"Your tits are so fucking perfect," he grunted and he pumped himself faster. "I knew they would be."

Harry slid his hand up and down his length. His thumb smeared the moisture gathering at his tip. God, he was slick for her, she was so wet for him, when he finally pressed into her, they were going to glide perfectly together like the last piece of a puzzle sliding into place.

"I can't wait for you to fuck me," she gasped and rubbed her fingertips faster too, then dipped down into her velvety entrance for more lubrication. She tipped her head back and her eyes fluttered closed as she pressed the back of her other hand against the side of her breast, feeling its familiar curve and heft. She couldn't quite bring herself to the audacity of cupping it or catching the nipple between her fingertips like she would when she was alone.

"Stop." His word was breathless, gritted out between his teeth.

Marion's eyes flew open and she snatched her hand away from her breast like she'd been caught out. Harry looked down at her, his chest flushed and his eyes wild. He was holding his cock in a tight ring of his thumb and forefinger. He looked wrecked.

"What's wrong?" she gasped as she drew her other hand to the safe, neutral territory of her stomach. Her fingers felt sticky.

"You look so fucking good like that," Harry grumbled, "and I don't want to come yet."

Her eyes widened with concern. "No, please don't come yet."

Harry's serious face split into a wide, affectionate smile. "It wouldn't be the end of the world."

"Strongly disagree," Marion replied. "I don't think I can wait five more minutes for you to fuck me, much less until tomorrow."

"Tomorrow?" Harry laughed. "It wouldn't be more than an hour, you looking like that. Maybe less."

Marion utterly failed to mask her surprise. In her prior experience, it took a lot of effort to get Joe up in the first place, much less twice in a night. Harry bit his lip and grinned. And finally — finally! — thank the Lord, he climbed onto the mattress and settled his weight over her. Marion keened delightedly and wrapped her thighs around his waist as their bare skin seared together. After so long letting the air between them grow thick with wanting, every point where his skin met hers felt electric. The sudden, overwhelming quantity of contact after so long denying it sent a flood of sensation that shocked her system, like being dunked into a cold lake but with the absolute opposite effect.

Harry pushed himself up on his elbows and then greedily pressed his mouth to hers. The heat of him was overwhelming, the pressure delicious, and Marion pushed her hips against his length trapped between them, gripping his waist hard with her thighs.

"You're so fucking ready for me," he said into her

mouth. She could feel the low timbre of his voice in her bones. She nodded eagerly and slid her pelvis against him in emphasis. She sucked his lip into her mouth and her hearing felt dampened by the spiraling pleasure of rubbing shamelessly against him.

Harry tilted his hips such that his cock slid along her folds and she bit down on his lip a bit harder than she'd meant to. He pulled back. "How close are you?"

"So close," she whimpered. She was too far gone to behave with any dignity.

He bent close and whispered in her ear, "How many times can *you* come in an hour?"

Marion's hands slackened on his shoulders. Her face felt like it was on fire. How could he make her blush with just one question while she was so shamelessly rutting against him? Maybe because the thing was, she knew the answer to his question. She'd tested it out. (Sometimes all the laundry was done and there were still hours to kill until the children came home. Sometimes pulp dime novels gave a girl ideas.)

"At least three," she managed to say over her thick tongue. "Sometimes more. There's a, um, compounding decline in the quality, though."

"Hm," he replied helpfully. And then he had the utter audacity to roll off of her.

"Hey, what's the big idea—" she started, but he grabbed her by the hips and pulled her on top of him. As she settled her knees on the either side of his waist, his calloused palms slid roughly over her hips, sliding up her stomach to indulgently caress handfuls of her breasts. His blunt thumbnails caught ever-so lightly on her nipples and they were so overly sensitive, the sharp sensation of it shot searing rounds into her groin. She moaned and chased his cock with her hips.

"Fuck me, fuck me, fuck me," she repeated desperately. The pressure of her cunt on his lower belly was not enough. He pushed himself to sitting with one hand, seizing a heaping handful of her breast with the other and enclosing its tip in his mouth. Marion cried out in surprise as she felt her thighs shake with tension. Her pleasure drew up tight, pressing in and coalescing. Harry's tongue flicked her nipple against his teeth, drawing her even tighter. She gripped his shoulders hard as her hips lifted and arched towards him. His hand came up and pinched her other nipple, twisting and rolling it in his fingers. Marion watched this with fascination as her breath caught in her throat and she felt her crest come within her reach. It felt ridiculous, but she was going to come. Just from this.

Harry looked up at her and his eyes smiled. He sucked hard and pulled her nipple back with him before he released it. It was slick and wet and tightened into a hardened nub. If he so much as touched her clitoris — or pushed his hot, bare cock into her, Jesus Christ — she'd come. She was so ready, teetering on the precipice. She could come untouched if he did that thing with his teeth just one more time.

"Please," she whined. He looked at her for a split second with perfect, blue-eyed clarity, before he flipped her onto her back, pushed her knees wide, and pressed his face into her folds. She must have screamed because her ears were ringing and her head felt tight, like it couldn't fit inside her skull, and she was coming harder than she had ever come in her life, harder than when he'd fucked her on her countertop two days ago. It ripped through her so that every muscle she had was shaking with the effort, seizing and pulsing as pure, keen sensation filled every gap in her body to overflowing.

Harry didn't let up. He used his lips and teeth and tongue to gather up every tremor, every drop of her pleasure until it was too much and she was swatting at him to stop. But he didn't stop. He kept pushing her, even as she squirmed with sensitivity, even as she thought she might cry, and then another crest broke over her. It all felt so incredibly impossible as she arched, her feet scrabbling at his back as her hands yanked hunks of his quilt in their search for purchase.

She was still quivering when he finally broke away, wiping his chin and leaning back over the end of the bed. She wearily pushed herself up onto her elbows as he drew the tin of rubbers from his pants pocket. The sight of it made her grin. Her heartbeat pulsed through her clitoris as if in agreement. Harry's face was ragged, his cock leaking a strand down onto her thigh as he broke the paper seal and pressed the condom over his tip.

"Yes," Marion breathed, spreading her thighs wider. She definitely had another orgasm in her. She was hungry for him to fill her, even if the rubber was going to keep the evidence well contained.

Sheathed, Harry got up on his knees and Marion tilted her quim eagerly towards him. Then he flopped onto his back next to her. "I want you on top of me. I want to see you use me to fuck yourself."

Jesus fucking Christ. He didn't have to tell her twice. Marion scrambled onto his lap and gripped his cock as she worked herself down over him. God, he felt so good filling her, stretching her. She hovered over him as she got the condom slick with her own wetness. Then she sat heavily on his lap, his prick spearing her, and looked down at Harry's face. His eyes were shot out with wide, black pupils, drinking her in. His lips parted as his breath came hot and fast, his chest flushing again as his hips jerked to meet hers. She'd never felt so beautiful. So powerful. She watched his face as she rolled her hips experimentally, searching for a rhythm that made her shiver. She drew an arm up and over her head, like a pin-up girl, just to see how he'd react.

A smile crept over his lips and his hands pushed up her ribs to cup her bobbing breasts. "Fuck, you're such a knock-out."

"So I've been told," Marion replied and her breath caught as she slid her hips just the right way.

"You look especially good riding my cock," he gasped as he squeezed his eyes shut and pumped harder up into her. Marion wished she had something to hold onto above her as she tried to match his increasingly erratic speed. She could tell he was close and she squeezed, willing herself closer too.

"You should see me with a cock in my mouth," she said experimentally. She'd imagined she'd be embarrassed to talk like that, but once the words were out of her lips, she felt a surge from her groin, a tremble in her thighs. Fuck yes.

Harry seemed to feel it too, because he gripped her thighs and hammered her from below, his lips parted and panting. Marion's hips stilted and seized with promise and she let him do the work as she chased her third release. She brought her hands down and cupped her own breast with one hand, squeezing the nipple hard between her thumb and forefinger, while she pushed her other hand between her folds and rubbed her clitoris hard with two fingers. The sight must have pushed Harry over the edge, because he gave a ragged groan and threw his head back. His own thrusts grew more harried and stilted as she rode out his release. Marion wasn't sure whether it was psychosomatic or real, but she could swear she could feel the searing heat of his release through the condom, filling its tip. And that did it. She was coming, a hot burst of pleasure squeezing around his quivering cock until it was too much for him and he pulled out. She collapsed on top of him and continued rubbing herself through her climax, shuddering as his hands came up to grip her shoulders and press gentle kisses to her hair.

When it was over, she decided she was never going to move from this spot again. In fact, she was so certain, she said so aloud.

Harry let out a long contented sigh. "No argument here."

"Won't it be difficult to finish my kitchen with a naked woman draped over you?"

"I'm sure I'll manage somehow." His hand cupped her jaw and he pressed more kisses to her cheek, her jaw, the sensitive spot just beneath her ear. "Stay here. At least tonight."

Marion slid onto one side, nestled in the crook of his arm, his side flush against her front, and let herself believe she could do that. At least for the next fifteen minutes.

Chapter 12

Thursday, December 8th, 1955
9 days until the Christmas party

When Harry woke up Thursday morning, it was to a cold bed with a pillow that smelled like Marion's hair. He swatted at his alarm clock, rolled over, pressed his face into the pillow, and inhaled. God, he wished she could have stayed. He'd driven her home and dropped her off like some sort of sneaky gangster in the alley with his truck lights all turned off. She'd gotten out of the truck and then looked back up at him with a small, secret smile before disappearing into the hedge. For some reason, out of all the exquisite moments of the previous evening, that smile was what he couldn't get out of his head.

He pulled himself out of bed and went to the water closet, brushing his teeth and staring at himself in the mirror as he tried to pick apart what to do next. They had an easy sort of dynamic that he couldn't stop yearning for. It was actually quite embarrassing. And maybe it was perfectly fine for him to continue working on Marion's kitchen and fucking her on his breaks. But he'd made a point to take her out on a proper date and, even though it had certainly ended with a somewhat misguided but extremely satisfying encounter, he meant to demonstrate that his interest was more than just physical. He wanted her, far beyond what a few weeks of banter and bedding could provide. It seemed like a foregone conclusion that a woman would want a fellow to go through the motions of propriety, so when Marion made it clear she wanted to hook up with him in secret, he'd been a little thrown for a loop. He couldn't be sure that he wasn't the fallen person in this interaction, the person whose finer feelings were being taken advantage of.

These thoughts made him squirmy, so he shut the medicine cabinet door on them. It was install day. He had a full suite of appliances to get running, and the electrician would be there in the afternoon to make sure he didn't blow any fuses in the process. Marion would be there in the morning, but she'd said she had errands to run before the children returned from school. So Harry steeled himself for a day of the more drudging sort of work, made more dreary by the lack of privacy with his new favorite person.

He stopped at the Tick Tock diner on his way to Marion's to make sure he wasn't too early again. As he turned the corner to return to his truck, a steaming paper cup of coffee collecting the lightly falling snow, he noticed a kid in a brown wool coat and a flat cap loitering in Phil's Place's parking lot. Harry paused and squinted. The boy was strikingly familiar, and it only took him a moment to realize it was Marion's son. Who was supposed to be at school, not poking around the empty parking lot of a dinner club.

Harry did hesitate. He swore he did. He knew Marion didn't want him to meet her kids yet. But he wasn't intervening as the boy's mother's boyfriend, or whatever he was, at least that was what he told himself as he started across the icy street. He was a concerned community member who'd spotted a child playing truant.

The kid noticed his approach from about thirty yards away and turned away, making to walk off in the opposite direction.

"Hey, Charlie," Harry blurted, waving his hand that wasn't holding his coffee cup.

The boy startled, looking furtively over his shoulder, then squinted.

"Who are you?" he said guardedly. "How do you know my name?"

Harry winced and barreled on in spite of the guilt growing in his chest. "I'm Mr. O'Conner, the contractor installing your mother's kitchen. I met you the other day on your way to school."

Met was a strong word. More like exchanged wary glances. That happened again now.

"Which," Harry continued, "is supposed to be where you are right now, if I'm not mistaken."

Charlie's eyes skittered away across the frosty pavement, and Harry caught him trying to erase a wince from his expression. He remembered the feeling of being caught out doing something he wasn't supposed to do. He remembered the flood of anger at being told all the ways his thoughts and feelings and priorities didn't matter. He wasn't about to do that to this boy. He sighed and adjusted his own cap.

"Maybe there's something — or maybe someone — you're not too eager to see at school today?" Harry ventured. Charlie intensified his glower, so Harry added, "I remember dealing with a bully when I was your age. It was awful. But I did learn that if I didn't face him, it only got worse."

Charlie's lip curled. "You have no idea what you're talking about."

Harry frowned. "I suppose you're right. I don't. But I'm willing to listen."

Charlie blinked a few times. When he looked up at Harry, he could see the poor boy was blinking back tears. Harry felt the flinching instinct to look away, to preserve the boy's dignity, but he remembered what that felt like at that age. Instead, he stepped forward and placed a bracing hand on the boy's shoulder.

Charlie hunched over himself for a moment, sniffed a few times, and then managed to fix his face back into a serious expression. "I wasn't going to play hooky. I just wanted to make myself scarce until all the other kids are inside."

Harry considered this. He wasn't very familiar with the neighborhood, but he did know there was a school only a few blocks from here. It was plausible. And Harry wondered, really wondered, what it would be like for a boy to be taken at his word instead of bulldozing over him with an inflated sense of knowing better. So he nodded. "Okay." He flipped his wrist to check his watch. "Isn't it about time for you to be heading back, then?"

Charlie shifted from foot to foot. It was cold out today. "Yeah."

Harry returned both his hands to the warm paper cup. "You need a lift?" He flicked his head toward where his white truck was parked on the street.

Charlie's serious expression regarded Harry for a moment, then looked back over his shoulder to the truck. The fact that the kid seemed to easily pick out which vehicle it was told Harry that he indeed remembered.

"Sure. Thanks."

Harry nodded and felt that sense of guilt inflate to the point that he was choking a little on it. Marion wouldn't like that he was talking to her son, but she also wouldn't like that her son was loitering around the neighborhood instead of being in school. He wasn't hurting anyone by intervening, and surely, someone needed to. It was too cold for an eight-year-old to be playing truant by himself all day. All sorts of trouble could be heaped on this kid's doorstep if Harry left him to himself, and at the end of the day, Harry couldn't stomach the thought of leaving him alone just because Marion told him she wasn't ready to introduce him to her kids. She wouldn't want him to leave Charlie to whatever it was he was going to do all day (because plausible as it was, he didn't believe for a second the boy was just waiting for school to start before heading back).

"Come on." Harry led the way across the street to his truck. The boy climbed into the passenger seat, where his mother had sat last night, and Harry swallowed against some sort of mutant emotion in his throat, guilt and discomfort and something else he couldn't begin to describe. Duty, maybe? Or longing? It felt wrong, whatever it was. Like he was pretending to be someone he wasn't.

He set his coffee cup on the dash and fished in his coat pocket for the key.

"Oh, yeah," he said and pulled out the bear claw he'd bought at the Tick Tock. "Do you want this?"

Charlie looked up and solemnly regarded the pastry with covetous eyes.

"Go on, take it," Harry insisted, setting the pastry on the bench between them before going back into his pocket for his keys. He kept his eyes on the wheel as he plugged the key into the ignition and turned it. He heard the crinkle of pastry paper and he tried not to grin as he clunked the truck into gear and lurched into the road, snatching his paper cup before it jostled off the dash.

The school really was just down the street and around

the corner. When he pulled up, the schoolyard was empty. Charlie held half a pastry in his hands, which he regarded before he looked up at Harry and said, "Thanks."

"Anytime."

"Please don't tell my mother."

Harry frowned. Keeping his connection to this boy's mother from him was one thing, but juggling a secret from her son as well was quite another. But … he'd also won a measure of trust just now, hard-earned and tenuous, and what would happen if he breached that and found out later that his way would have been eased had he not? He knew now he was serious about Marion. That meant he needed to be someone her kids could trust.

"Fine," Harry rumbled. "But I don't want to hear or see you do anything like this again."

Charlie let out a breath he apparently had been holding. He nodded. "Thanks for the pastry, Mister."

"Don't worry about it," Harry said. "Study hard, okay?"

God, he sounded like his Uncle Pat. Next thing he knew, he'd be ruffling the kid's hair and making outrageously bad puns. Charlie gave a serious nod and pushed the truck door open, then slid out and made his way towards the school whose bricks stood out dark against the snow flurry.

Harry waited until he'd gone through the door before he put the truck into gear and headed towards Marion's.

✦

The door snicked shut behind the electrician and Harry felt a crack of frisson zoom up and down his spine. They'd spent the whole morning wrangling electrical wattage for the new appliances, going down and up the stairs to the basement endlessly trying to figure out whether Mrs. Milner needed a new breaker or not. The bad news was that she would indeed need a new breaker. The good news was that that meant there was nothing more for the electrician to do until he could get the parts and return on Monday, leaving Harry and Marion blissfully alone once again. He leaned on the shiny new countertops as Marion turned the corner back into the kitchen.

"How're you holding up," Harry asked.

Marion shrugged. "A new breaker will be best in the long run. It's not so much extra, all said and done."

She crossed the room and pressed her hands over his chest, pushing her fingers under the bib of his overalls. He hoped she could feel his heart race under her touch. She looked up at him regretfully. "I should probably get some lunch together."

"Or," Harry replied slowly, "we could work up an appetite."

All it took was the twitch of a smile on her lips before he took the liberty of claiming them with his own, letting his hands settle into the cradle of her waist and pulling her against him.

"You are terrible," she murmured with absolutely no malice whatsoever.

"You don't really think that," Harry replied and sucked her lip in between his teeth until she moaned. He had a hundred ideas of what he wanted to do with her and was annoyed that he could only do a few of them at a time. Her fingers pulled at the fasteners on his overalls, pushing them free enough to loosen his inseam against his hardening prick. He seized her hips and pulled them into his own to inform her of his condition.

"I was going to run errands," she murmured.

"Nothing that can't wait for tomorrow?" he replied. "After all, there won't be anything to do for the kitchen until Monday now."

She tipped her chin down to smile up at him. God, he wanted to seize either side of her blouse and rip it off, sending the buttons flying all over the room. Instead, he chased her mouth and kissed her fiercely while his hands pushed under her skirt to knead at her generous thighs.

"You're eager," she murmured against his mouth, her lips stretching in a smile.

"Would you rather I take my time?"

"Maybe … I don't know." Her breath was in his mouth and his nose and he felt drunk on her scent. "Maybe we have time for both?"

He grinned. Quick fuck before lunch, then a torturously long one after. He could get behind that. He rumbled his approval into her mouth and enjoyed the play of teeth and tongue and lips for a few more minutes. Then, he seized her hips and whirled her round so she faced the countertop. Her hands naturally went to brace against the laminate. The edge wasn't too high — at her waist — but he was fairly sure this position would be more accommodating for his height when it came to the final act. He pressed his erection against her round backside to make her think about it.

"Oh, Harry," she gasped and her fingers curled against the countertop. He seized great handfuls of her skirt and shoved it up around her waist, pressing himself into the soft cleft of her ass with only the flimsy satin of her panties — well, no, not quite because his overalls were still half up. He didn't hate that though, and he rubbed the rough denim over the backs of her thighs, enjoying how her skin pinked after a few rolls of his hips. He wanted to see the flush of her sex, see it glisten for him, but she was strapped and hooked within an inch of her life by her girdle and stockings, making it impossible for him to just yank her panties down.

"Fuck these things," he growled, snapping the panties over her left buttock.

"Just cut them off," she gasped. Harry froze for a moment as her directive surged in his ears and all the blood in his body dropped directly into his cock.

It took him a moment to return to himself, to scrabble at his toolbelt (which was why his overalls hadn't dropped to the floor yet) for his side cutters. They were better used for cutting errant nails or wires than for slicing off a lady's underwear, but they would do to get through the elastic so he could rip the rest. Yes. This was good. He was ecstatic at the prospect of ripping her clothes off of her. After seizing the cutters in his right hand, he unbuckled his toolbelt with his left and let the whole thing crash noisily onto the linoleum. His overalls slumped down further, but were sort of caught on his erection as he carefully let the cold, metal jaws of the cutters slide over Marion's hip. Her breath was coming in gasps and her thighs trembled. *God*, this woman. He pulled the elastic of her panties up enough to slide in between the jaws of the cutters, then paused. "You sure?"

"Yes, yes, please get them off already, God dammit." Her voice was thin and desperate. He squeezed the cutters hard and cleanly sliced through the elastic and the filmy satin that encased it. He set the cutters on the counter, and she whimpered as he gripped the edges in his hands and tore the fabric clean across the grain, revealing a swath of her creamy smooth skin. It stopped firm at the elastic hem at the opposite edge. His grip had pulled the fabric tight between her legs, into her cleft. He gave that end an extra tug before he released it and she hiccoughed an involuntary moan. Her right buttock was on full display and he gave it a firm caress before reaching for the cutters again. He snipped the opposite elastic with the cutters and set them back on the countertop as he admired the bare swath of her backside, a milky expanse of flesh with a deep cleft, strapped on each side by the garters that held her stockings up.

"Fuck, Marion," he growled, filling his hands with her flesh. He deeply enjoyed the idea that he could flip her skirt back down and she'd look for all intents and purposes fully dressed. He imagined an occasion where she might dress to the nines for a nice dinner date, but omit the panties. He imagined having her against the wall in the swanky restroom of the restaurant. He'd only have to unzip and pull her skirt up and she'd be ready for him. God, it was everything he could do to resist pushing into her right now, enveloping himself into the hot welcome of her flesh. The only reason he resisted, he reminded himself, was because then it would be over. And despite the fact that she'd suggested they go quick, he loved the exquisite torture of this too much. So instead of burying his cock into her, he dropped to his knees and pressed his face into her cleft instead.

This must have been unexpected, as it made her scream. He grinned as his tongue found her slick cunt and pressed into it. He prodded her a few times before he pulled back, his hands pushing her legs wide so he could admire how flushed and wet she was for him.

"Fuck, Harry, fuck, please," she babbled.

"Please what?" he replied and took another firm lick, this time over her clit.

"P-please, just, please—" he pressed his tongue harder against her clit, let it flick with pressure, "— please, God, please, Harry, I'm-I'm —"

The groan she delivered sounded more like she was lifting a truck than having an orgasm, and her thighs seized around his head with such force it made him dizzy, but he carried on licking and kissing and sucking until her legs trembled with the effort and she sagged against the countertop. Harry sat back on his heels and watched her pulsing cunt, framed by her generous ass and ample, gartered thighs. It was a view he intended to save forever.

Harry got unsteadily to his feet and shoved his overalls down to his shins. He pushed his hand against the small of her back and lined himself up. The height was much better this way. He grinned.

Now he would fuck her.

He pushed in. Marion's fingers scrabbled at the countertops. She sank compliantly under the pressure of his hand. She moaned aloud again, her hips squirming for a better angle, pressing towards him. He pushed up on his toes and drove in. She was crying out for him with every thrust, pushing back in rhythm, slick and hot and deep and he couldn't string thoughts together anymore because he felt his edge come up on him as fast as he had feared.

Which was also about the time he realized he hadn't stopped to put on a condom. In a hysterical panic, he pulled out and stepped back. He was already pulsing so he gripped himself in his hand and brought himself to his finish all over the brand new linoleum floor. He made a desperate sound, his head spinning with pleasure and danger and relief in a deadly cocktail that frightened him, because it was the most incredible orgasm he'd ever experienced and he couldn't deny how much the notion of truly compromising Marion had played into that. Even the shame of that desire was an ingredient.

"Harry," she whimpered. She was still draped over the

counter, her buttocks laid out like a feast. "Harry, please, I'm so close."

He hesitated. He couldn't decide whether he should appease her first, then apologize, or if he should take immediate responsibility. He had no idea how she might react. He'd had sex with Alice without a condom, pulling out before his moment of release, and they'd never had any trouble. But he didn't know how Marion would feel about that. Had she noticed? God dammit.

"Marion, I'm so sorry," he blurted. "I forgot the condom, I'm so sorry."

Her attention was immediately caught. "But you didn't —"

"No, no, I, uh," he gestured uselessly at the mess he'd made of the floor. "I pulled out."

"Oh." She surveyed the mess. "I see."

"I'm sorry, Marion, I have them right in my pocket. I just got caught up — I know, it's no excuse — but I'm sorry."

Marion bit her lip then slid delicately off the counter, pushing her skirt down in the process. Fuck, but she did look just as put together as she always did, albeit more flushed and her hair a little rumpled. If he wasn't such a monstrous fuck-up, that dinner-date fantasy could have been his. When she spoke, her voice was carefully measured, spread thin. "Does that work?"

"What?"

"Pulling out?"

"I, uh," Harry pulled his shorts and overalls back up self-consciously and licked his lips. "It has, in the past. For me. As far as I know."

"I thought it felt different." She flushed. Then she pressed her face into her hands and sucked in a breath. "What would you do if it didn't work?"

"Do you mean if you got, uh —"

"Yeah." Her face was still covered with her hands.

Harry's heart surged. It was the uncanniest thing. Here he was, mortified with himself, feeling like the worst kind of cad, and all he wanted to say was "Marry me, Marion," which was absolutely the least romantic proposal in the history of man, but it didn't make him want it less. Instead, he said, "I'd do right by you. However you decided."

Marion looked up at him again. Her expression was not particularly readable, but it definitely wasn't the look of a woman who was holding back an uncontrollable desire to marry him.

"I'm sorry," he repeated. "It won't happen again."

Marion nodded, her eyes on the floor.

"Good. Let's get some lunch, shall we?"

Harry pushed his hand over his head and hesitated for a moment. "Alright. I'll just, uh, clean this up."

Chapter 13

Marion wasn't sure what to make for lunch. Probably because she wasn't sure how she felt about the entire situation that Harry was cleaning up in the kitchen. She pulled out four slices of bread from the bread box on the dining table and began the rote of preparing peanut butter and jelly sandwiches while her thoughts rioted inside her skull.

She hadn't noticed there wasn't a condom. But she'd also known there wasn't. Did that make any sense? The rubbers pulled a little unpleasantly before they were, well, slicked, which took a few strokes. In fact, she'd never used one before Harry had introduced them of his own accord when they'd started this whole thing. She hadn't really thought to ask. She knew how children were made, of course, she'd had two of them for Chrissakes, but to be honest, when she'd begged him to fuck her that first time, she'd assumed he would pull out. She'd been half-stupid with lust, but she imagined she would have said something to that effect at some point if he hadn't been so prepared with the rubbers already.

Fact was, ten minutes ago when she'd been fucked over her new laminate countertops, she'd known he'd been bare and the only thought that had crossed her mind was how hot and smooth and velvety his cock had felt. She'd fully known he didn't have the condom and it hadn't occurred to her to be concerned about it. What kind of reckless idiot did that make her?

Even now the idea of him filling her up made her squeeze her thighs together and remember sharply that she was not wearing any kind of underwear because he had *cut hers off* and — *fuck*. A smarter, wiser woman would feel betrayed or call things off. But Marion found that she just wanted to get through lunch so she could ride him in her bedroom. Because at the end of the day, she was indeed the wanton sex-crazed divorcee everyone feared she was.

Or perhaps, she just trusted Harry. Even as he was literally cleaning up the mess he'd made, clear evidence of his fallibility, she still wanted to trust him wholly. It felt so good to let him have his way with her. She didn't want to lose that. She really wanted to believe it had been a mistake.

Harry came in and assumed a rather chastened pose in one of the dining chairs as Marion cut his sandwich in half and set his plate in front of him. She took a seat next to him at the end of the dining table that wasn't covered with pots and pans and pantry items in her makeshift kitchen.

"Did you truly forget?" she ventured as she picked up her sandwich tentatively.

Harry blinked at her. "Yes."

"Okay. I mean … well, okay. That is to say, I did notice you didn't have the rubber."

Harry's brow crumpled. "Why didn't you say anything?"

Marion's mouth opened, but no words came out. She shrugged. "I'm not sure. Honestly, I think I just … um, trusted you."

His mouth tightened to a flat line. "I'm so sorry, Marion. I don't deserve that trust—"

"—But I think you do." Marion winced and hoped she wasn't being a complete fool. "You made sure you didn't, you know…"

"Right."

Marion felt a tiny laugh burst out of her. "Oh my God, Harry, look at us. We could do all that in the kitchen moments ago, but we can't even talk about what we already did." She giggled. "And even as I say that, I still can't make myself say it."

Harry reached over and took her wrist, drawing her hand away from her face. "Marion. I want to deserve your trust. I swear I will do everything in my power to take care of you. I messed up today. I got cocky and I didn't think. I swear on my mother's grave I didn't do it on purpose, or because it was convenient. I was careless. I won't be so foolish again."

Marion bit her lip. "Good." The word sort of gushed out of her, the first in a deluge. "Because I love how you take charge of me and the way you make me feel like some sort of, I don't know, goddess? That sounds so egotistical but—"

" —No, it's not. I worship you." He said it so seriously, it made her embarrassed, and she couldn't help but flush and giggle.

"But I want to trust you. It feels too good. So …" she thought for a moment, "I need you to do everything you can to deserve it."

Harry stilled and considered her very soulfully for a moment. Then, he nodded. "I will." He looked down at his untouched sandwich. When he looked up at her again, his expression was steeled. "I will always use a condom. I will handle that. If you want it a different way,

I'll wait to hear from you."

Marion pressed her lips together against the unsolicited disappointment of having to use those rubbers. He was absolutely right that it was the best course. She just wished there was another way. She nodded.

"Thanks, Harry."

"Thank you, Marion."

She scoffed. "For what?"

"For being magnanimous. I don't deserve it, but I plan to earn it."

Marion pressed her lips together. "Good." Her cunt reminded her with a pulse that it was still bare and wanting underneath her skirt. "Because I'd like you to get a head start after lunch."

✦

Harry was as good as his word. After lunch, he took Marion to her bedroom, pushed her skirt up around her ears, and used his tongue to make her come in two or three waves that made her very glad her tenants upstairs were out for the day. Then, he took off her skirt and blouse and bra and directed her to ride his rubber-sheathed cock in her girdle and stockings. It was absurd the way being almost naked felt so much more exciting than actually being naked, but Marion wasn't about to ask any further questions. By the time she had to get up to dress for meeting the kids' bus, she was boneless and exhausted and blissfully happy.

Marion stood in her bedroom and plucked at the shredded remains of her panties as Harry lolled on her pillow. It would smell like him later, and she had every intention of making the most of that with her own fingers after the children went to sleep.

"You're ridiculous," she informed him, pulling the satin out from under her girdle as evidence.

"Excuse me," he replied. His bicep under his cheek was perfect. "I believe that was *your* idea."

"A means to an end," she sniffed and turned to consider the issue in the vanity mirror. Her nipples were an almost angry red from the relentless attention he'd paid them, and the skin around them was chafed pink from his stubble. Her cheeks flushed with pleasure from how debauched her reflection looked. There was nothing like the thatch of dark hair at the apex of her thighs where her panties should be, peeking out from under her girdle.

"You like to look at yourself," Harry murmured.

Marion crossed her arms across her chest. It just made her breasts swell together between her arms. She shrugged.

"I'll have to remember that for next time."

God, she needed to get him the hell out of here if she wanted to keep a clean pair of panties. "Quit it," she chided and yanked on the remnants of her panties once more before, in a fit of decisiveness, she pulled a pair of snips from her drawer and cut them all the way off at the side seam. She tossed them into the wastebasket.

"Sorry about that."

"*Please* don't be," she replied as she dug into her bureau for a fresh pair. "There's more where these came from."

Harry snickered and stood, pulling his shirt back on. Marion turned and smiled admiringly.

"See, everyone looks good dressed only to the waist," she pointed out.

Harry grinned and waggled his hips at her. She squealed and he seized her by her shoulders. He kissed her, slow and deep. She expected it to feel like a prelude to something. It did, in its way, but whatever it was, it wasn't sex. It made her breath go out of her like a popped balloon.

Tentatively, she pulled away. "I have to go meet the kids. And you need to go."

Harry sighed and pressed his forehead against hers. "I know."

Then he squeezed both halves of her buttocks and like that, the moment was over and she was giggling again.

Marion watched Harry drive off in his truck through the window of her great oak front door and wondered for a long moment what on earth she expected to come of this. Everyone in the neighborhood expected her to remarry. In fact, there were many (her mother included) who thought she was well past the time to remarry. But even with Harry in the fantasy, Marion couldn't imagine it. What she had with Harry was lovely, revelatory in many ways, and with him, she felt like herself. Maybe it was her past experience talking, but she worried that would go away if she became his wife.

She was out on the corner to meet the bus right on time. Linda hopped off first with a giant construction paper snowflake in her hand, grinning with pride. Charlie stood at the head of the aisle for a moment and glared harshly at someone toward the back of the bus before he stomped down the steps to the street behind her.

"How was school?" Marion recited, accepting the proffered snowflake with a grin.

Charlie shrugged as the bus pulled away. A shout leapt from one of the rear windows and Marion looked up with bewilderment.

"What was that?" she wondered aloud, but no sooner had the words come out of her mouth than Charlie was sprinting into the road, shouting cuss words at the retreating bus for all the neighborhood to hear.

"Charles Frederick Milner!" Marion screeched. "What is wrong with you?"

Charlie turned on his heel and grimaced at her. His mouth was grim, his eyes wide and angry. His nostrils flared for a moment before a tear leaked out of his eye and his face just *crumpled*. Tears started to flow and Marion hurried toward him with horror.

"Oh, honey, no, come on now, don't cry," she babbled in hushed tones.

"Momma, Charlie's sad," Linda declared, hopping into the street after Marion. It was a quiet neighborhood and there were no cars coming, but it scared Marion for a jolt nonetheless.

"Yes, I see that Linda," Marion said as she tried to herd Charlie toward the house, looking over her shoulder to make sure none of the neighbors could see him. God dammit, shouting obscenities and then crying like newborn babe? What on earth would the bullies at school make of that if they got wind of it? She hoped he wasn't doing that at school.

"Charlie, stop it," she hissed as they approached the opposite sidewalk. "You said bad words and you're going to be punished for it. If you didn't want that to happen, you shouldn't have swore to begin with."

Charlie sank into his shoulders and shook his head. He was clearly trying and failing to get a hold of himself. He gave a mighty sniff and pushed through the gate into their backyard.

"Hello, Milners!" came a call from across the street.

"Sorry, Edna," Marion called back. "We've got a bit of a situation just now."

Marion winced, worried that she'd been unspeakably rude.

"Been there!" Edna replied easily, then turned and headed into her house. Marion blinked after her for a moment. She wasn't sure what she'd expected, but apparently, it hadn't been solidarity.

Charlie was standing on the stoop with his head hung, waiting for Marion to unlock the door.

"It's open, honey," Marion said as she hustled Linda through the gate.

Charlie pushed inside and let out an unholy wail as soon as he was indoors. Marion's shoulders sagged. It was times like these, when her children acted incomprehensibly, that she missed Joe the most. He had this unearthly calm about him (that was probably due to the fact that he didn't really know what to do with any of them, but it had been steadying nonetheless).

Marion herded Linda through the door and shuffled over the shoes in the entryway.

"Charlie?" she called, not seeing him immediately.

"He's in our room," Linda pointed out. The children shared a bedroom off the sitting room that had probably been an office or music room or something when the house had been one big residence, but now that it was a duplex, it was the second bedroom. Marion cracked open the door and saw Charlie had bundled himself underneath his blankets.

"Charlie, come out of there. I need to talk to you," Marion said.

"No dessert," Charlie said, parroting back the usual punishment for bad behavior in their house. "I understand. I won't do it again."

Marion sighed. "But I want you to tell me why you did it. What's going on?"

"I don't wanna talk about it," Charlie muttered, pulling the blankets tighter over his head.

Marion stood in the doorway for a long moment. She cycled through all the things she could say. When cross-referenced with all the things she had already tried in the last few weeks, she was coming up with nothing. Perhaps it was high time she tried waiting for Charlie to be ready. To trust him to come to her when he needed her.

"Alright," Marion said quietly and shut the door.

Chapter 14

Monday, December 12th, 1955
5 days until the Christmas party

On Monday, Harry was sitting at the counter at the Tick Tock, reading the paper and waiting until he could get into Marion's house. She had a Sokol Ladies Auxiliary meeting this morning and the electrician wasn't able to be there until after lunch, so there was nothing for Harry to do at the house except get foolish ideas about an idyllic domestic future he had no right to fantasize about.

The counter at the Tick Tock was just inside the door and it stretched from the front to the back, with an extension that ran right along the front window. Harry sat there now, watching the cars pass by on West 7th Street and letting his mind wander as he sipped his coffee. Impressively, his imagination didn't require the scenery of Marion's cozy house to inspire insipid flights of domestic fancy. Harry shook the paper and forced himself to read the sports section.

Out of the corner of his eye, he caught sight of a person much too short to be walking the sidewalk at this hour of the day. He folded the paper down and frowned as he saw Charlie Milner picking his way around an ice patch just outside the cafe. Harry stood abruptly, his stool squealing on the tile floor. The kid had promised he wouldn't pull shit like this again. God dammit.

Charlie looked up from the ice patch, saw Harry through the window, and gave a tentative smile that looked much more like a grimace. Harry frowned and crooked his fingers. Charlie's grimace lost all remaining remnants of forced merriment, and he nodded curtly as he hustled to the door of the cafe and came inside.

The bell rang and the fellow working the cash register behind the counter frowned at Charlie.

"Ain't you supposed to be in school, fella?" the cashier said. Charlie's shoulders rounded and Harry took a few steps toward him.

"He's with me," Harry said to the cashier, then shook his head at Charlie. "I thought you weren't going to pull this kind of thing anymore."

Charlie's lip quivered for a moment, his brows slowly crumpling as he tried with all his might to keep himself together. God dammit all. Harry rubbed his hands on his overalls and sighed. "It's alright, come on now. Sit down." He herded the boy onto a stool, then looked over to the cashier. "Say, can we get a pastry over here? And a glass of milk?"

The cashier nodded and ducked into the bake case.

Turning his attention back to Charlie, Harry felt his brows furrow at how the boy's chin trembled, his eyes cast shame-facedly at his hands in his lap. "Hey. What's happened?"

Charlie's mouth pressed into a thin line. He shrugged.

The cashier quietly slid the glass of milk and a plate with a Danish on it in front of the boy. Harry nudged the glass toward him. "Whatever it is, it looks like you need a stiff drink."

That made the boy crack a wan smile. He reached up

and took the glass in two hands. His hands were so small. The knuckles were scraped up and bloody. He let the kid take a drink before he said anything more.

"Wanna start with what happened to your hands?" Harry said when the glass was set back on the counter.

Charlie curled his hands into his coat and shook his head. Harry frowned and turned to his coffee. He lifted the heavy earthenware cup and took a long sip while he waited. Twenty different things he might say to encourage the boy to open up popped into his head, but he squashed them down and forced himself to wait.

Several minutes passed. Charlie picked at the Danish and took another sip of milk. Harry was humming with agitation at first, but after a minute, he began to feel his own energy and patience smooth out. He was starting to cobble together a gentle suggestion to get the kid back to school when Charlie said, "I got in a fight."

Harry could crow with triumph. Instead, he gave a curt nod and, continuing to regard his coffee cup, said, "Oh?"

"There's this fifth-grader who likes to make fun of my mom," Charlie said. He was shredding a scrap of pastry onto his plate. "And other kids think it's funny, so they join in too. I can't walk through school without them saying stuff to me. It's every day."

Harry nodded. "Hm."

Charlie looked at his lap and squeezed his eyes tight. "Today they just crossed a line. That's all."

"Did they?"

"Freddy deserved it, okay? He's had it coming for months now. I don't know what I'm supposed to do. I know I'm s'posed to turn the other cheek, but I just *couldn't*."

Harry swallowed around some kind of feeling and nodded. "Sure."

"And there's only so much a fellow can take," Charlie said resolutely, nodding like he was convincing himself as much as he was Harry. His chin began to tremble again. Harry reached out and put his hand on the boy's shoulder.

"What did the teachers do?"

Charlie grimaced. "I didn't stick around to find out."

"I mean, before. When the kids were all saying … all the things they were saying."

Charlie looked up at Harry for the first time then, his eyes skeptical under his brows. "They pretended not to hear. Because they agree, I think. They'd say it too if they could."

Harry frowned. He felt a swell of protectiveness in his chest. "What have they been saying?"

Charlie looked at him a long time before he took a breath, looked over his shoulder, and whispered, "That my mother's … loose. That she's been trying to steal their fathers away from their mothers. That she's a hussy and a … I can't say it. But you know what I mean?"

Charlie flinched a little when he looked up at Harry again. It occurred to Harry that he might look rather imposing, given he was grappling for control over a wave of hot rage. "I do."

"It makes me so *mad*," the kid said, his fists tight in his lap. "She works so hard, she's never done anything wrong, and my Dad just up and left us and I don't know why everyone can't just *leave us alone!*"

Tears started to spill over Charlie's cheeks. Harry's hand on his shoulder squeezed. He wanted to pull the poor kid into a tight hug. But he didn't. He wasn't this boy's father and he had that feeling again — that twist of self-consciousness that made him feel like an imposter — even as he was also supremely proud and honored that

Marion's son had trusted him with this.

Harry pulled his handkerchief from his pocket and offered it quietly to Charlie.

"Well," he said at last. "Sounds to me like that little snot deserved it."

Charlie snorted around his sniffle as he wiped his face with the handkerchief.

"Thanks for telling me," Harry said solemnly.

Charlie gave a curt nod. "I don't know what to do now. They're gonna call my mother and I just … I don't want her to know what they're saying about her. Every time we go somewhere, they whisper and I can see how much it bothers her. She doesn't deserve a bit of it."

Harry gave his shoulder a pat and drew his hand away. "That's kind of you, but you don't deserve a bit of it either. And you might be surprised how strong she really is."

Charlie narrowed his eyes. "You think so?"

"I know so. I've been working on your kitchen for almost a month and I can tell you, your mother is the bravest lady I've ever met."

"Brave?"

"Sure. Listen, sometimes being brave doesn't look stoic or proud or confident. Sometimes it looks like facing something head on, even if it scares the pants off you, and doing it anyway. Because it's right. Your mother could have hidden away but she hasn't. She faces everyone straight on. She knows she ain't got anything to be ashamed of." Harry's chest puffed a little with pride.

Charlie frowned. "She shouldn't have to, though. None of these people should be saying all these mean things in the first place. They're *wrong*."

"You're right. They are very wrong. And your teachers should know better than to let them go on slandering any of you."

"How can I make them?"

"Did you tell your father any of this? I'll tell you what, if you were my son, I'd be in that principal's office giving him an earful he wouldn't soon forget."

Charlie shrank somehow. "I can't. He'd just get real sad, say he's doing everything he can — which he *isn't*, Mr. O'Conner, he really isn't — and buy us ice cream to make himself feel better."

Harry had wanted to clock Joe Milner before, so this sensation wasn't new. "What about your mother?"

Charlie sank into his chair. "Aw, I really don't wanna tell her."

"I know. But she's tough."

"She ain't, though. And I can't watch her cry no more."

"Crying isn't the opposite of tough. Listen, kid, I been in the airforce and I seen lots of grown men cry. And I'll tell you what — they're the tough ones. The ones who run away don't cry. They're too busy hiding."

Charlie seemed to chew on this. "Can *you* talk to my principal?"

"What?"

"Well, you just said, if I were your kid, you'd go and tell the principal what's what."

"Yeah, but you're not my kid. It's not my business. I'm sorry, Charlie. I can't do that. I'm — I'm not even supposed to be talking to you. Your mother said she doesn't want you all meeting me—"

"Why not?"

"Uh. I — Well, I'm just a laborer… and she's — well. Yeah."

"Hm." Charlie considered him calculatingly. "You like my mother a whole lot, don't you?"

Harry cleared his throat and investigated his coffee

with more care than any cup really deserved. "Sure I do."

Charlie smirked.

"I don't know what's got you smirking like that, but you can wipe it right off your face. I'm just fixing the kitchen."

"Sure, Mr. O'Conner."

Harry glowered at him.

Charlie put his hands up. "Whatever you say! But you know, Mr. O'Conner. My ma's favorite restaurant is The Lexington."

"I don't know why you think I should know that."

Charlie just shrugged. But he was grinning.

Harry sighed and took the last swig of his now-tepid coffee. "So, what are the odds of you getting clocked if I bring you back to school?"

Charlie slumped out of his stool. "Do you have to?"

"It's either that or I call your mother."

"No, no, don't do that. I'd rather go to the principal's office."

Harry pulled his wallet out of his pocket and counted out a dollar and a few coins. He sighed. "You do need to tell your mother about this."

"No, I can't, Mr. O'Conner. Please don't make me!"

"Listen, kid, either you tell her or I will. And I'd really rather she hear it from you." God, he'd give anything for her to hear it from Charlie. She was already going to be furious that he was meddling with her kids against her wishes. Come to think of it. "Actually, why don't we tell her together?"

Charlie's expression sagged like dropped ice cream melting on a sidewalk. "Can't you just take me back to school and we can do it later?"

"Are you telling me you'd rather go back to school and get your clock cleaned by this Freddy Schmukster than go home and tell your mother what happened?"

"I just don't want her to be upset! She's gonna do that thing where she frowns and gets real sad in the eyes and tells me she's not mad, she's just disappointed, and that's worse than getting in trouble!"

Harry stood as he remembered his own mother's sigh of disappointment. "Fair point. It is worse. But it doesn't mean you should let the school tell the story. If you think this Freddy character isn't gonna turn everything around and make it all your fault, you got another thing coming."

Charlie stuffed his hands deep in his pockets. "Fine."

✦

Marion was just wondering where Harry was when the knock came at the door. She threw the percolator on the hot plate and dashed to the front, straightening her blouse and making sure her tits were well distributed in her bra before she opened the door with a grin.

"What took you so long—"

Harry's expression was tentative, like he was bracing against something. And in front of him, coming up no farther than Harry's armpits, was Charlie.

"Charlie!" Marion exclaimed. "What are you — why aren't you at school?" Charlie had his eyes cast petulantly on the ground. Marion looked back up at Harry as wariness set into her eyes. "Would someone please tell me what's going on?"

"Why don't we go inside?" Harry suggested, looking down at Charlie. Marion felt a sense of foreboding settle over her shoulders. She stepped aside and let them into the vestibule. When she glanced up, she saw Mrs. Dvorak plain as day standing in her living room window with a phone receiver up to her ear. Oh, for cripe's sake.

Charlie and Harry toed out of their boots and hung their jackets on the hat tree. The percolator was rolling and Marion hustled to remove it from the hot plate before her nerves tore right in twain. What the hell was Charlie doing with Harry? She'd told him she didn't want them to meet yet. She'd really thought he'd respect her wishes. Something serious must have happened to make him break his word.

"Coffee, Har — Mr. O'Conner?"

"That's alright. I just had a cup at the cafe."

"Oh." Marion looked at the percolator for a moment. At the cafe. He must have just run into Charlie and brought him home. Steeling herself, she poured a cup for herself and carried it back to the living room with her. She sat on the armchair and regarded Charlie and Harry sitting side by side on the sofa, Milly's head in Harry's lap demanding her requisite ear scratches. He provided them automatically. As though he belonged there. Marion felt her chest clench. She took a bracing sip of too-hot coffee. When she opened her mouth, words tumbled out. "Would someone please tell me what on earth is going on? Why aren't you at school? Why are you with Mr. O'Conner?" She gave Harry a pointed look.

Charlie looked up at Harry deferentially. Marion's brow rose. Harry lifted his brows at Charlie, in an almost chiding way. What the hell was going on here? Marion could feel herself getting angrier by the minute.

"Go on," Harry said to Charlie. "Tell her."

Charlie's jaw worked for a moment. "I got in a fight, Ma."

Marion stood up again, a little coffee sloshing over the edge of her cup. "What?"

"It's alright, Marion, he's not hurt."

"Mrs. Milner," she murmured.

He winced. "That's what I said."

She tried not to roll her eyes at him and to focus instead on Charlie. "Who did you fight with, honey?"

Charlie looked like he was trying to sink into the sofa. "Freddy Schebesta…"

"Oh, for crying out loud. Charlie, I don't care what that boy says, you do not fight —"

" — I think he was provoked," Harry cut in.

Marion glared at him. When she spoke, her voice was tight and sharp. "The electrician should be here any minute. Mr. O'Conner, could you please take a look and make sure everything is ready for him in the kitchen?"

Harry frowned at her pretty firmly considering this was none of his damn business. But he stood, hesitating over Charlie for a moment, before sulking off to the kitchen. Marion glowered after him for a moment, one hand on her hip. For Chrissakes, what the hell was this all about? She turned back to Charlie and set her cup on the coffee table before sitting next to her son on the sofa. She took a deep breath.

"Charlie, this isn't like you. If something is going on at school, I need you to tell me. I can't help if I don't know what's going on." She was pretty sure that sounded like something Doctor Spock would say. Right?

Charlie clearly hadn't read Doctor Spock and burrowed further into the couch cushions. "Nothing's wrong, Ma. Freddy was being mean so I made him stop."

"Violence is not how you make people stop being mean, honey."

"I know."

"Do you? Because your knuckles are telling me otherwise."

Charlie pulled his sleeves over his hands and shrugged. What the hell was this? He wasn't even ten yet; why was he acting like a teenager?

"Mind telling me why Mr. O'Conner brought you back home before school is even out?"

Charlie shrugged again and it made her bite down on her back teeth. "He's nice."

"That's not what I asked you. Does the school know where you are?"

A third shrug and Marion thought she might scream. "Charlie, I don't know how you expect me to make sense of any of this. What am I supposed to think? Mr. O'Conner of all people brings you home in the middle of the day with bloody knuckles? You hit Freddy Shebesta? Is this the first time? Or should I expect a call from the principal telling us you need to find a new school?"

This tack wasn't working, but Marion was too frustrated. "I don't understand, Charlie. What have I done to teach you that you can't trust me?"

That got some kind of reaction. Charlie frowned and looked down at his hands in his lap. "I trust you, Ma. Freddy's a bully. Mr. O'Conner said that if I don't face up to him, he'll just keep picking on me."

"Did he now?" Marion crossed her arms and glared toward the kitchen.

"And they were starting in on Linda, Mama. You said I gotta look out for her."

Marion felt the blood rush in her ears. What bastardly ten-year-old picked on a little first-grade girl? What the hell was this dumbass saying? Betty Schebesta was getting an earful.

"I did say that, but I don't want you getting into fights over it. Why didn't you tell your teacher what was going on?"

That got another shrug.

"Charlie, this is so disrespectful. You need to tell me what's going on this instant, young man. No more talking me in circles. This is serious."

"I'm sorry, Ma. I shouldn't have hit anyone. I know that. I'm sorry."

"That's not the whole of it, though, is it? I need to know you're going to stay in school. I need to know you're safe."

Charlie snorted. "I'm safe, Ma."

"Are you? How did you end up with Mr. O'Conner, then?"

"He's usually at the cafe so I went to find him."

Marion slowed. "Usually? Why would you know that?"

Charlie took a deep breath. "Ma, promise me you won't be mad."

"I will do no such thing."

"Please? Mr. O'Conner said I gotta tell you the truth or he will."

"I'm all ears."

"I just … I been waiting to go into school until after all the other kids are inside."

"Because Freddy's been giving you trouble?"

"Yeah, but it's not just Freddy. It's everybody."

"What are they doing?"

Charlie's eyes widened and he avoided her gaze. "They just say stuff."

"About me and your father?"

"Well, um … yeah."

"Charlie, we talked about this already. 'Sticks and stones will break my bones…'" She waited for him to finish.

"I know, but they *do* hurt me, Ma! If you only knew

what they were saying, it'd hurt you too."

"What are they saying?"

"Ma!"

"No, come on. What are they saying? You won't get in trouble for saying it, I just need to know what they're saying."

Charlie shook his head firmly.

Marion glanced up and saw Harry sticking his head out of the kitchen door. She sprang to her feet and stalked towards him. If her son wasn't going to give her any answers, Harry damn well was going to.

She pulled the swinging door shut behind her and hissed, "What the hell is going on here?"

Harry's face was the picture of guilt. "I couldn't just leave him out there —"

"He said you're usually at the cafe. How does he know that?"

"I've seen him. He avoids the schoolyard when he can and he walks near there."

"How long has this been going on?!" Marion forced her voice under control, because she felt like screaming. "Harry, you told me you understood why I don't want you to meet my kids yet. I told you I didn't want them —"

"Getting too attached?" he finished bitterly.

"That's not what I was going to say."

"But you were thinking it."

"No! I wasn't — dammit, Harry, don't put words in my mouth. That's not what this is about."

"Isn't it? You don't want them getting attached because you don't think anything is going to come of this, do you?" Harry's arms folded over his chest.

"I didn't say that," Marion backpedaled. "I want to see where things go before involving them. I'm not some hopeless romantic who thinks we're going to live happily ever after because we had one nice date."

"Nice?"

"Really nice, I mean, Harry! I don't know what you want me to say." Marion glanced over her shoulder at the kitchen door and hoped Charlie wasn't eavesdropping. "You're the one who's been talking to my son behind my back. What the hell do you think you're trying to pull here?"

"Nothing. I'm not pulling anything. Marion, I saw him at the parking lot by Phil's Place last Thursday and drove him back to school. I told him never to do it again or I'd tell you. So when he showed up at the cafe today, I made good on that promise."

Marion froze. Thursday. That was ... that was before he'd promised to earn her trust. He'd been keeping that from her even when he'd been imploring her to trust him. "Why didn't you tell me in the first place?"

"He asked me not to."

"He's eight years old, Harry. And you promised me you'd wait until I was ready to introduce you."

"What was I supposed to do? Just leave him out in the cold running truant all over the neighborhood?"

Oh God, how many people had seen him wandering the neighborhood? Did her mother know about this? "No, of course I don't want that. But you should have told me right out the gate."

"I know," Harry pushed his hand through his hair. His coppery red hair that he was self-conscious of and God knew why. "I know. But he begged me not to tell you and I..." He shrugged. She waited for more. For the earnest apology, like he'd made last Thursday. But he didn't. And it occurred to Marion that he wasn't repentant. He wasn't horrified with himself or regretful for lying to her.

Marion let out a frustrated growl and threw her hands into the air. "I think you should leave."

"What? But the electrician will be here any minute."

"Fine. Then I'll leave my own damn house, I guess. I'll just take Charlie to …" Where? Back to school? Her mother's? Her sister's? Joe's?? Marion was mortified to feel tears prick into the corners of her eyes.

Harry's hands twitched towards her, but he didn't touch her at all. "That's not what I meant. I can just …" His shoulders drooped. "I can just show the electrician what needs doing and then head out. If that's what you want."

Marion's teeth gritted. "It is. You do that."

She turned on her heel and stalked back to Charlie on the sofa.

"Last chance to tell me what's going on."

Charlie's eyes looked like a sad dog. Marion felt her resolve crumble, and she fought hard to keep the pricking in her eyes from resolving into full tears.

"I don't want to tell you. I don't want you to get hurt."

"It's too late for that, Chuck. I am already hurt by you refusing to talk to me, over weeks and weeks of me asking and trying. You are eight years old. It's not your job to protect me — it's mine to protect you. And if you don't tell me what's going on, I will not be able to do my job."

She was not going to cry in front of her son. She was not going to cry in front of her son.

Charlie looked down into his lap. He did not have the same self control.

"Oh, honey," Marion cooed. She brushed her hand over Charlie's hair, felt the soft strands against her fingertips. She experienced a sense of timelessness, the memory of his cotton candy baby hair a phantom touch on her skin. A tear leaked down her cheek.

"They're awful, Mama," Charlie choked between hitching breaths. "They say Dad's got too many girl-friends to have time for us, that you're trying to steal away their dads from their moms, that Linda and I must be awful children to make our Dad run away like that."

He was sobbing now. Marion wasn't far behind, but she just held her boy and let it wash over her. It was what she'd feared. But none of it was a surprise. "I don't need to tell you that they're wrong, right Chuck?"

Charlie nodded and sniffed hard. "I know they're wrong. I know they're just saying it because they think it's funny to hurt me. But that doesn't make it stop hurting. It hurts all the time, Mama."

Marion clutched him tight. "Me too, baby."

Charlie shrank away and turned his tear-stained face towards her. "Then why did you do it?"

Marion held her face immobile, her jaw so tight it made her feel like she was choking. The bottom fell out from beneath her and she felt like she was free-falling for a moment. Why *did* she do this to her children? How could it possibly be worth it? If she loved them, she should have stayed with Joe, found a way to force him to stay, even though it had been making them both miserable shells of themselves for six years. It was no less than her duty to her children. If she didn't like it, maybe she shouldn't have brought them into the world.

Charlie twisted his face and looked down at his hands. "I'm sorry. I shouldn't say that. I know you didn't have a choice."

Marion took a sharp breath through her nose. "No," she confessed. "Honey, I did choose. And I chose to stop trying to squeeze blood from a stone. I … I know this is so hard for you. For Linda. It's not normal and it has drawn a lot of attention to us that we never wanted. But Charlie — it wasn't fair for your father and I to keep pretending." She looked at her beloved son and wondered if he'd learned to chastise himself the way she did. It filled her with a fierce surge of protectiveness. "I don't want your life to end when you have children. I want you to live a life as full and as long as you can. And ... and what would I be teaching you if I didn't show you what that looks like?"

Charlie pressed his mouth into a hard line and whimpered. "I just want things to be like they were before."

"I know, honey," Marion pulled him into her arms and squeezed him tight. A thousand platitudes swept across her mind — *Your father and I still love you just as much* or *This isn't your fault* or *God has a plan for us all, just wait and see* but none of it would bring relief to the shit-slog this was. And in spite of all the hurt, Charlie still clung to her sleeves, let her hold him close, let her hurt with him. And for the first time, it felt like enough.

Chapter 15

Harry left as soon as the electrician arrived. Marion was holed up in the children's room with Charlie and didn't come out to say goodbye. Harry wasn't surprised by that, but he couldn't say he wasn't disappointed.

He got in his truck and started driving without really knowing where he should go. He had no idea what he should do now. All he knew was that he'd bungled things up in a big way and he deeply regretted it. Of course, he should have told Marion about Charlie cutting school as soon as he possibly could. Just because he'd done it when he was a kid didn't mean it wasn't a big deal (although, to be fair, he'd been a teenager and not an eight-year-old), or that Marion didn't have a right to know about it. God, he was such a grade-A fool.

He ended up back at the Tick Tock, which unlike his apartment, wasn't a source of endless reminders of Marion's presence. Here was the thing — in spite of the very physical turn their affair had taken, Harry was absolutely head over heels. The thought that he might have messed everything up so bad that she wouldn't want to see him again made his guts wrench. He wallowed in a cup of decaf coffee and stared out the window for the rest of the afternoon until it was a socially appropriate time to go to the bar.

He drank two beers at the Coney Island Tavern near his apartment before Gerald showed up. Gerald didn't like to drink alone, so if he was up for a happy hour, he almost always haunted the Coney because he knew if Harry was similarly inclined, they'd meet up. Heaven forbid they simply make a routine of it so they didn't waste their time hoping the other might show up. But these happy hours were stolen time and by keeping things unofficial, Gerald was able to safely say that he was prioritizing his family.

It occurred to Harry as Gerald slid in the door of the long, narrow bar that relations between men and women might be significantly smoothed if they actually just talked to one another. This provided Harry with a fresh pang of guilt as Gerald grinned and took the stool next to him at the bar.

"Fancy meeting you here," Gerald said with a friendly bump of his shoulder to Harry's. "Say, what's got you looking so blue?"

Harry frowned into his beer.

Gerald rolled his eyes as he called for a beer from the bartender, whose name was Tom and was well-known as the grouchiest son-of-a-bitch who ever sidled behind a bar. (It was sort of a puzzle as to why, if he was so averse to people, he'd choose to run a bar, but no one dared bring up the subject.)

"Come on, Harry, don't play coy. I know you've been seeing someone."

"What on earth would make you think that?"

"Because you're never here anymore. I had to drink with Don all last week." Gerald flicked his chin towards the red-nosed middle-aged man at the end of the bar. Harry had never been in the Coney without Don occupying that first stool. He couldn't rule out the possibility that the fellow just simply lived there. "So ... what's her name?"

Harry tipped his head back, and then let it flop forward so that he groaned into his beer. He declined to elaborate because, one, as good of a pal Gerald was, he couldn't be sure he wouldn't get fired for getting involved with a client and, two, none of it mattered anyway because it might not even be a thing anymore anyway.

"jeez," Gerald said. Harry was grateful that he had a friend who could understand his meaning completely without him needing to say anything. "That bad, huh?"

"I was a big idiot," Harry lamented, again into his beer. "I wasn't up front with her and she found out and I think it's over now."

Gerald frowned. "Did you not tell her about your ex-wife?"

Harry grimaced and hoped that would be enough for Gerald to jump to wrong conclusions and not the right ones.

"Damn. Maybe you're better off. A girl that jealous wouldn't be a walk in the park if you ask me."

"You don't think your wife would be uncomfortable if you'd had a different wife who left you?"

"Well, no. Janey loves other women."

Harry looked at him flatly.

"Well, she's got nothing to worry about anyway. And it's pretty obvious the baby is mine."

"Why, did he grow a sleazy mustache since the last time I saw him?"

Gerald gave him a thump on the arm, which made him crack the tiniest of smiles.

"So who's this chick? Do I know her?"

"No." Harry probably said it much too fast, but Gerald didn't seem to notice.

"Well, there's lots of other fish in the sea."

Harry peered into his beer and sighed. That's what everyone always said and it made sense, because it had only been a few weeks. Didn't make it feel any more discouraging, though. "I s'pose you're right."

"You deserve a girl who likes you and trusts you. Just because you had a shotgun marriage before enlisting doesn't mean you're broken forever. Unless … is she Catholic?"

Harry wanted to hide inside his pint glass. He *was* doing a pretty good job climbing into it considering his size relative to the glass. "No. It's not what I did as much as the fact that I took pains to hide it from her."

Gerald sighed. "She's not entitled to your entire life story on the first date."

"No, but I promised her I'd be a man she could trust."

"jeez Louise, this sounds pretty serious for a two-week old tryst. Is she someone we know?"

"Nope. No. She is not." Harry was not going to be winning any awards, for lying well or for telling the truth. Now he was trying to pull the wool over his best friend's eyes too. God, what would his life be like if he just lived it and stopped going along with what everyone else wanted?

"It's Marion Milner," Harry blurted.

"Who?"

"The, uh… the divorcee who's getting her kitchen redone down by West 7th Street."

"The … what? *What??*" Gerald squawked, then huddled towards Harry and hissed, "Are you telling me you're stepping out with a client?"

Harry winced. "Yes?"

"Holy shit," Gerald pulled a hand over his face. He didn't look upset, though. More devastated, but also thoroughly enjoying it. "You *dog*, you! If the boss finds out, you're on your own pal. Jesus Christ. I'm almost impressed."

Harry shrugged miserably. "Well, it doesn't really matter one way or another now. I don't think she wants to see me again."

"How're you gonna finish the job?"

"I'm just gonna go and try to do it and if she tells me to leave, I'll just … I dunno, call my dad or something to finish things off."

"You're not gonna tell your *dad* you were trying to get fresh with a client?" Gerald reeled. "I can't even imagine what he would do."

"Drop my body in the river, is what."

"That's ridiculous. But also accurate." Gerald pinched his chin between his fingers and Harry took the moment to process that he'd told Gerald the truth and it hadn't blown up in his face. (This was perhaps a lesson he should have learned four days ago.) "Okay, so you're sure she's through with you?"

"Well, I dunno," Harry pushed his hand through his hair with a sigh. "She told me she didn't want me in her house and so I left."

"When she found out about your ex?"

"Well, no … when she found out I'd had a chat with her son after she told me she didn't want me to meet her children."

Gerald peered at him for a moment. "You overrode a mother's wish for her child? Damn, you're done for."

"When you put it like that…" Harry buried his head in his hands with a miserable sigh.

✦

Charlie seemed to be feeling much better after he'd finally opened up to Marion. She should have been feeling proud about it. But instead, she felt like a limp, three-day-old koláče that had been left out on the radiator. This did not calculate into the evening's plans, unfortunately. Sunday dinner had been rescheduled, so she was at her mother's house on a Monday.

Marion sat on the sofa with her ankles neatly crossed and watched Charlie and Linda scurry through the sitting and dining room playing some sort of elaborate game of make believe involving the tortoise and the hare, which one of them must have read at school. Marion's sister, Evelyn, sat across from her in Mother's floral upholstered armchair. She looked as distracted as Marion felt.

"Well, I suppose I'd better ask you how the kitchen is going?" Evelyn forced out into the silence thickening between them.

"Almost done," Marion replied. "We had the new breaker installed today, and tomorrow they'll have all the appliances up and running."

"That's going to be such a relief to have access to your kitchen again."

"I'm going to have a dishwasher," Marion said to cheer herself up.

"Not that you're bragging or anything."

Marion sighed and didn't reply. Evelyn fidgeted in the chair for a moment before she rose and said, "Well, I don't know about you, but I'm going to see if Mother needs help in the kitchen."

Five years ago, Marion would have jumped to her feet to join her, all the while feeling guilty that she hadn't thought of it. But now, she understood that this was a sort of projected passive aggression that Evelyn pulled out when she was feeling either jealous or vindictive. Marion suspected both might be occurring right now.

Evelyn swept into the kitchen and got waylaid by the hoard of children jumping up and down like bunnies. This did very little to set her at her ease. Marion struggled to care.

"Marion!" Mother called. "Can you please get the girls to set the table?"

Marion stood and dragged her feet to the kitchen. What she would give to be anywhere else right now. If she hadn't just fallen out with Harry in the most disappointing, anticlimactic way, she might have comforted herself with fantasies of his apartment, but they fell flat now that he had made clear he wasn't as trustworthy as he'd worked so hard to make her believe. Just like everyone else, he didn't trust her judgment, so he'd overridden her wishes when it suited him. Her mother and Evelyn did this all the time, but she had no choice to put up with them.

Dinner was impeccable. Marion's father sat at the head of the table and carved slices of ham for everyone like a Norman Rockwell painting. He'd parachuted out of a plane over Normandy through several thousand feet of smoke and bombs and bullets and spent the winter of '44 mired in a fox hole. He'd returned to his homeland in Czechoslovakia to liberate Pilsen from the Nazis, and seen the city of his childhood flattened to rubble. Marion supposed he deserved a Norman Rockwell painting after all that.

The children settled down after dinner, Charlie helping his younger cousin set up some toy soldiers while the girls dressed paper dolls. Marion's mother served coffee with perfectly flaky strudel.

"So, Marion, how is the kitchen coming along?" she asked lightly.

"Great," Marion replied after accepting her delicate china cup. "Appliances will be up and running tomorrow, and if all goes well, we'll be ready to move everything back in."

Marion's mother sucked her teeth when Marion said 'we.' Marion tightened her grip on her cup and braced herself.

"That builder man is there *every* day?"

Marion swallowed. "Yes. His name is Mr. O'Conner. He installs for G–E."

"O'Conner? Irish Catholic?"

Marion shrugged, deflecting. "I guess."

Charlie walked through the dining room, and Marion's mother put out a hand and brushed his arm. He stopped. "Babi?"

"What do you think of Mr. O'Conner?"

Marion's stomach dropped like a stone. She shouldn't have eaten that second helping of casserole.

Charlie looked at his mother and then back at his grandmother. He shrugged. "I dunno. He's fine, I guess."

Marion's mother gave Marion a tart, pinched look over Charlie's shoulder. "He seems very friendly indeed, if you ask me."

Marion could feel a betraying flush creeping onto her cheeks. Did Mrs. Dvorak call her? Did someone see her get out of Harry's truck on Wednesday? *What did she know?*

Charlie shrugged and went into the kitchen for a blue tea towel to arrange toy naval ships on. Marion forced herself to take a sip of coffee and pretend like she wasn't experiencing a horrible urge to blurt out everything. The worst part was that Marion wasn't sure, if her mother did know Harry was interested in her, whether she'd be angry at Marion's indiscretion or delighted by the prospect of marriage as the solution to the Marion Problem. Marion doubted the latter. Mother had doted on Joe. She was surprised he hadn't gotten her in the divorce. Lately, she sometimes wished he had.

"I suppose you must be so nervous about the Sokol Ladies Christmas party," Marion's mother said sympathetically.

"Yes," Marion admitted. She was spinning her coffee cup on its saucer and she couldn't make herself stop.

"It's a lot of work to get that kitchen back up and running and get ready for the party and the holidays at the same time," Evelyn said. "You're so bold to take it all on."

Marion nodded. Bold was her middle name.

"First thing when you get that kitchen working, you have to do a test run of all the food you're going to serve," Evelyn pointed out.

"Have you decided what you're serving?" Mother asked.

Marion barely shook her head before the onslaught began.

"You should absolutely serve vánočka," said Evelyn. "It's not Christmas without sweet bread —"

"—But who knows how it'll cook up in an electric oven," Mother put in.

"Oh, that's true."

"That's why she has to dry run the whole menu."

"Well, she could maybe have some potato salad and a relish dish to cut down on the cooking prep. Marion — did you do refrigerator pickles?"

"I … no." Marion's tongue felt too big for her mouth.

"You can have some of mine. Or wait — Frances! Did we finish all those pickles?" Her husband nodded. "Oh, dear. Well, I'll get you my recipe anyway."

"I have the recipe," Marion said despite knowing it was futile.

"Many of the ladies will probably bring some sort of dessert," Marion's mother said. "So you should make sure you don't make any Linzer tarts because Mrs. Novak would be embarrassed if you made her signature treat. Besides, yours aren't anything to write home about and wouldn't it be embarrassing if the hostess made sloppy cookies? Better to avoid it completely."

Marion felt her throat tighten and wondered why she hadn't even thought about the menu for the Christmas party until now. Well, she had, abstractly. But they were right. She had no plan. And she did need to practice cooking on her new range before the party. She had so much to do. She should have started writing down menu ideas as Evelyn and Mother fired them off, but now it was too late and she'd forgotten what they said. Other than don't make Linzer tarts. She'd heard that loud and clear.

A warm and heavy hand fell over her own.

"Don't worry, Marion," her father said matter-of-factly. His voice still carried the ghost of an accent despite having lived most of his life in Minnesota. "I like your Linzer tarts."

And this entirely innocuous comment, of all of them, was the one that made her eyes swell with tears.

"Marion, whatever can be wrong?" Mother demanded.

Marion took a steadying inhale, blinking hard to force the tears back into her head where they belonged. Her mother was looking at her like she was alarmingly distressed. Which, to be honest, she couldn't entirely deny.

"Nothing, Mother," Marion said. "I'm just tired."

Evelyn scoffed. "Tired after a month of not having to cook?"

Marion's nostrils flared. "I cook every day. On a hot

plate."

"Oh, that sounds awful."

How was it that Evelyn could make her feel both lazy and foolishly overworked? Her sister was the passive aggressive eighth wonder of the world.

"Well," Marion said and stood up. "I had better get the kiddos back home before bedtime."

"So soon?" Marion's mother frowned. "I haven't even had a chance to spend any time with my grandchildren."

Marion blinked and tried not to show her frustration on her face. "Oh." She sat back down. "In that case."

Marion's mother frowned. It didn't matter if Marion stayed another hour or three. She'd already suggested leaving earlier than Marion's mother deemed acceptable and she would carry that ding for the rest of the night.

Luckily, Mother moved on to perfecting Evelyn's pastry recipe. Marion slumped in her chair and stared at the china cabinet with what must have been a petulantly vacant expression. All she wanted to do was to leave. But she couldn't. She didn't even have anything left to look forward to anymore, now that Harry had turned out to be just like everyone else. Or maybe it was her, being overly sensitive and unreasonable again.

She'd been so angry with Harry earlier that afternoon, but now it felt like nothing more than exhaustion. She was embarrassed — deeply — by how easily he'd lied to her. After everything. They'd had that whole conversation about trust and he'd pledged himself to do right by her. And at that same moment, he'd already talked to Charlie and taken him back to school in secret. She'd been an idiot. She'd been taken in, hook, line, and sinker, by his charming earnestness, but at the end of the day, he'd overruled her judgment, just like everyone else did. It didn't matter how good he made her feel if he thought she needed to be managed. No way was she bringing someone like that into her children's lives. Or her own, for that matter.

It hurt. It hurt because she'd really believed Harry was different. She thought he respected her, cared for her desires, and respected her commitment to her family and her judgment. But apparently not.

The dessert hour was so brutal that by the time Marion was walking her bundled children two blocks back to their house in a flurry of snow, the only thing she had to look forward to after bedtime was crying herself to sleep in her big, empty bed. It was a good thing she'd changed her pillowcase. She wasn't sure she had it in her to resist the temptation of burying her face in it and recriminating herself until sleep found her.

It was about 10 o'clock when she stared up at the darkened ceiling from her bed and thought maybe Harry had been right all along. Maybe she was ashamed of him. It was an awful notion, but the way she flinched away from people knowing about him made her wonder if it was true. In which case, what did it say about her that she was prioritizing what Mrs. Dvorak thought over the regard she had for Harry?

Maybe she'd made much ado about nothing, and she shouldn't have been so stingy about introducing him to her children. But then she kept coming back to the feeling that he wanted to ingratiate himself into their lives in a way she simply wasn't ready for. She liked Harry. And she had to admit, she especially liked keeping him to herself. She had no interest in playing house. Charlie and Linda already had enough to adjust to without needing to negotiate a second father figure trying to usurp the father they missed. A hasty replacement would do nothing to alleviate the grief of losing their actual father anyway.

Maybe she was wrong, and Harry had every right to make in-roads with her kids. But that interpretation demanded that Marion wished to marry him. And she simply didn't, as much as she enjoyed the time they'd spent together so far. She wasn't sure she ever wanted to marry anyone ever again.

God. She was just as morally bereft as everyone thought.

Chapter 16

Thursday, December 15th, 1955
2 days until the Christmas party

Harry finished the job on Thursday. Despite having been at the house all day every day in the interim, he hadn't had a chance to talk to Marion at all. He was almost certain she was avoiding him. When he arrived at Marion's house Tuesday, she let him in, showed him where to help himself to coffee, and sprinted off to shop for the Christmas party on Saturday. Wednesday, she was in disarray, juggling recipe cards and demanding to know when she'd be able to start using her appliances. Harry replied she could do so any time. She glowered at him and then ran off to a Sokol Ladies meeting.

Now it was Thursday. Marion was gone again — Harry didn't have the heart to pretend he had a right to know where — and the kitchen was … finished. The glossy cabinets glittered under the light of the new fixture he'd just finished installing. The linoleum floors provided bold contrast to the turquoise green cabinets and appliances. It was as clean as a whistle. It could have been a television set.

Harry felt his pride in a job well done significantly muted. He couldn't help but mark the room with the moments that had contributed to its creation. Laying linoleum while Marion knitted and chatted, joking with her while he installed the sink, kissing her against the counters. A … number of other things. He should be proud, and he was, but mostly he was just sad.

Outside the window, snow was falling in big, fat flakes. There wasn't anything he could do about it now. It'd been three days since Marion had told him to beat it and she hadn't said anything to indicate she was interested in patching things up. He knew where he stood. There wasn't anything he could do about it, and it wasn't his place to ask even if there was. She'd decided to cut things off. So cut off they were. Just like when he'd got back from Korea.

His eyes tracked the snowflakes through the wavy window glass. There was a tempest inside of him, and he couldn't help but notice he was bracing himself. He wiped his mind as clean as he could and focused on the snow, until the storm passed. He'd weathered worse. Much worse. This was just disappointment.

The back door banged open.

"Harry! Are you still here?" Marion called out breathlessly. Harry told his stupid heart to stop jumping in his chest and turned around.

"Yup," he replied.

Marion's face appeared through the doorway. She was flushed and out of breath and harried. Her eyes were darting around the room like she was looking for something she'd forgotten.

"I got a Christmas tree and they just delivered it and drove off without as much as a word and now I can't get it in the house by myself. The angle is too sharp and there's no room between the stair rail and the door and — God, I'm sorry, I'm being ridiculous. This isn't your problem.

I just … I need help."

She stood in the doorway with her hands gripped together, chastened eyes cast onto the floor.

"No problem," Harry said, with more feeling than he'd meant to. "I'll get it in here in a jiff."

Marion trailed behind him as he walked out the door and into the backyard. The snow was falling gently, but it was fat and heavy and accumulating quickly. Already, the Christmas tree that was wedged half into the entry and half out on the stoop was gathering enough snow to make clean-up a headache once it got inside and melted.

"I'm sorry," Marion continued as he began to angle the tree around the corner, pine needles pricking his knuckles. "I know you're trying to get everything finished in the kitchen and —"

" —No, it's done," Harry said and lifted the tree up so that the trunk didn't catch on the door jamb.

"Done?" Marion breathed. "Oh my God, and I didn't even notice. I'm such a rat, Harry, I can't believe —"

"Don't worry," Harry cut her off. "You can take a look once we get the tree inside. Do you have a stand?"

"Yes." Marion paused long enough that Harry looked over his shoulder at her, concerned he was being too terse. But she just stood there, looking at him miserably. When she saw she was being observed, her expression neutralized and she said, "I'll go make sure it's ready."

Harry felt her absence like chill. He chided himself and got the tree inside with a wiggle and a jerk. He carried it all the way down the hall and into the dining room so it didn't drop quite so many needles or scratch the new linoleum. The dining room was in a state of chaos, as Marion had clearly taken a crack at putting everything back into the kitchen last night but hadn't finished yet.

"Do you want me to take the hoosier with me today?"

Harry asked consideringly. Marion, who was fiddling with the tree stand in the sitting room, looked up at him.

"That would be wonderful. Can you move it, though?"

Harry frowned. "Probably. Do you think the fellow upstairs could be persuaded to help?"

"Maybe, but I don't think he's home until later. Edna across the street could help, though."

"I don't want to trouble her."

"She won't mind. Housewives move lots of things when husbands are busy at work. We're not so helpless, present situation excluded — There, it's ready."

Harry wished she would stop being so self-castigating. He'd never seen her quite so overwhelmed, and he figured it was because of the Christmas party. Truly, he'd never meant for installation to take so long, but he'd lost significant time last week for … reasons. He carried the tree into the sitting room and carefully lifted it so the trunk clunked into the center of the tree stand. "I don't think you're helpless."

"Well, I wouldn't blame you if you did," Marion joked, but her voice was flat and thin. "It's not even that big of a tree."

"It was a tricky corner. Besides, you've got a thousand other things to worry about right now."

"Don't make excuses for me. I am making such a bungle of this Christmas party. I haven't brought out any of the decorations. I only just got the menu squared away, and I have no idea whether I'll need to cook differently on my new appliances."

"They have all the temperature settings in the manual," Harry assured, kneeling to help twist the screws tight into the tree trunk. "I tested the temperature in the oven too, so the knobs should get you the right heat. And you got the built-in thermometer. It'll turn itself off when the meat is done."

Marion sniffed hard and sat back on her heels to wipe her eyes. "Stop it, Harry. Just stop."

"What?"

"Being nice to me."

Harry frowned. "Why? I like you."

"That's another thing! You don't."

"I'm pretty sure I know when I like a girl."

"Well, maybe you like me. But stop treating me like I'm some sort of calm, capable woman. We both know I'm not, so it's ridiculous to pretend like you believe in me."

"But I do believe in you." She laughed incredulously around a throat tight with tears. Harry's chest clenched with frustration. "I do, dammit. I do believe in you. And like you. Could maybe even love you, if given half the chance, I don't know. Marion —" He grabbed her wrists. "I'm not just saying these things to be nice."

Marion looked up at him with wide, glistening eyes. Her chin worked hard to stay firm. She pulled her hands back from him and crumpled them against her chest. "Then why did you lie to me?"

Harry's resolve chastened.

"Seriously, Harry, I need to know. Because as far as I can tell, as much as you might like me, you didn't respect my judgment. And I have no idea how incompetent you think I am. I've spent the better part of this week talking myself in circles, but I have no way of knowing what was real and what was a line to get me to go to bed with you."

Harry sat back on his heels, horrified. He felt angry and guilty and frustrated and despondent, all at the same time, hurling up like vomit in his throat and at that moment, all he wanted to do was shout. He gritted his teeth and said, "All of it was real."

"Except for when you talked with Charlie after I told you not to?"

"Yes, actually."

"You *told* me I could trust you. You convinced me that you would earn it. And at the same fucking time, you were lying by omission and undermining me to my son!" Marion apparently did not have any aversion to shouting.

"I said I was sorry!" Why was it when a woman shouted, she sounded righteous, but when Harry did it, he sounded belligerent?

"Sorry you did it or sorry you got caught?"

Something sort of cracked inside of Harry. He *wasn't* one of those assholes who thought they were entitled to whatever woman they took a fancy to. He didn't want a woman who was so passive she couldn't say what she wanted or deliberately put aside her own wants for her man. He only ever just wanted to please. Alice, his mother, his family, his friends. Everyone. What was the point of striving, of trying to do right by oneself and others if it all ended in disordered disappointment and degradation and death anyway? Honestly, none of it mattered. There certainly wasn't some Godly force working to ensure he was rewarded for his efforts. Fact was, he'd already given up on himself for far too long. It was high time he stopped calling his ambivalence 'respect'. Marion wasn't going to turn around and suddenly want him back for respectfully keeping his distance. If he didn't say what he wanted, he wouldn't have the ghost of a chance of getting it.

Fuck it.

"Sorry I did it. For Chrissakes, stop putting words in my mouth. I never planned to lie to you. I was trying to do right by your son because I thought maybe I'd get a chance, once the job was done, to date you properly and I wanted —" It was so humiliating but he was damned if she was going to misunderstand him, "I wanted him to like me. I'm not just trying to get you into bed, or whatever disgusting turn-of-phrase you used. I like you. A lot. I also like your kids. I want to be *real* to you. I want to be someone you are proud to step out with, someone you trust with not just your house or your pleasure, but with your family and friends and your whole life. I understand it's not my place to decide that timeline, but I … I see real potential in what we've got here. I want to go for broke with you."

Marion looked blindsided.

"But what I don't want is to be some sort of guilty pleasure. I'm serious about you. And if that's not what you're looking for, then that's fine. I can't say I'll like it, but I'll respect it. I just can't leave here today and never know whether there was a shot left."

Marion's mouth opened and then closed.

"Harry," she said quietly. "I don't know what to say."

Harry gathered his dignity, or what was left of it. "Okay. Do you mean you're speechless or you just don't want to say what you mean?"

"It means what it says. I don't know what to say." Marion shoved her face in her hands. "I have so much running through my head at once. I don't know what I want, I don't know what I think about all this. I need some time to think."

He nodded mutely.

"I just need to get this Christmas party out of the way."

Harry felt his heart sink into his shoes. "Right. The party."

"Then, afterwards, can I call you?"

Harry desperately wanted to believe her. But her priorities were pretty clear. He had no preconceived notions she would actually call. He shrugged. If he could have wrapped his shoulders around himself like a shield, he would have. "Fine."

They both rose awkwardly from the floor. Harry turned and walked to the kitchen. "Might as well come take a look."

Marion followed him. As he flipped on the lights, she watched the room illuminate with round eyes.

"Harry. It's beautiful."

Harry nodded. He didn't look at her. He didn't think he could without losing whatever scraps of dignity he had left.

Chapter 17

Saturday, December 17th, 1955
The Sokol Ladies Auxiliary Christmas Party

Marion wasn't sure how she'd managed it. She stared down at the dining table laden with potato salad and vánočka bread and schnitzel and five different kinds of *not* Linzer Christmas cookies. She'd been cooking for the past forty-eight hours. She wasn't entirely sure it was Saturday until someone knocked on the door.

Not only did the spread need to meet muster, but so did the house. It was spic and span, thanks to a little assist from Edna, and the kitchen shone like a movie set. The children had turned themselves out well, too. Marion's mother had made them little matching gingerbread outfits, which looked both adorable and entirely like she was trying too hard. (It didn't matter, it wasn't like she could ask them to change. Her mother would be supremely offended.)

Marion herself wasn't sure what she looked like. She wore her green sweater, which felt audacious, but it was the only Christmasy colored sweater she had clean right now, and she *certainly* hadn't had time to do the laundry this week. She also wore a brown skirt and a red novelty Christmas apron with flat loafers, and damned if she was going to begrudge herself for not wearing heels after the hell week she'd endured.

"Mother?"

Marion looked up at Charlie and realized she'd just been standing in the dining room staring at the table.

"There's people at the door." Charlie gave a bemused smile.

Marion compulsively wiped her hands on her apron even though she'd just washed them. "Wonderful. Why don't you let them in."

Charlie nodded and trotted towards the door. "Linda! You offer to take their coats."

Linda followed in her adorable brown pinafore bedecked with white ric-rac and sang out, "Okay!"

Milly gave out a half-hearted "Woof" in lazy lip-service to her guard dog duties.

The Sokol Ladies Auxiliary began to flow in the door. Within twenty minutes, all of the expected guests had arrived with their families and the house was packed to the gills. Children helped themselves to the toys in the nursery, shepherded there by Charlie and Linda. The husbands congregated around the sitting room sipping coffee and trying to outdo one another with speculation about Communism behind the iron curtain (or something — Marion honestly wasn't tracking much other than the fact that they kept saying things like "Marxist despots" and "damned Khrushchev"). The ladies huddled around the dining table cooing over one another's offerings as they tried to squeeze in a dozen platters of Christmas cookies along the edges of Marion's spread.

"Oh for cute, Marion!" Betty Schebesta gushed, swathed in a red and green block dress. "Everything looks just perfect."

"How did you find the time?" said Helen Blaha. "Didn't

you just finish your kitchen?"

Marion smiled placidly and said, "Yes, but it's a wonder how those appliances save time! Why don't you all take a look—"

"—Mary, did you make your famous Linzers?" exclaimed Betty. Marion waited for everyone to finish complimenting Mary Novak's baking and tried not to be resentful even though she'd only made one tray of cookies while Marion had made a whole menu of food.

While she was waiting for the group to return to the topic of her kitchen, Marion felt someone nudge her shoulder. She looked over at Helen Blaha.

"So I understand congratulations are in order?" Helen murmured in a conspiring tone.

Marion blinked. "Um, yes. The kitchen is—"

"Not the kitchen, you silly goose. I mean the fellow," Helen waggled her eyebrows. "I hear you've got someone lined up to be the next Mr. Marion."

Marion opened her mouth. "I don't … know what you mean?"

"Oh, come on," Helen gave a little secret grin. "Your mother was saying you've been seeing someone discreetly."

"My *mother*?"

"We've all been dying to know who it is."

Betty Schebesta joined at this juncture. "Oh, yes! Marion — who is your new beau? Is it that fellow who was doing your kitchen? I heard he was always getting here early."

Marion's lip curled in a confusion that belied her extreme discomfort with her privacy being thus invaded.

Helen Blaha sort of squealed, which she was about ten years too old to pull off. "Oh, isn't that so romantic! No wonder it took so long. I'll bet you never wanted him to leave."

How the *hell* did they know all of this? And what did Marion's mother have to do with it?

"It's really about time you remarried," her sister Evelyn put in, turning from the main conversation.

"And you couldn't have picked a cuter fellow," Helen reiterated. "I've seen him at the Tick Tock diner a few times and he's just a darling. Bright red hair, though." She giggled.

Marion was experiencing a somewhat dissociative, out-of-body experience. She'd spent significant time in the past few weeks worrying about these people finding out that she was having an affair with Harry. She'd expected them to condemn her for a loose woman, for endangering her children with her wanton behavior, for betraying her marriage vows again by letting another man catch her eye. That had been the thrust of the rumors she'd overheard ever since her divorce. If she had known that openly engaging with a new beau would have quieted that gossip rather than fueled it — well, hell, she would have saved a whole lot of money on a new kitchen and just gone on a date with Harry that first day instead.

More ladies began to pile on with insights on Marion's rumored love life. Weren't they embarrassed to say all of this to her face? Did they think they were being kind or encouraging? Marion reeled. She couldn't very well tell them all the truth. *Oh, no, I'm actually not attached at the moment, though you're right that I was seeing the contractor for my kitchen. It didn't work out, but he gave me a very good run, if you know what I mean.* What the hell had she been so worried about this whole time? Sneaking around the alley just to go on a date, pulling curtains, telling lies and trying to pull the wool over her children's eyes. Well, that last part was more for their own sakes than anyone else's, but still. Had she bungled this whole thing up just because she'd assumed it would be perceived a certain way, only to be wrong?

"Ladies, ladies." Marion's mother joined the fray and immediately silenced the group. The older women across the dining table were frowning at them all. "Certainly it isn't polite for us to pry into Marion's private affairs if she's not ready to talk about them."

Marion stared at her. What angle was her mother trying to work this time? She hadn't told her a goddamned thing about Harry; why was she inserting whatever it was she thought she knew now? Was she trying to get Marion to patch things up with Harry? How would she even *know* anything needed patching up, much less that it was there to begin with?

"No. Yeah no," Marion found herself saying. "It's not polite. I don't think it's okay for any of you to assume you can speak to me about my romantic affairs."

Eyes among the Sokol Ladies widened. It incited something in Marion, something resentful and angry and silenced for much too long.

"In fact, none of you have any right to speak of my romantic affairs to anyone at all. I've had an awful year. My children have had an awful year. And everyone in this community who has thought it was okay to cast judgment on our affairs — which, I might add, none of you know enough about to judge anyway — is responsible for the hardships we've continued to endure as we've tried to start a new life and figure out what it means to have a family outside of a failed marriage. It is *none* of your business — none of you. You should be ashamed of yourselves."

Marion's mother looked like she'd been blown out of glass. Marion's hands shook with anger, or anxiety, or both, as she waited to see what fresh hell awaited her on the other side of this particularly mortifying speech. But even as she was terrified, she couldn't manage to regret it. These women *deserved* it.

Betty Schebesta looked at Helen with her mouth open. Evelyn averted her eyes to the cookie spread and twisted her fingers. Edna, who was standing across the room, raised her fist at Marion and nodded.

Marion's mother cleared her throat. "Well. Marion, why don't you show us this kitchen we've been hearing so much about?"

Like nothing had happened. Marion had half a mind to throw them all out on the street, send them and their cookies and their fake concern out into the snow. But then what would she do? Never speak to any of them again? Walk through her neighborhood in angry silence, pretend like none of them existed in perpetuity forever? She couldn't stop them from being petty or nosy or jealous. She couldn't force them to be anything at all.

A thought occurred to her and it quieted the chaos in her mind. She couldn't force them to behave politely, but she could stop letting them run rampant over her life. She could stop worrying so much about what they thought or what they would say. She could stop letting those worries drive her decisions.

Marion looked them all in the eye fiercely, one by one, before smoothing her apron and saying, quite tightly, "For sure. Come and see my new kitchen."

The Sokol Ladies let out a cumulative exhale and a hum of overly enthusiastic voices agreed on their eagerness to see what had become of Marion's kitchen.

Marion led them through the swinging door and the dozen or so ladies crammed in as best they could, half of them sidling into the back hall or otherwise craning over the shoulders of those in the doorway to see. Marion had imagined this moment many times over the past few months. This kitchen was the kind most of these ladies could only dream of while paging through a magazine. The satisfaction she'd imagined seeing their envy was anticlimactic in reality. The envy was there … it just didn't make her feel the way she had expected.

"Jeez Louise, it's so shiny!"

"Is that an automatic oven timer? Just built in?"

"Marion! The dishwasher! Are you in hog heaven?"

The comments were what she'd dreamed of. But it all fell flat because all Marion could think was that they were trying to be nice to her after she'd called them out. Did they really like the kitchen? Or were they just trying to gloss over their own bad behavior?

"I can't believe what a contrast. It's very nice, Marion. What a wonderful color choice."

"It looks like a spaceship just landed right in your house!"

Fucking hell. She'd spent so much time and effort trying to be above reproach, hadn't she? Most of her life, in fact. She thought she'd managed it too, before Joe had dropped a bomb of reality on her. It was high time she admitted that she had no earthly idea what would make these people like her. She'd jerked Harry around six ways from Sunday trying to keep him a secret and apparently, all they wanted was for her to marry the first fellow who'd have her. She could have stepped out with him at any time, and apparently they would have thought it worthy of celebration.

"This linoleum is so bold. It's like we're in a little space-age beehive."

"That's quite a lot of green between the appliances and the cabinets. Were you worried about it being too much?"

Except, she knew that wasn't true. They wouldn't have just celebrated her going on a date with a new fellow. No matter what she did, they'd find something to gossip about. It wasn't about her, or whether she was doing the right thing, or the wrong thing. It was about them. Being bored. Building themselves up by tearing others down. If it wasn't Marion's divorce, it would be Betty's sixth pregnancy, or Helen's drinking, or Mary's husband's wandering eye.

Fuck. It struck Marion that she'd made a horrible mistake. She'd thought that Harry talking to Charlie and keeping it secret had been a judgment on her character, a measure of his true opinion of her and her fitness as a mother. But she had assigned him — and everyone else in this damn neighborhood — a lot more credit than he deserved in that regard. The simplest explanation was the most likely truth. And Harry had said it clearly — he'd made a mistake, for which he was sorry. For weeks she'd known him as a careful, thoughtful, considerate person. It didn't make sense for all that to be fake so his one mistake could represent his true character. He really did just want Charlie to think well of him. Because he was interested in Marion. Long term. For real.

What was she so afraid of?

Marion's Christmas party ended early. No one seemed particularly upset about it. Even still, it was the longest and most arduous two hours, preceded by the most nerve-wracking week of Marion's life. After everyone had gone, Marion put the children to bed with one knee bouncing impatiently. All she wanted to do was to call Harry.

After the children were settled, Marion burst into the kitchen and picked the new phone up off the receiver. It was teal, to match the rest of the kitchen, and she loved it. She flipped through her phone diary with trembling fingers and spun each of Harry's numbers on the rotary dial. It rang once. Twice. Three times.

Goddammit, he was out, wasn't he?

She hung up. She picked up the receiver again and called Edna.

"Oh hi, Marion. Did I forget something at your house?"

"No, sorry. Say, do you think your oldest would mind coming over for a few hours? The kids are already asleep, but I have a bit of an emergency I need to take care of."

"Oh! I'm sorry — is everything alright?"

"Yes, everything is fine. It's just … I can't wait until tomorrow."

"So everything is fine, but it's an emergency?"

Marion paused, twisting her fingers in the cord. "…Yes."

She swore she could hear Edna shrug. "None of my business. Right. I'll send Johnny over in a few minutes. He thinks he's going to save up for a car, the dear, so he'll do almost anything for a few bucks."

"Thank you so much," Marion gushed. "I can't tell you how much I appreciate it." She paused. "And Edna?"

"Yeah?"

"I *will* tell you what's going on. I'm sorry I've been so obtuse, but you're a good friend and I'd like to confide in you."

"Oh, thank God. I was terrified you thought I was just like the rest of those Sokol hens and the idea was mortifying."

"No, no, you're the exception. I'm sorry I was such a nag tonight —"

"Do not apologize. They all got what was coming to them. I just wished I had half the guts you do, telling them off like that. Did you see Mary Novak? I thought she was going to lay an actual egg."

Marion laughed. Relief flooded over her. "Once I get everything figured out, I'll stop by."

"I will have cookies and coffee waiting for you."

A quiet knock came at the back door. "Oh, Johnny's here already? That was fast."

"I told you. He thinks he's going to buy a car."

"I'll make sure to tip him then."

"You really don't have to."

"Thanks, Edna."

"My pleasure, Marion."

"Bye."

Chapter 18

The closer Marion drove her disused Ford Anglia toward downtown, the more she questioned her plan of action. She called Harry again before she left, but there was still no answer. Her hands clenched the steering wheel tight as she inched through the intersection at Seven Corners. The roads were icy and there was a lot of traffic near the Auditorium.

What was she doing? She didn't need to see Harry right this minute. She could call him tomorrow. He didn't go to church; it would be easy to get a hold of him in the morning. A rational woman could simply wait for a more reasonable time. It wasn't as though she were going to throw herself at him and declare her undying love forever. She just needed to know that they were okay. But this sense of urgency wasn't going away. There was no way she'd be able to just go home and go to sleep. Maybe she didn't have undying love to declare, but she did have a sizeable apology to deliver, not to mention an enormous amount of affection he deserved to know about. A whole garden bed full of seedling feelings filled with potential. Harry was like no one she'd ever met before. He was patient and considerate. He listened to her and made her feel like the most beautiful woman on earth. She was an idiot to push him away.

She needed to fix this. Right now. She couldn't stand the thought of Harry going to sleep and thinking she didn't want him. So her only option was to supremely embarrass herself.

She found a parking spot outside the Church of Assumption. She skittered down a slick sidewalk to the corner of Wabasha and 9th Street, where she looked up at the old 1890s building Harry lived in. The streetlamps reflected off of his darkened second-floor windows. She dithered in the street, shivering in her green wool coat. He wasn't home. She knew that, she'd called and he hadn't answered. He could be anywhere in the city. Doing whatever he pleased, which was no less than he deserved given she'd left him hanging so awfully on Thursday.

God, she was so selfish. She'd been so tied up in knots about the Christmas party and what the Sokol Ladies would think. She thought she had been trying to think about her children and her responsibilities. She wanted to do things Right. But she should know better by now. There was no Right, and she was fooling herself if she thought that she could get close. At the end of the day, she'd ignored the people who cared about her in order to curry the favor of people whose approval she could never earn. She had to find Harry — right now — and prove to him that she had her priorities straight. That she'd acted as soon as she'd figured it out.

It still didn't excuse why she couldn't just call him on the phone.

This was Harry's fault for not having an answering service.

Marion looked around the streets. The city was mostly darkened buildings, quiet in the night, dotted with street lamps and the occasional glow of a bar window. The neon sign at Mickey's Diner flashed a block back west, so she started walking in that direction without giving it much thought. She didn't know whether she'd find him lurking at the bar of some nearby watering hole or what. It was too cold to sit outside his building and wait for him to return. But she'd come all the way out here, she couldn't just give up now.

At the corner of 9th and St. Peter, she paused again, facing down the reality that she would need to walk into a place and look for Harry among the patrons. Explain to the bartender that she was just looking for someone. Which would cause people to be concerned about her state of agitation and urgency. A woman roaming the city at night looking for a man all on her own. She started to craft the story she imagined they would tell about a woman like that, but quickly snapped down on her thoughts and resolved to try. She felt foolish, but she'd feel even more foolish if she went home. It was perfectly possible that she might appear ridiculous in the eyes of strangers. It was worth the risk to find Harry and be able to talk to him tonight.

"Mrs. Milner!"

Marion jumped about a half foot off the sidewalk and yelped. She turned, expecting to see Harry, her heart slamming against her ribs even though mere hours ago, she'd been turning mental gymnastics trying to tell herself that he wasn't the man she'd thought he was. Instead, she saw the G–E salesman, tall and thin with a narrow mustache, hurrying down the sidewalk towards her.

"Mrs. Milner, I'm sorry to startle you. It is you, isn't it?" the salesman asked eagerly as he caught up with her at the corner.

Marion nodded and then said, "I'm sorry, you have me at a disadvantage."

"Stinson," the salesman supplied readily. "Gerald Stinson. I sold you your kitchen a while ago. I was just about to head home when I saw you. Are you looking for Harry by any chance?"

Marion hesitated. "Um, yes. Actually. Have you seen him?" She twisted her scarf in her gloved hands.

"I was just with him!" Mr. Stinson exclaimed jovially. "He's at the Coney Island Tavern, just there. He's probably not far behind me — just finishing up his beer. Would you like me to show you?"

"Oh, no, you can't stay out in this weather longer than you have to. I can find my own way just fine," Marion said. She was impressed with her own ability to sound like a calm, functioning adult when her entire body was vibrating with anxiety. "Does he — well, that is, do you think he'll be upset I've crashed his evening?"

Mr. Stinson hesitated at her question. She experienced a brief panic, imagining Harry was out with some other girl. Someone younger and more available and less selfish than her.

"Not at all," Mr. Stinson replied with a gracious smile. "It's just there."

He pointed to a tiny storefront, no more than a door and a single window. Warm light glowed from the window strung with Christmas lights, permeating the subzero night outside. Marion murmured her thanks, and Mr. Stinson tipped his hat and went on his way. She turned, took a deep breath, and walked maybe fifty feet to the bar's entrance.

A glance through the front window showed a warmly lit galley bar. The stools were mostly occupied by men of a working class sensibility. She spotted Harry's red hair toward the front, talking to another fellow next to him. He laughed and Marion felt a strange sense of voyeurism.

Not to mention a strong urge to run away. What if she just waited? Called him in the morning? If she made it known she was so eager to speak to him, to patch things up, surely it would put him in an awkward position. What if he'd already written her off? But, she reminded herself, he'd said he wanted to go for broke with her. If he could be so honest with her, it was only fair that she return the favor.

Marion wasn't sure how she got herself to do it, but she rapped her gloved knuckles against the glass of the window. It took three tries for anyone to notice, and it was the fellow sitting nearest the window, the one Harry was chatting to. His attention conveniently drew Harry's too, as a matter of course.

Harry's face stilled when he saw her through the window. It took him a moment to answer his conversation partner's quizzical expression. Then he looked at Marion, held up one finger, and dug in his pocket for a few bills to leave on the bar with his mostly empty pint glass.

It was the longest minute Marion had experienced. She twisted her half-frozen fingers in her hands and tried not to crawl out of her own skin while she waited. When the door to the bar swung open, she looked up at Harry with a thump of apprehension.

"Hi," Harry said, pulling his cap over his head. His face was a sight for sore eyes, his block jaw and that earnest brow and a 5 o'clock shadow glittering orange and gold in the blink of the Christmas lights decorating the Coney Island Tavern window.

"Hi," Marion replied.

"What happened to your party?" Harry asked. He shoved his hands deep into the pockets of his trousers. He wasn't wearing overalls. Just normal slacks. Marion's gaze stuttered over his knees before she forced herself to look up at his face.

"It ended early. I guess the Sokol Ladies weren't having quite as good a time after I told them all to mind their own business."

"Oh God, what were they on about now?"

Even now, he was engaged with what she had to say. Marion twisted her hand in her scarf now. "You, as a matter of fact."

"What?"

"They seemed to have it in their heads that you were my new … beau."

Harry's brows furrowed in confusion. "But how —?"

"I have no idea, Harry. Honestly. I think my mother had something to do with it. I can't imagine it was anything more than wish fulfillment and a monstrous coincidence."

"So … you set them straight?"

"Yes." She wished she hadn't.

"Then why are you here?"

Marion felt suddenly self conscious. "Well. I, uh…" At this rate, she was going to twist the fingers right off these gloves. "I just thought that maybe…" She looked around. Anywhere but at those relentless blue eyes. God, she was such a coward. There was snow and brick walls and neon lights blinking red and blue at Mickey's Diner across the street. "Maybe, you'd like to get dinner with me?"

"Right now?" Harry asked incredulously. "It's 9 o'clock at night."

Marion shrugged with a wan smile. "I'm sorry, it's too little, too late, I know."

"What happened to calling me after the party?"

"I did call you! I called you twice, but you didn't answer."

Harry nodded.

Marion took a deep breath. She opened her mouth. She couldn't do it.

Harry waited.

"I was wrong," she finally said. "I was scared and I left you hanging. I spent the last week worrying about a flock of hens whose regard I'll never earn anyway because that's just how they are, you know, they just want to pick at anyone who crosses their path for the fun of it. I thought I could somehow trick them, or beat them, put myself above reproach, but I can't. It's a waste of energy to try. And I convinced myself you were like them because you didn't tell me about Charlie, but I was wrong. You're not."

Harry blinked. His brows turned up and the expression turned his eyes soulful. "I'm sorry. I should have told you right away."

Marion nodded. "I know. I realized there's a difference between an error in judgment and a mark of bad character."

"So …?"

"So, I accept your apology, and I want to take you on a date. A real one. One where we don't have to hide or sneak around."

A wide smile crept across his face. "I did kind of like sneaking around."

Marion felt her cheeks heat. "Well. Um." It would be so easy to take his hand, lead him to the diner, to leave it at that. But it felt cowardly.

"I don't want to get married again," she blurted. She watched his feet because she was too chicken to look him in the face.

"Okay."

"I don't know if I'll ever want to get married again." She dared a glance. His brow was furrowed. He was confused. Of course he was confused.

"What does that mean?" he asked. "Do you just want to keep things casual, or…?"

Marion winced. "I don't know. No. I don't want to 'keep things casual.' I like you tremendously. I want more than to," she lowered her voice to a discreet whisper, "go to bed with you. Like you said, I want to go for broke too. But I just … It feels only fair that I tell you now that I don't know if I can get married again."

Harry tipped his head to the side. "Can I ask why?"

Marion huffed a mirthless laugh. "Yes, but it's not going to produce an accurate answer. I'm not sure I know myself. I just know whenever I think about it, of me at the altar with all those biddies in the pews, it makes me feel like running to Canada."

Harry nodded as though that made any sense at all. "Sure."

She took a deep breath. "It makes me feel a sense of … doom? I don't know if I can go through it again. I was a terrible wife. I could never get anything right. My mother had to help me keep my house clean until Linda was three. I … I don't think I'm any good at housework and I—"

"Marion," Harry interrupted. He put his hand heavily on her shoulder. "You're not responsible for your marriage ending."

She looked up at him. "I know that."

"But do you believe it?"

She squirmed under his gaze hand shrugged.

Harry looked at her for a moment with something — not pity, not that, but … maybe compassion? Then, he nodded his head curtly and sighed. Oh fuck.

"Regardless of what lies ahead," he said simply, "what I'm hearing is, right now, you'd like to get dinner."

"Yes, well, actually, I'm not at all hungry, but that's the general gist of it."

"So you want to go on dates," he ventured. She nodded. "Go steady?"

She nodded again.

"Then I think we're on the same page," Harry said. "You don't owe me some abstract commitment of marriage someday."

"I'm sorry, it's so childish —"

"No, it's not. I understand."

"Do you?"

"Yes. I know what it's like to feel unsuited to the institution. That doesn't mean I'm going to mess it up if I try it again, but none of that matters now, because at the end of the day we just met maybe a month ago and how would we know if that's what we wanted anyway?"

Marion nodded. He was giving her permission to kick the can down the road.

"Life's too short," he added with a shrug.

She tipped her head up and took a step towards him. "Too short to be scared?"

His hands settled on her waist. "Damn right."

She bit her lip. He was right. She was no fortune teller; she couldn't expect to know what tomorrow would bring. Maybe she would be able to see a future with him. Maybe she wouldn't. But she couldn't throw the fragile potential of what they'd found away because it might fail later. She had no guarantees. Just a heapful of hope.

Marion pressed her lips to Harry's. It felt a little bit like coming home.

And for now, that was enough.

EPILOGUE

St. Paul, Minnesota
Wednesday, June 29, 1956

"Harry!" Marion's voice rang out from the kitchen. The tone and volume indicated to Harry that he could expect to be assigned some sort of task in the form of a question. Shifting the dog's brick of a head off his knee, he rose from the sofa and walked through the dining room.

The kitchen, with its robin's egg cabinets and yellow hive linoleum, was as bustling as the honeybees that inspired it. Linda was sitting at the narrow kitchen table with one of the leaves up, writing carefully in a composition notebook, while Charlie was crawling on the floor trying to reach under the dishwasher. Marion was standing with the turquoise refrigerator door open, staring into its contents with some consternation.

"You rang?" Harry said, leaning against the doorframe for only a moment before Charlie sprang up and squeezed under his arm, scampering towards the sitting room.

"Momma," Linda called from her place at the kitchen table, legs swinging under the chair, "how do you spell 'machine'?"

"M-A-C-H-I-N-E," Marion spelled automatically, then looked up at Harry over the fridge door. "Can you tell me what exactly General Electric means by a freezer with frost protection?"

Harry lowered his brows from consideringly open to thoughtfully furrowed. "Well, it's perfectly normal for some condensation to form, especially now that it's getting humid out." He stepped into the kitchen to join Marion standing in front of the refrigerator door. "You haven't had to defrost it yet?"

"Mom! Have you seen my matchbox cars?" Charlie shouted from somewhere in the vicinity of the living room.

"Did you look in the cigar box?" Marion called back. Then she leveled a brow at Harry and opened the door to the ice box. "I've only had to do it once so far. It's been frosty before, but this is a whole other level, Harry. I thought this freezer had frost protection?"

"It does," Harry insisted. "Well, it should."

"Momma, how do you spell 'mansion'?" Linda had lost both of her front teeth earlier that month and her voice sounded adorably younger than it had before her teeth had gone.

"M-A-N-S-I-O-N. I just defrosted a month ago and it's already like an igloo again," Marion exclaimed, gesturing indignantly at the thick layer of snowy white frost curling around the edges of the ice box.

"S-I-O-N?" Linda's 's' came out as 'eth'. "Are you sure it's not S-H-U-N?"

"No, it's S-I-O-N," Marion said.

"Although, you do have a point there," Harry put in. "S-H-U-N would make a lot more sense."

"Harry, don't encourage her to change the English language. She'd take you up on it if given half the chance."

"I'm just saying that it *would* make more sense if mansion was spelled M-A-N-S-H-U-N. It's more phonetical."

"Regardless, it's not correct."

"Momma, which is it?"

"It's M-A-N-S-I-O-N. Harry, stop confusing her."

"Sorry," he apologized with a laugh.

"I thought Gerald said that this had frost protection, so why am I having to defrost it twice in two months? I would think I'd at least get a season out of each time."

Harry leaned in and scratched the layer of frost with his fingernail. "I wonder if we're just opening the door too much and letting all the humidity in."

"Mom, it's not in the cigar box." Charlie had reentered the room.

Marion frowned. "Kids, did you hear Mr. O'Conner? You have to stop opening the fridge so much."

"If we can't open the 'frigerator, how are we gonna get the food out?" Linda asked.

"You mean we need to stop doing what you're doing right now?" Charlie waved a hand at the pair of adults standing with the fridge door wide open. Harry looked down at Marion, and they exchanged a sheepish look before she hastily shut the fridge door.

"Regardless, Harry, can you call Gerald and ask him to come fix it?" Marion implored. "Everything is still under warranty—"

"—If I call Gerry, he's just going to turn around and ask me to fix it," Harry sighed. "But you're right, it is under warranty still. I can just—"

"—That's ridiculous. Why would I call my sales rep to call the repairman if he just turns around and calls my partner to do it anyway?"

"Well, it won't log as a repair under warranty if I don't call Gerry first —"

"Mom!" Charlie was still standing in the doorway of the kitchen with his hands on his hips. "Have. You seen.

My matchbox car?"

Marion's eyes narrowed. "Last time I saw them, they were in the cigar box—"

"Well they're *not.*"

"I don't know what you want me to do about it, then. This is why you have to put your things away, otherwise you'll never be able to find anything when you need it."

"Ugh, I know, I know." Charlie spun out of the kitchen with a frustrated growl.

"Watch how you speak to your mother!" Marion called after him.

This was maybe the wrong time to ask the question, but Harry couldn't help but ask it anyway. "Is there a reason we can't just defrost it again?"

"Harry! If there's something wrong with the model, we should get it fixed before the warranty runs out."

"I know, but I really think it's just because it got hot out this week and the kids are leaving it open too long while they're making a snack." Harry stuffed his hands into his pockets and tilted his head. "And that's what I would tell you if I called Gerry and then Gerry called me and I came out to look at it."

"Momma, how do you spell 'cemetary'?"

"C-E-M-E — wait a minute, Linda, what are you writing, a gothic novel?"

"What's a gothic novel?"

"C-E-M-E-T-A-R-Y," Harry cut in, trying to get back to the task at hand.

"Oh, that makes sense." Linda's version of 'sense' sounded like 'thence'. "'Cept for the C. What's the point of C? All it does is make the 'S' sound or the 'K' sound."

"What about C-H?" Harry pointed out. Linda's eyes lit up with the well-taken point, and she flashed her gap-toothed grin at him before turning back to her notebook.

"Can you just call G-E directly, Harry?" Marion plead-ed, leaning against the refrigerator door with her arms resignedly folded. "Then call Gerald if it sounds like it's actually a problem?"

"FOUND IT!" Charlie shouted from halfway across the house. Footfalls thundered towards them.

"Yeah, sure, you bet," Harry shrugged.

"It was in the desk drawer!" Charlie declared, holding his matchbox car aloft in triumph.

"What was it doing in the desk drawer?" Marion asked.

"That was the carwash," Charlie replied as if it were painfully obvious, then ducked into the back hallway and started pulling on his shoes. "Can I go play across the street?"

"I suppose, but you probably won't have more than a half hour before dinner."

"That's okay!" Charlie was already dashing out the door.

"Make sure you're back for dinner!" Marion shouted down the hall. Harry reached over Linda and the kitchen table, took the receiver off the wall-mounted cradle, and started spinning the number to the local General Electric retailer.

Marion stepped towards Harry as he spun the last few numbers and squeezed his arms. "Thank you," she said, both earnest and a bit sheepish.

"Of course," Harry replied, then leaned down to kiss her on the cheek. He lingered for a moment, pulling in her scent, the softness of her skin against his five-o'clock shadow.

"Everything alright, Mrs. Milner?" came a voice from the back stairway. Harry straightened and glanced round the corner. Mrs. Jessup, the upstairs neighbor, was standing in the frame of the back door, which Charlie must have left open. She had a hat and purse in her hands and looked very sharp.

"Oh, yes, sorry—" Marion turned and let her fingertips slide down Harry's arm before she strode down the hall towards Mrs. Jessup. "Charlie just had a bee in his bonnet about something. What are you all dolled up for?"

"Hello?"

Harry startled and yanked his focus back to the receiver in time to realize he recognized the voice on the other line.

"Oh, it's you."

"What do you mean, 'it's you'? Who's this?"

"Sorry Gerald. It's Harry. Harry O'Conner."

"What do you sound so cut up about? You know I never see you around the Coney anymore. Too good to hang out with your oldest pal?"

"No, of course not. But you know how it is. I'm a family man now."

"No kidding. Welcome to the club. What can I do you for?"

Harry leaned against the wall as he watched Marion ask her tenant about where she got her dress. He probably looked unspeakably fond. Luckily, he no longer had any reason to try and hide it.

"What exactly does it mean for the freezer to have 'frost protection'?"

Mr. Milner Gets Divorced

Chapter 1

Thursday, January 7, 1954
Minneapolis, MN

Stephen Vincelli had a weakness for tall men. He also had a weakness for the bathhouse when he was feeling especially sorry for himself. His greatest weakness, however, was falling for married men.

He was at the Hennepin bathhouse because he was currently indulging his weakness for feeling sorry for himself. He liked to go to the bathhouse and catch the eyes of strangers on him and feel like he was real. Their hands and mouths didn't hurt either. It was, all in all, a strong counterargument to the intrusive notion that he was entirely invisible, a ghost wandering a world that had no use or care for him. Visiting Kreuger's bar also helped assuage this feeling, but it had been particularly bad the past few weeks, what with Christmas and New Year's Eve with no one to kiss. So he'd left his scruples behind and taken the streetcar all the way to Minneapolis.

The Hennepin bathhouse, with its sprawling steam rooms and communal bathing pools, fortified Stephen's humanity like nothing else could. Made his hands solid and his blood thrum with life. All his mundane qualifications, his pertinent details, his almosts and not quites, didn't matter. His underwhelming resumé, his dead-end job, even his dismal high school GPA was null. At the bathhouse, he was a warm, virile body. He could be anyone he wanted to be.

Today, he was Shorty, christened by the fellow who'd whispered in his ear. It wasn't an inaccurate nickname, and nicknames were best for this sort of situation, so Stephen accepted it with a good-natured nod and followed the guy to the locker room. When it became evident the fellow had something more than the dark room in mind, Stephen got excited in spite of himself. It was a gamble to go to a second location with someone new, but Stephen couldn't resist the siren call of unspooling potential.

The January air was biting cold, a shock after the heat and steam of the baths. Stephen followed the guy across Hennepin Avenue. There were a number of hotels surrounding the crumbling Lumber Exchange Building that housed the Hennepin Baths. The guy suggested the Milner Hotel, which Stephen tried to casually dissuade him from. He certainly wasn't in a position to pay for a hotel room, so he was at this fellow's discretion, but turning tricks at the Milner Hotel felt a little too raw. Which was completely stupid, because it had been the better part of a decade since Stephen had talked to Joe Milner. He'd just rather not see his childhood friend's surname emblazoned on the pillowcase while he was getting cornholed.

They ended up at the Hotel Vendome next door, which had the virtue of being slightly closer than the Milner, and the guy didn't seem too bothered by it anyhow. It was his money. Stephen couldn't be too picky. Things proceeded quite nicely as clothes were re-shed, which was actually frustrating because ideally, Stephen would like the baths to stop providing so much positive reinforcement. It wasn't the kind that lasted, the kind he really needed.

Stephen felt like an apparition returned to his tangible body as the trick ran his hands over his skin, his eyes sharpening and his mind clearing, like seeing in focus for the first time in weeks. He was real. He was alive. He was desired. The guy was really eager, desperate almost, but not in a pitiful way. He was generically good-looking, tall like Stephen liked, with a charming smile that suggested he did a good deal of glad-handing in his real life. He sucked Stephen's cock like it was a sacred relic.

Afterwards, Stephen laid out on the shabby bedspread next to the guy. He'd come to think of him as Stew, since he sort of sounded like Jimmy Stewart when he talked. Stephen turned towards him and caught Stew looking at him consideringly.

"Can I see you again?" Stew asked. His voice had a persistent nasal tone, and his smile was fully confident in Stephen's anticipated reply. As well he might, with a mouth that greedy. Stephen bit his lip. So much about this was surprisingly encouraging. Usually, Stephen ended up in bathroom stalls or the bathhouse dark room for a furtive hook up that was always more about release than any sort of connection. The hotel room was a splurge, one that made him think Stew might be looking for something more, like Stephen was. Being able to see Stew laid out on a bed in the waning afternoon light had been liberating. Made him feel less like a dirty secret.

"That could be arranged," Stephen shrugged with a smile. He leaned in and put his palm to Stew's cheek. He glanced at Stew's lips then moved to close the remaining space.

"Uh," Stew said, flinching back. "What're you doing?"

Stephen felt his stomach drop like a rock. He flinched back too. "What?" Like he didn't know.

Stew gave an uncomfortable frown and sat up. "I, uh, I'm sorry if I gave you the wrong idea…"

"So you *don't* want to see me again?" Stephen clarified. It sounded pathetic in the stark brightness of the room. Stephen felt himself flicker insubstantially.

"I'm married," Stew scoffed, like that explained everything.

"Sorry if I didn't see your ring," Stephen sneered, glancing toward Stew's conspicuously bare ring finger. Perhaps all of Stephen's weaknesses were interrelated, because the tall men he met at bathhouses were almost always married.

"I don't see how my being married has anything to do with meeting up again," Stew said with an exasperated expression. "There's already enough pressure in every other part of life. You seemed to enjoy yourself well enough. Why couldn't we help each other blow off a little steam from time to time?"

Stephen got up and retrieved his underwear and worn wool trousers, dismissing several retorts. What he really wanted to ask this guy was whether he'd ever considered the possibility that homosexuals could find companionship, or domesticity, or—heaven forbid—love. Whether they could exist outside of bathhouses and basement toilets, the dingiest of forgotten shadows. Whether their desires could ever be anything more than "blowing off steam."

"How many kids you got?" Stephen asked, because he was a glutton for punishment.

"I don't see how that's any of your business."

Definitely at least one, then. Stephen shrugged his shirt back on and buttoned it up. His undershirt was in need of a wash now, so he stuffed that in his pocket. "It's nothing personal. I just don't step out with married guys."

Stew snorted. Stephen's hands faltered as he fastened his belt. He braced.

"Who said anything about stepping out?" Stew laughed then. "God, next thing I know, you'll be asking for my pin."

Stephen sucked on his lip for a moment to stop himself from saying something bitchy, but it didn't work. "You were already begging for my dick, so I don't see how it's that big a reach."

Suffice to say, Stephen wasn't too broken up about it when they left the hotel and went their separate ways. After riding the streetcar back to St. Paul, he went straight to Kreuger's. He ambled up to the shabby building on Wabasha between 5th and 6th Streets with his hands in his pockets and shouldered through the door with his chin tucked below the collar of his jacket. The warm galley bar was welcome after the biting January chill. It only had one small, oval window at the front, filled with a neon "Liquor" sign. The bar didn't have any other signage to distinguish it, nor did it need any. That one sign told you everything you needed to know. Mr. Kreuger was a silent sentinel behind the bar, and Stephen dutifully stopped there first, ordering a beer. There were no free rides at Kreuger's.

The place couldn't be more non-descript, an honest, simple, dingy blue-collar bar—a perfect sanctuary for queers. The Kreugers put up with them too, as long as they kept it discreet and always bought something. Stephen craned his neck to inspect the occupants of the back corner booth while he waited for his beer. Mae West was holding court with Frank Atlas, Walter, and Dickie. Marge was there too, he presumed, because the smoke was coming up from the near side of the booth like a chimney.

When Kreuger sloshed his beer on the bar, Stephen seized it and sidled down the long, narrow dive toward his friends. Oh god, Carol and Jack were in the adjacent booth again. Stephen quickly averted his gaze and hustled into the back booth.

"Vinny, there you are," Frank Atlas said. "Tell them—"

"—I'm not helping you try to get Dickie to lift weights with you," Stephen cut him off. "We all know you're just trying to corner him in the locker room, and the only reason you keep trying is because Walter can't kick your ass without help. Did you see the Two Blind Mice are here?"

"Bless their sweet, simple souls," Mae West crooned. He was a sweet sort of sissy with bottle-blonde hair and hands that flopped off his wrists like noisemakers at a New Year's party.

"You'd think they'd give up after striking out so many times," Walter sighed.

"Oh, now he has an interest in sports," Frank groused. "You know, when you all waste away with porcelain bones in your old age, don't say I didn't try to help you. I'm heading out."

"Not on my account, I hope," Stephen deadpanned.

"No, I'll take that honor," Walter said, glowering at Frank over crossed arms. "Tell all the gymnasium boys we said 'hello'."

Frank snorted and stood. He was a hulking fellow, tall with big shoulders. Stephen had been interested when he first met Frank, but things had fizzled out pretty quickly when he realized Frank was less well-endowed in other areas. Chiefly intelligence, of course. Chiefly.

Frank charged past the Two Blind Mice and gave a

manful nod to Kreuger as he headed out the door.

"Where have you been?" Dickie turned to Stephen with a curl of his upper lip. Dickie was an elegant bitch who would never be caught dead somewhere as smelly and sweaty as a gymnasium. His tastes ran more to expensive silk scarves, finely tailored wool trousers, and shiny polished shoes. Walter was the only fellow in their set who could afford to be his boyfriend. Dickie had creamy skin and delicately carved features in perfect symmetry—objectively, a beautiful man. He and Frank would make a fine-looking couple if Frank didn't waste all his money on subscription Charles Atlas guides. And if Dickie wasn't so awful at covering up how head over heels he was for Walter.

Stephen squirmed in the booth and busied himself with a long draught of his beer.

"Stephen," Walter intoned. "How's that New Year's resolution going?"

"Fine. Just a teeny tiny, minor setback," Stephen confessed around the rim of his glass.

"I thought you weren't cruising anymore," Marge said with a tobacco smoke sigh. She was a glowering bull dyke dead-set on compensating for her delicate bone structure by letting her eyebrows grow together. She and Stephen had hit it off immediately a few years ago by virtue of the fact that they were both Italian.

"I'm not," Stephen said, but his voice curdled like it was a question.

Dickie scoffed. "What happened to true love?"

"I'm still looking for it. I just … didn't find it at the bathhouse." Stephen winced into his beer.

"What *did* you find at the bathhouse?"

Stephen grimaced. "Another tall, dark, married man."

"Wow, you sure can pick 'em," Mae West sang.

"Maybe you should pick up the Two Blind Mice? At least then the wife knows she's getting cuckolded."

"Dear god, I'm a poof, not a pervert," was Stephen's requisite reply.

"You're quite right," Dickie said. "Frank let them pick him up once. He said he couldn't walk straight for a week and it weren't on the fellow's account."

"I'm sorry, what?" Marge exclaimed. Any suggestion of penetration made the bridge of her nose wrinkle.

"I'm not one to air someone else's *private* business," Dickie replied with relish. "Only that I understand the husband isn't the only one with queer tastes."

Two Blind Mice indeed. Fact was, though, it was slim pickings this time of year. Everyone was hard up after Christmas and it was cold as a witch's tit. Things wouldn't pick up at all until Winter Carnival at the end of the month, and Stephen was loathe to wait that long to meet someone he could be serious about.

The bell above the door that was chipped with enough layers of oil paint to prevent nuclear fallout chimed as a burst of frigid air barreled down the galley. Stephen, seated in the best spot for casing the door, leaned out the booth a-ways, then made his report to the table. "It's just Red."

The rest of the group sagged. Red, a bespectacled man in his forties, perched on his usual stool at the bar and took to chatting with Mr. Kreuger. He was a notorious cruiser, often flitting in and out of the bar to "check his traplines." The old fairy held no interest to the back booth crowd at any rate—beyond being a perfectly decent middle-aged man, he was plain as could be, and had a long-term partner at home besides. It made Stephen spitting mad, to be entirely honest. Red got the best of both worlds, and he didn't even have any looks to make it make sense.

"Well, true love eludes the hopeless romantic once more," Mae West declared sorrowfully with a sweep of his hand.

"I think that's giving him a little too much credit," Walter commented. "It wasn't all that long ago that he was waltzing in here bragging about his latest conquests."

"You know, I'm right here," Stephen said churlishly. "You don't have to talk about me like I'm not."

Dickie ignored him and replied to Walter, "You're right, darling." Then, he turned to regard Stephen. "What inspired your noble change of heart?"

Stephen glowered at him. "You all make me sound like a chippy-chaser."

"I'm sorry, are you not?" Dickie again, his naturally sarcastic voice positively dripping.

"I'm not! I was seeing Dale for six months, I don't know why you're slandering me like this." Stephen crossed his arms and pouted. The bell for the bar chimed again and he glanced over at the door. "King Crab."

"Oh bless his heart for coming back here," Mae West cooed. "Surely he must know by now his reputation precedes him?"

"I mean, it's preceded him for years," Walter said. "How does anyone know he still even has crabs?"

Glances ranging from offended to bewildered to exhausted (that was Dickie) ricocheted across the booth. Apparently, no one had a ready answer to that question.

"Listen," Stephen said, trying to steer the conversation back to his own miserable love life. "I admit, there was a time when I enjoyed playing the field. I didn't know any other gay fellows growing up and I'll admit, I've been enjoying sowing my wild oats."

"'A time,'" snorted Dickie. "Try the better part of a

decade."

"Shut up," Stephen gave him a shove with his shoulder, eliciting a yelp from Dickie. "This place has lots of potential tricks, but how's a guy supposed to come in here day in and day out, see idiots like you setting up house together, and not want something like that for himself?"

"Awe, hear that Walter?" Dickie crooned. "Vinny's jealous of our quaint domesticity."

Walter grinned at Dickie like he was the only person in the room, and it made Stephen want to crawl under the table, although he wasn't sure if it was the envy or of the fact that everyone could probably see it on his face.

"Fine," Stephen said before Walter could start reciting poetry or something. "Maybe I am a little jealous. But most guys out there don't think there's anything more for men like us than anonymous encounters in men's bathrooms. It's pretty evil of you all to make me hope."

Now even Dickie looked moony. What a nightmare.

"I want to invest my time and energy into someone who cares to know my real name," Stephen barreled on. "Someone on my side, through thick and thin—"

"Oh, darling, you want a *husband!*" Mae West declared.

A husband, a companion, someone whose touch could reinforce that Stephen was still flesh and blood and hadn't winked out in a blink of loneliness like a dying star. Not to be melodramatic about it or anything.

"Well, maybe," Stephen hedged, "not in so many words, but yeah. And why shouldn't I want someone like that? Companionship isn't a purely female occupation. Plenty of men have found lifelong partnership together, whether or not they were having sex."

"Absolutely," Marge agreed with a jab of her cigarette. "We all ain't any different from anyone else. In fact, we're doing the world a favor by not contributing to overpopulation."

"Cheers to that," Mae West said, raising his glass.

"Love is too expansive to be limited by these piddly man-made ideas like marriage," Stephen continued. "I want something bigger. I want to have a great passion before I die. Is that so much to ask?"

The bell at the door chimed again. Stephen trailed off as he leaned over to see who'd come in. Like the previous new arrivals, he recognized this man, but unlike the others, it was the last possible person he'd expected to see.

"Holy shit," Stephen said.

"And lo, his prayers are answered," Dickie quipped, but his smile faltered as Stephen's jaw continued to wag. He leaned forward, almost pushing Stephen out of the booth as he craned for his own look.

"I don't know what he's all worked up about," Dickie reported to the group. "It's just some run-of-the-mill 9-to-5er."

To anyone else's eye, Dickie would be correct. The man was tall, with sandy blonde hair and a smart hat. He had a camel wool overcoat with a suit underneath it. Shiny patent leather shoes. But Stephen knew his face like the past eight years had never happened, like they were still sitting on the last row of bleachers with their thighs pressed together, laughing as Stephen talked shit about the football players on the Central High School field. Joe Milner, his face still as round and shiny and sweet as ever, was in Stephen's bar. He was *in Stephen's bar.*

"For cripe's sake, Vinny," Marge said, "put your tongue back in your mouth and tell us what's wrong with you."

Stephen looked back at the table of his friends. His real friends, the ones who knew him and still stuck around.

He wrinkled his nose.

"It's no one."

"Bullshit," Mae West leveled in a timbre much lower than he usually used. "Give it up."

"Well, it's..." Stephen's face twisted into a full grimace. "...my soulmate."

Dickie looked like he wanted to bash his face through the table, but also like he might strangle Stephen if he didn't keep talking.

Stephen couldn't even hold a straight face through that. "It's a guy I knew growing up. We were real good friends, and we told each other we were soulmates. But he was never interested in me and got married straight out of high school. So yeah, it's my soulmate, but also, not at all." He laughed, to give them permission. They didn't.

Pity dawned one by one on the face of all the boys. One had to live under some sort of rock or look like Dickie to not have one of those unrequited coming-of-age stories.

"He must have a hefty pair to be showing up around here like that," Walter said, craning over the back of the booth to get a look. It was nice to be defended, even if Joe Milner was about as threatening as a wet noodle.

"Are you going to go talk to him, Stephen?" Marge asked. "Go on, go offer him a smoke and catch up."

"Are you insane?" Dickie admonished. "Stephen can't take that kind of risk. What if the guy's a snitch?"

"He probably has no idea where he is," Marge dismissed. "He looks like one of those city government guys. Probably just wants a beer on his way home."

Everyone in the booth was now on their knees on the cushions, craning up to get a good look at the newcomer. Stephen buried his face in his hands, mortified. But he couldn't quite manage to stop looking at Joe through his fingers.

"City government guy? All the more reason to treat him like *persona non grata*," Dickie said. "Besides, he threw Stephen over. What kind of friend calls you a soulmate and never talks to you after getting married?"

"The kind who harbored a little more than friendly affection," Mae West surmised, a lifted brow directed at Stephen.

"Stop it, you're torturing me," Stephen said miserably. "He didn't leave me in the lurch. I stopped talking to him. I just couldn't do it anymore."

Walter leveled Stephen with a serious expression. "That's damn hard to do. Good for you, Stephen."

"Thank you, Walter," Stephen said, straightening a bit at the acknowledgement. "It *was* hard. He kept calling my mom, asking for me. Wanting me to come to his wife's dinner parties."

"Two Blind Mice?" Marge snorted.

Stephen cast her an impatient look. "*No*. The calls stopped after I got my own place. As far as I know, he still calls my mom now and then. She loves it." Except he never managed to get his own place and he was so embarrassed, he was still lying to his friends about it. So every time Joe called, he got to listen to his mother chat him up. He only had enough strength to refuse the call; he still sat on the steps eavesdropping on every ounce of information he could glean from one side of the conversation. That hadn't happened in years. Not since Marion had their second baby. Fuck.

"Oh, he's looking this way!" Walter hissed, and they all ducked down at once in the most glaringly obvious display of Not Looking at Someone in the history of the world.

Stephen had nowhere to hide, seated at the end of the

booth as he was. From where Joe Milner stood at the bar, Stephen was clearly visible. And he was looking this way, a sort of puzzled expression on his face, which made sense considering that he'd just caught a whole booth's worth of slack-jawed yokels staring at him. His eyes met Stephen's, and Stephen was very sorry to report that the effect those green eyes had on him had not waned one bit in the past eight years. Stephen looked sharply away at his own hands, unable to hold the connection. When he got the guts to look up again, Milner was no longer looking their way.

"Did he see you?" Mae West hissed.

"Yeah, he definitely saw him," Walter reported, peering round the edge of the booth like a film noir villain.

"Is he coming over?" Dickie asked.

Marge rolled her eyes. "Just go offer him a smoke and say 'hello.' The longer you hide over here like a ninny, the more awkward it's going to be. Just get it over with."

Stephen looked at her and then back at Joe Milner. He was half sitting, half leaning on a barstool and sipping his beer awkwardly, like he'd never drank at a bar by himself before. Like he was an approximation of a normal man, dressed in the costume and lurking in all the usual places. Except this wasn't one of the usual places. What was he *doing* here?

Stephen entertained the possibility of getting up and saying hello. He scarcely managed to imagine walking up to Joe Milner, heart in his throat, before he had to shut the whole operation down.

"Nope," Stephen said as he scrubbed his face in his hands. "I'm not going over there. He didn't recognize me."

"Well, I'm sure he will once you say, 'Hi, remember me? I'm Stephen Vincelli, your soulmate, from high school,'" Dickie pointed out.

Stephen groaned and buried his face all the way in his arms. If Joe glanced over, Stephen certainly wasn't going to appear to be nonchalant, well-adjusted, or better off without him. He pushed himself upright and inhaled deeply.

"I'm going to the toilet."

Mr. Milner Gets Divorced, the prequel to *Mrs. Milner Gets a Kitchen,* is out now in eBook and paperback. Learn more at www.janehadleywrites.com.

FOOTNOTES

This story is very close to home for me. Literally.

I live in a 1915 Craftsman duplex in the Little Bohemia neighborhood of St. Paul. The inspiration for this story came from my own 1959 G-E appliance suite. Honestly, the appliances were what sold me on the house. When you walk into my kitchen, you can tell that these appliances were carefully maintained for decades and still operate well given their age. The original manuals were also passed down to me in pristine condition (providing the inspiration for the cover design). Historical research on the house turned up that owners during the 1950s were a cabinet-maker and homemaker, respectively. The cabinets are all custom and the countertops are so short, we had to get a special dishwasher to fit under them. I can only conclude that the lady of the house was short of stature. She's not short of resolve, though. She's still here — I can feel her presence often in that kitchen. She doesn't like people to use her appliances; in fact, for the first month or two that we lived here, I was the only one who could cook without burning things. My imagination was caught by the kitchen she left behind.

Important sources of historical inspiration came from the oral histories of my grandparents (the story about stealing the car is almost verbatim my grandfather's words). I enjoyed a brief and sort of rabid obsession with long-line bras and girdles after reading *In the Mood for Munsingwear* by Susan Marks — did you know that Minnesota has one of the largest collections of underwear in the world? — and I got good and mad after reading Betty Friedan's *The Feminine Mystique*. I really loved researching the Silent Generation of midcentury housewives. It was remarkably cathartic (and a little demoralizing) to see so many of the same worries I have about my roles as Wife and Mother reflected in the experiences of women who came before me. I spent an inordinate amount of time trying to figure out what restaurants were on West 7th Street at the time by paging through old City Directory photos shared by a neighbor, as well as tracking the historical weather record (the weather on Thursday, Dec. 15 in this book is dead wrong and I'm still agonizing over the decision to not correct it). Details and design inspiration were further pulled from a G–E catalogue and informational pamphlets my spouse saved from his grandmother's basement. I lurked at the fringe of Sokol Hall events and studied the Czech section of *They Chose Minnesota* by June Drenning Holmquist, as well as *Christmas on West Seventh Street* by Jerry Fearing.

Researching the mid–20th century can be a little challenging at times. Many folks don't consider the period properly "historical," perhaps because they know people who lived through it or did so themselves. But as far as I'm concerned, if a student can do a National History Day project on a time period, it's ripe for a historical romance. Unlike the nineteenth century, studying the 1950s allows the researcher to straddle both formal historical sources and the memories of elders in the community. (And it's a little awkward to admit to those elders that you're hoping to leverage these facts to write about fictional characters going on spicey dates.) Lots of survey texts tend to gloss over the period, as it is neither properly Historical nor is it Contemporary. For books like *They Chose Minnesota*, which was originally published in 1963, it's extremely challenging to get a good sense of the period and I spent a very stressful couple of days wondering whether I had to rewrite the Sokol crowd as Catholics. (It turned out that despite the fact that the Czech Catholic church and the Sokol Hall in Little Bohemia are literally 50 feet apart, they did not actually mix much. I think. I'm still trying to corroborate this with Sokol Hall elders.)

Finally, I worked hard to imbue this manuscript with the dialectical patterns of Minnesota and the Upper Midwest. From the usage of words like "ain't" and "gotta" and "don't got," to the avoidantly noncommittal ways of the passive aggressive Minnesota Nice, I really enjoyed thinking about the ways language I've always known to be "normal" actually highlights our culture, for better or worse. Uffda.

ACKNOWLEDGEMENTS

Many thanks are owed to the communities of readers and writers who inspired me to get this book out into the world, including the Romance Salon, Not Quite Write to Market, and write what you may. To my betas, Louise Mayberry and Alivia Fleur, who have been absolutely invaluable in orienting me to the self-publishing world. To the Old St. Paul Facebook group for unwittingly aiding and abetting historically accurate smut with 1950s West 7th diner recommendations. To Allison for being my Czech Checker and cheerleader. To my spouse, for being the most encouraging alpha reader a gal could ask for and for helping me work out all the kitchen logistics. Finally, to the ghost who haunts my 1959 G-E kitchen — thank you very much for letting me use your appliances. I will provide annual gin and tonic offerings in the double oven for the foreseeable future, providing you don't start any electrical fires.

Also by Jane Hadley

Secret Soldier Series
Fort Snelling, Minnesota. 1861.
A woman dresses as a man to enlist in the Union Army only to fall in infuriating infatuation with her strapping bunkie.
A Fine Looking Soldier: Volume 1
A Right Honorable Soldier: Volume 2
Out now.

Oh! You Pretty Things
Minneapolis, Minnesota. 1970.
A closeted genderfluid university student joins a proto-glam rock band and gets drawn into a messy love triangle that pushes him to find and claim his own queer identity.
Out now.

Mr. Milner Gets Divorced
St. Paul, Minnesota. 1954.
An upstanding husband, father, and city official reignites an old high school friendship at the 1954 Winter Carnival and proceeds to blow up his life.
Prequel to Mrs. Milner Gets a Kitchen. *Out now.*

<u>A Rogue's Gallery</u>
St. Paul, Minnesota. 1929.
An aimless flapper contrives a fake relationship with the queen of the St. Paul gangsters to shake off a persistent ex-boyfriend, only to find herself longing to convince her that it could be real.
Coming soon.

About the Author

Jane Hadley writes historical romance teeming with footnotes and feels. She lives under seven layers of blankets where she can comfortably survey the cold tundra of Minnesota through wavy glass windows which she refuses to replace because old things are inherently valuable.

jane@janehadleywrites.com
www.janehadleywrites.com

www.ingramcontent.com/pod-product-compliance
Lightning Source LLC
Chambersburg PA
CBHW012039140726
47991CB00011B/3199